Logan sprang up, crouched, and caught the time jumper with his shoulder, just as the man rebounded. This time, when he hit the window, it shattered around him, and he teetered at the edge of the frame. Logan dived for him, but the man sidestepped—aside and out. Nine hundred feet above the pavement of Fifth Avenue, the time jumper toppled from the window. Around him, fog swirled and coalesced as a wormhole in time opened to receive him.

At the broken sill, Logan clenched his teeth. "Missed!" he muttered. Whenever the traveler came from—somewhere in the future, probably Logan's own time of 2007—he was back there now, out of TEC's reach. But he had gone back empty handed.

Logan got to his feet, glanced at the time, and scowled. There was less than a minute remaining. Somewhere in this building was a suitcase containing $18 million in bearer bonds—money lost in history. And in just a few seconds all hell was going to break loose.

By Dan Parkinson
*Published by Ballantine Books:*

*The Gates of Time*
THE WHISPERS
FACES OF INFINITY*

*Timecop*
VIPER'S SPAWN
THE SCAVENGER
BLOOD TIES*

*forthcoming

# TIMECOP

## The Scavenger

# Dan Parkinson

Based on the Universal Television Series
created for Television by Mark Verheiden.

Based on the characters created by
Mike Richardson & Mark Verheiden.

A Del Rey® Book
THE BALLANTINE PUBLISHING GROUP • NEW YORK

This book contains an excerpt from the forthcoming edition of *Faces of Infinity* by Dan Parkinson. This excerpt has been set for this edition only and may not reflect the final content of the forthcoming edition.

A Del Rey® Book
Published by The Ballantine Publishing Group
Copyright © 1998 by Universal Studios Publishing Rights, a Division of Universal Studios Licensing, Inc. All Rights Reserved.
Excerpt from *Faces of Infinity* by Dan Parkinson copyright © 1998 by Siegel & Siegel Ltd.

http://www.randomhouse.com

Library of Congress Catalog Card Number: 98-92818

ISBN 0-345-42196-5

Manufactured in the United States of America

First Edition: November 1998

10   9   8   7   6   5   4   3   2   1

## The Superstition Mountains
## Arizona, 1873

The Yaquis were everywhere, like shadows among the rocks. Stover had killed two of them almost immediately, but in the burning hours since then, he had been unable to get even a single clear shot. They moved like ghosts, he thought. A glimpse of a dark head above a boulder, seen again thirty yards away as a shadow crossing a slanted crevice—it might be two Indians, or the same one moving fast.

Maybe there were only two or three out there, or maybe a dozen. It didn't matter, Stover told himself. One or a hundred, it makes no difference how many if you can't even get a shot at them.

Up on the tumbled rise where a faint trail led toward Weavers Needle, there *was* a visible target, but the Dutchman was far beyond the range of Stover's repeating rifle. "Walz, you old devil!" Stover rasped through sun-cracked lips. "You're enjoying this!"

Snapping a quick shot at a flick of movement off to his right, Stover turned and looked again. Even at this distance, he could see the Dutchman's snowy beard split in a malevolent grin. The Dutchman was just sitting up there, watching! He felt secure on that shelf of stone, well above the tumbled landscape of the desert below. The Yaquis couldn't get to him up there. The cliff was a fortress, and Walz controlled it.

But Stover had no such cover. He had come a mile or so since that first attack, leaving behind two dead mules and one dead Mexican—a mile of duck and run, dodge and shoot—and always the Yaquis were with him. Like silent, darting shadows they were all around him. An arrow had gouged his rifle stock, and another still protruded from his backpack.

He drank the last few drops of hot, acrid water from his belt canteen and rasped a curse as the bit of moisture only compounded his thirst. His back to a sheer surface of sun-baked stone, he lay still for a moment, listening. Then he rolled to his left, got to his knees, and flung the empty canteen away from him. The full-arm throw sent the container arcing high, above the climbing boulders below him.

He saw its silhouette spinning across the sheet-copper sky and fixed his slitted eyes on the rocks below. Something moved there, and he leveled his rifle and fired. Fifty yards downslope a savage figure leapt out of hiding, whirled around in a shower of spurting blood, and fell.

"Three," Stover muttered.

Echoes of the shot still dwindled among the tumbled stones as he spun around, raced from his cover, and scrambled up a fan of loose pebbles. He heard shouts, and a flashing arrow whisked past his ear to explode shards of stone just above his head. He rolled to the right, found a foothold, and climbed another eight or nine feet to dive into the shade of a low overhang. Another arrow followed him, clattering against the stone at his back.

Distantly, drifting down on the desert wind, he heard cruel, cackling laughter. The Dutchman knew the Indians couldn't reach him, and the Indians knew it, too. So they were going after the one they could get to. Himself. May the devil take you, Jacob Walz, Stover cursed silently. I'd have helped you with your find, if you had let me. I'd have been a good partner. I'd have settled for a share of the gold. But no more, Dutchman. I'm coming for you, and I'm not dead yet!

Gravel rattled below him, and Stover brought the rifle up and fired point-blank. The Indian was hardly more than a child, but the short-ax in his hand, poised to throw, was no toy. The Indian staggered backward, sagged, and slid down the gravel fan.

"Four," Stover whispered, fitting a fresh cylinder into his rifle.

He waited a few seconds, then flung himself over the sheered stone above him and rolled into the shadows beside a standing rock. More seconds passed, becoming a full minute, and Stover moved again, more deliberately. Nothing responded but the desert wind; nothing moved but a pair of buzzards circling lazily above.

He raced to new cover, still higher on the slope, headed around a jagged boulder, then cut back and went around it the other way. And then he knew that the Indians were gone. As changeable as desert storms, they had simply gone, vanishing into the arid rifts and broken stones of the desert.

It was the way of Yaquis. Primitive and unpredictable, they could be deadly, but they were seldom persistent. They came into these mountains sometimes, following the old trails. They took what came handy, then when they felt like going on, they simply went.

Easing around an outcrop, Stover looked up the mountainside. The shelf above was empty. Jacob Walz, too, had gone. As though tiring of the entertainment below, he had gone on his way, onward toward that secret trove where the nuggets were as big as marbles and the bits of ore were almost pure gold.

Stover had seen the nuggets. Half of Phoenix had seen them and heard the white-bearded old German's drunken boasts about the rich discovery he had made. And Stover wasn't the first to follow Walz when he headed out from Phoenix. Back there at the foot of the mountains lay the bodies of two Phoenix men, with the Dutchman's bullets in them.

Looking around now, Stover felt a shiver of excitement. I must be close, he thought. Deep in the Superstitions, the trails were few and hard to follow. He could see the landmark called Weavers Needle from here, and his intuition told him that the mine was very near. Beyond the peak above the Needle, other canyons opened out—canyons far easier to reach by other routes than this.

With a prospector's instincts, he gazed around, fixing landmarks in his mind. Ahead was the serrated peak, and below it Weavers Needle. Nearer, midway between here and that next slope, wind-scoured stones like bizarre castles shadowed a smaller, crack-riddled crest where a lone, weather-beaten old paloverde tree stood, stripped of its bark. A single, skeletal limb jutted from it, pointing away from the Needle.

He saw something else, too. In a shadow of overhanging rock, just beyond the old tree, something white moved slightly in the wind.

"That snowy beard betrays you, Dutchman." Stover nodded. "So that's your game, is it? An ambush? Well, we'll just see about that." Keeping out of sight, he circled high around and found a ledge within fifty yards of the little cave where the white whiskers waited. Easing to one side for a better view, he rested his rifle on a stone and cocked its hammer. Sighting carefully, holding on the dark shadows just below the white beard, he fired.

In the cave, a dry stick shattered and toppled outward into the slanting sunlight. Stover gaped at the thing lying on the ground there—a white rag, a piece ripped from a linen shirttail.

Directly behind him, metal clicked on metal as the hammer of a big rifle was hauled back. Stover turned, gaping. The last thing he ever saw was the white-whiskered face of Jacob Walz, and the last sound he ever heard was the Dutchman's cruel, cackling laughter. Stover was dead before the thunder of the old man's rifle reached his ears.

Atop a weathered spire, not far away, Jack Logan shook his head slowly, controlling his impulses. Old Jacob Walz had just added one more victim to his private graveyard on the mountain. No matter how you cut it, it was murder, pure and simple. Again, as so many times before, the TEC agent felt that surge of frustration, the aching need to go down there and arrest that man for what he had done.

But what Walz had done was beyond Logan's jurisdiction. Murder, yes. The killing of Eli Stover by Jacob Walz was cold-blooded, willful murder, with intent. But it was a murder that had occurred nearly a hundred and forty years ago. And it involved no alteration of history. It occurred just as it had always occurred in 1873, and thus it was out of Logan's jurisdiction. As a timecop, an agent of the Time Enforcement Commission, Logan's purpose in life was to track down temporal perpetrators, to keep history from being changed.

History wasn't always pretty, he reminded himself again, but changing it was unthinkable. Every alteration of past time reflected itself in changes down the timestream, to the present and into the future.

Jacob Walz killed Eli Stover in 1873. Now Jack Logan had witnessed the crime, and could find no fault with the sequence. Whatever had started the ripple on the so-called Dome of History, the big overhead Eventuality-Wave Resonance Projector display in TEC headquarters, this wasn't it.

Still, E-warp registered a level-two ripple centered at this date in history, and the historians gave it a 90 percent probability that it had to do with the Lost Dutchman mine in the Superstition Mountains in Arizona.

Out there in the broken desolation of that rocky slope, Walz went to retrieve his mules. He returned with his own animals and Stover's, too. With only a glance at the dead man lying in the sun, the Dutchman headed back to his mine.

So far, nothing anachronistic had occurred. But Logan knew that if he returned now to 2007, the ripple would still be there, blending into the timestream, becoming part of the fabric of history. And history would be different then, by that much. Some change, happening here and now, would snowball down through the years, and some significant alteration would be forever uncorrected.

*"For want of a nail,"* Logan muttered, *"the shoe was lost; for want of a shoe the horse was lost; for want of a horse the rider was lost; for want of a rider the battle was lost, and all for the want of a nail."* He frowned. "Now

where did *that* come from?" he growled. "Flotsam! Damned speed-brief, it always leaves clutter behind."

In the distance, he could see Jacob Walz poking around a crack in the broken stone—a crack that seemed too narrow and too shallow to mean anything. Yet now and again, the old man seemed to disappear into that crack, carrying tools or bundles, and reappeared carrying different items. It was an optical illusion, Logan realized. What seemed to be only a narrow crack in a rock was actually a cavern, where lapping stone hid an accessible entrance.

No wonder the Lost Dutchman mine was lost, he thought. You can't see it until you're in it.

The sun was slanting from the west, barely topping the hills there, when Logan noticed movement in the rocks across the narrow canyon from Walz's camp.

Logan's eyes narrowed. He studied the area, and the movement came again, in two places. There was someone in the rocks over there, a dark figure hiding in deep shadow, scanning the Dutchman's camp through binoculars. And just below the watcher, a file of walking men came into view.

Indians! Not the same Indians, though. These were of a different order—better equipped and better attired than the primitive Yaquis—but definitely Indians. He thought for a moment that they were heading for the Walz camp, then he realized they were just passing through. They moved warily, following an ancient trail across the mountains, but they seemed only careful, not hostile.

The trail they followed was out of sight of Walz's diggings, and for the moment they were out of sight of the dark watcher up in the rocks. Logan studied them carefully, noticing their manner of dress, and the crash course he had received before launching—central Arizona Territory in the 1870s—scrolled through his mind. The sublimator, nicknamed speed-brief, was a new tool for TEC, and Logan had his doubts about it. It was shallow data, implanted by holographic stimulation of the mind. It was imperfect, usually lasting only a day or two except for odd bits of flotsam, and it could make a person clumsy if he wasn't careful—all those neurons loaded with raw data not assimilated into personal reflexes or logic patterns.

Still, speed-brief could be useful. He knew instantly what he was seeing.

These Indians were Pimas—six of them traveling with an Apache guide—and their mission was peaceful. They wore ceremonial garb and carried eagle amulets. As they rounded a shoulder in the slope, directly below the lurking figure up in the rocks, Logan turned his attention there again, suddenly realizing what he had just seen. Binoculars! There were few binocular telescopes in the 1870s, and none with vinyl casing! He had been so absorbed in his speed-briefed recall that it had blinded him to the obvious.

Instinctively, Logan shifted his weight, his reflexes sluggish from his concentration on subliminal data. His boot slipped on the stone of the spire, and a little shower of pebbles fell from the crest to cascade into the gully below. Their rattle was loud in the silence, echoing here and there among the rocks.

Above the Indians, the lurking figure turned, looking around for the source of the noise. Logan still couldn't see many details of the figure—a fairly tall, lean man in dark clothing, obscured by shadows. But one detail stood out. The gun in those gloved hands was no weapon that had existed in 1873. It was a short, authoritative blowback automatic with a curved clip and a laser sight.

The laser was live. Where it pointed, a tiny, bright dot of scarlet light danced across the rocks below.

"Clumsy," Logan muttered, angry with himself. If he hadn't slipped, the man might never have seen the passing Indians below him. Whatever was going to happen now, Logan's own presence had contributed to it. He had left tracks in history. Dropping from his perch, he drew his sidearm and headed for that rise. He had probably done what he had come for by distracting the sniper. The old Dutchman wouldn't die now. That thread of history was salvaged. Jacob Walz didn't die this way in real history—not out here on the sunbaked slope where he had found a fortune. Jacob Walz had lived long enough to commit at least three more murders, one of them his own nephew, Julius. The old man had died in bed, in the town of Phoenix, confessing his crimes but never revealing the exact location of his fabulous mine.

But in saving the old murderer, Logan had opened probability doors to a dozen other paradoxes. If only those Indians would pass by without seeing the time travelers so near them . . . if only he could catch that other jumper over there before he did real damage . . .

Logan raced for the ledge where the figure had emerged. Rounding a jagged boulder, he heard voices ahead—a shout, then several other voices. A gunshot rang out.

Logan skidded around the boulder just in time to see that telltale shimmer of the air that was the mind's interpretation of something beyond conscious grasp—the opening of a multidimensional wormhole in the fabric of time. Just for an instant, the shimmer was there, and the figure in the stones' shadows disappeared into it.

Higher up the slope, a rifle cracked and a bullet whistled above to ricochet off rock somewhere up the mountainside. The angry, unintelligible voice of Jacob Walz drifted down, and in the rock field ahead of Logan, Indians crouched in shelter.

All but one. A young, dark-haired man with a white headwrap lay sprawled among the rocks, dead. Killed by the stranger—the time jumper who had tried to kill the Dutchman. He had been surprised by the Indians and killed one of them, instead.

And TEC Agent Jack Logan felt again that sickening reality that too often faced the policemen of the timestream. By his presence, he had averted a major change in history, but his presence had caused secondary changes. He had left clumsy, new tracks in history.

Maybe that nameless Indian would have died anyway, Logan told himself, even if I hadn't alerted the killer in the rocks. Maybe both Jacob Walz and the Indian would have died, and maybe others, too. But that was too many maybes.

Shaking his head in frustration, Logan touched his "retrieve," the temporal controller at his wrist, and the air around him shimmered and swallowed him up.

### Time Enforcement Commission Headquarters
### Washington, D.C., 2007

"What do you mean, the border is wrong?" Eugene Matuzek demanded, coming around his littered desk to look over Logan's shoulder at the stained United States map hanging on the wall.

"I mean, I changed history," Logan said. "Before I launched, the Arizona and New Mexico southern borders ran due east and west. Lordsburg was a border town, and Tucson was in Mexico. It's changed now."

A few feet away, Dr. Dale Easter, the nominal chief historian of TEC, looked up from a scrolling chronology that occupied two screens of his ChronComp link. "I can see how that happened, if the dead Indian's name was Joseph Moon," he said. "Word had it in 1873 that the Navajos were sending a Pima orator to negotiate for the Apaches, Papagos, Zunis, and some other tribes at the First Statehood Conference. Some kind of Indian alliance, with territorial demands. Joseph Moon never showed up. If he had, though, he might have upset things enough for the Mexican Army to march in and establish protectorate rights to Apacheria. That could have brought about a boundary dispute between the U.S. and Mexico. Maybe the U.S. ceded some territory."

"If you're trying to cheer me up, Easter," Logan growled, "forget it. I left tracks."

"All right," Matuzek snapped, "you left tracks. It happens." As TEC's first and only captain, Matuzek had seen enough of historical paradox to know that there was no end to the twists time travel could take. "The point is, who was that jumper you saw there, and what did he want? Why was anybody trying to kill Jacob Walz, for God's sake?"

Others gathered around now, drawn by the discussion. "Maybe the old man killed somebody's great-grandfather," Bob O'Donnelly offered. "Generational vengeance . . . that's a neat idea."

"Neat, but not likely," Amy Fuller said. As usual, when the third member of TEC's crack history team spoke, all eyes turned toward her—if not to listen, then to look. Privately, among the predominantly male contingent of the world's first time police force, Amy Fuller was considered one of the seven sights worth seeing in this most secret of places. Along with Claire Hemmings, TEC's systems analyst, and two or three of the female agents such as Julie Price, Amy ranked right up there with the timesled and the E-warp dome.

"More likely," she said now, "it's somebody who thinks Walz's fortune could have been put to good use if somebody else had owned it."

"But nobody else ever knew where the mine was," Easter objected. "Walz killed everybody who ever found it."

"There was one he hadn't killed, yet," Amy pointed out. "His nephew, Julius. Check *him* out with ChronComp. Julius was a braggart, an accomplished liar, and an unscrupulous swindler. And when he was sober, he was a talented public speaker. In other words, the perfect politician. Imagine what he might have done to history, with all that wealth behind him."

"If his dear old Uncle Jacob hadn't killed him," Bob O'Donnelly said, nodding.

Matuzek started toward his desk, then glanced up at the big, swirling dome above—the Dome of History, displaying the patterns of eventuality in the timestream. "You can sort it out later," he said. "Right now we've got another ripple." He looked around the squad room and swore audibly. Six field agents on duty at the moment, and only one was available for assignment. Two agents were presenting cases before Timecourt, and the systems analyst, Claire Hemmings, had the other three busy recalibrating vector readouts.

"I guess it's you again, Jack," the captain said. "You up to another sled ride?"

"Sure." Logan shrugged. "I hardly ever sleep, anyway."

The techs had scattered to their monitors, and the historians to their screens. Logan pulled on a blast suit, checked his hardware, and ran his fingers through his thick, dark hair. The techs reading the E-warp adjusted the ripple intensity at 0.4, and tension mounted in the squad room as ThinkTank ran files through ChronComp, trying to match significant events or situations to the Dome's time vector—the exact time of origin of the anomaly slicing into the timestream patterns overhead.

"I've got a match!" Bob O'Donnelly's adolescent-sounding voice echoed across the squad room. "Maybe more than one. Significance ratings uncertain. Track me, please."

"Got you," Amy Fuller said, locking on. She read the screen and brought up cross coordinates. "You're right, there are multiple possibilities. Highest significance attaches to the collision. It's our best probability, according to ChronComp. Some other things happening, too, though. T-time is 9:41 A.M. eastern, on E-warp. That matches to within four minutes. It's a little strange, though. E-warp's target time is *ahead* of ChronComp's event, by maybe three or four minutes. Is that possible?"

"Theoretically, yes," Dale Easter intoned, putting on his professorial voice. "In theory, it could indicate a secondary event that triggered the ripple, before the main event occurred."

Claire Hemmings wandered by, her arms loaded with data discs. "That theory is outmoded," she said. "Secondary events in a temporal continuum don't cause ripples. They *are* the ripple."

"Not if they're primary in the sequence." O'Donnelly grinned. "Primary secondaries can predominate in a sequence of resonant pluralities."

Claire stopped at the door, turned, and pinned the young historian with a no-nonsense glare. "You really *are* strange, aren't you, O'Donnelly!"

"Primary causation only applies to single-source sequences," Amy chipped in. "Let's not assume that preliminary means primary."

"For God's sake!" Matuzek erupted. "Can we get to the point? We have an event with a T-time discrepancy. Why?"

"Maybe you're looking at the wrong event," Claire said, heading for the ChronComp vaults.

"We still have a time and place, and a ripple to match," Amy pointed out. "Whatever is distorting history is doing it there and then. Are we agreed?"

"It's our best shot," Dale Easter agreed.

"Wilco!" O'Donnelly sang out.

The others glanced around at him. "What?"

"Wilco," he repeated, grinning. "You know. Roger? Wilco? A-OK? It's period slang. It means, 'yes, I agree.' "

"Then why not just say so?" Easter snapped. "We're agreed, Captain. The ripple fits the collision of an army bomber with an office building . . . and whatever else was going on there and then."

"Where and when?" Matuzek asked.

"Lower midtown Manhattan," Amy read. "New York City. Vicinity of Fifth Avenue and Thirty-fourth Street. E-warp shows T-time to be 9:41 A.M. Saturday, July twenty-eighth, 1945."

"Give or take a few minutes," Easter corrected. "Chron-

Comp shows a major event, same location, at 9:45—that's when the airplane hit the building."

"Fifth and Thirty-fourth?" Matuzek crowded in to read the screens for himself. "Isn't that the—"

"The Empire State Building." O'Donnelly nodded. "A United States Army B-25 bomber ran into it, and all hell broke loose there."

"What are the other events?"

"Take your pick, Captain." Easter shrugged. "We've got a five-minute slice of daily life in a big city. Two unrelated deaths within a hundred yards or so of these vectors, a deal cut to build three submarines at the Groton Shipyards, a guy on the observation deck threatening to jump, an artist completing a will-be classic in an adjacent building, a diamond collection in security transit . . . it goes on and on, and who knows what ChronComp doesn't have because there's no record?"

"Claire's setting up your speed-brief, Logan," Matuzek said.

Amy Fuller turned, her dark eyes slightly worried as she gazed at the timecop. "This will be a critical-time jump. Fast in, fast out, or you'll be in serious jeopardy."

"That's putting it mildly." Bob O'Donnelly's young face held a very real concern. "Whatever this is about, if you get delayed, you're going to be an eyewitness to a really bad accident."

"Thanks for the assurance," Logan muttered. "And for those really precise leads."

Victor Baker Niner took off from Bedford, Massachusetts, that morning under a high overcast, bound for Newark, New Jersey. It was the final lap of a cross-country transit flight from the Air Corps bomber's home base at Sioux Falls, South Dakota.

Lieutenant Colonel William F. Smith brought the Mitchell B-25 to cruising altitude, came to heading 240 degrees, and trimmed the flaps. Beside him, Staff Sergeant Chris Domitrovich ran a finger down a USAAF chart, and glanced down at the hazy Atlantic coast dwindling to the west. "This'll put us right over Manhattan Island," he said. "Did you see the flyby memo, Skipper? Th' brass says Mayor La Guardia's raisin' hell about flying over his city."

"Beware of stray B-25s," Smith chuckled. "We've had memos like that ever since they snafued that Texas exercise and dropped chalk poppers on some town in Oklahoma."

"Yeah, Boise City." Domitrovich nodded. "I was at Amarillo when they put up that poster: 'Remember the

16

Alamo, remember Pearl Harbor, and for God's sake, remember Boise City.' "

"We'll follow the coast from Montauk Point," Smith
said. "Should be VFR all the way. Hard right at Coney Island, and across the Narrows. ETA at Newark about
0940." He checked his gauges, listened to the thrum of the
two big engines, and eased back in his seat. Visibility was
closing ahead, the cloud ceiling dropping steadily. They'd
have to drop to a lower altitude soon, he decided, to maintain visual.

On the console, a needle spun crazily, then dropped to
the peg. "Note for the flight log," Smith said. "Before this
aircraft flies again, I want that gyrocompass repaired."

### Lower Manhattan
### 8:37 A.M.

It was a gray morning. Thick clouds hung low over
Manhattan, shrouding the tops of the taller buildings.
From the street, less than half of the soaring height of the
Empire State Building could be seen. The rest of it—
everything above the fortieth floor—faded into nothing-
ness, obscured by thick fog and drizzling rain.

Salvatore Mancuso stood in the doorway of his hole-in-
the-wall pastaria, his hands in the pockets of his alpaca
overcoat, which was open in front, exposing his white
apron. He stared sourly out at the street. Dreary weather,
he thought. Everything looks dismal in weather like this.
The low, sullen clouds, the black streaks of mildew on the
buildings, the dull, dirty gleam of wet pavement, they
were all dismal. Dismal and depressing and lonely.

Being Mediterranean by descent, Sal Mancuso loved

crowds. To be Mediterranean and alone is to not exist, his friend Moishe Rubinstein had told him once. Sal could only agree. Yet these days, with all efforts focused on the war, the city seemed a solitary place—especially at a quarter to nine on a Saturday morning.

The only people in sight were rain-soggy women hurrying to their jobs, a few delivery trucks passing on the street, a couple of stray sailors in pea jackets looking for a missing buddy, some leftover drunks down by the alley, and a smattering of civilians in dripping hats and trench coats.

A police car cruised by, turned at Fifth, and then came back, creeping along in first gear. It pulled up across the street, and four uniforms got out, strolling off in both directions to plant themselves in the shelter of recessed entryways. Sal shrugged, disinterested, and stepped out of his doorway. He turned the crank, hearing the rolled awning creak as it disengaged and descended.

Trapped rainwater sagged the striped canvas and sloshed from the ends of the roll, and a little waterfall splattered Sal's head and ran cold down the back of his neck. Muttering, he shuffled aside, then turned to look as heavy tires squished on the pavement behind him. A boxy-looking enclosed vehicle with the inscription ATLAS ARMORED ESCORT SERVICE eased to a stop just across the street. Two brown-uniformed men emerged from its rear hatch and proceeded smartly to the divided glass panels beside the Empire State's revolving doors. Harvey the doorman stood aside to let them pass. Inside the panels, a gray uniform looked the browns over, then unlocked the panels and let them in.

Jewelry, Sal decided. He looked up at the rising tiers of windows above. A section of windows displayed lights behind drawn curtains and a sign in gold script: SUITE 4-B, I. BIRNBAUM, DIAMONDS AND FINE JEWELRY.

Sal started to lower his gaze, then gasped and looked higher. A hundred feet above the ground, a ten-foot section of the Empire State Building seemed to swirl and flow, distorted as though seen through uneven glass. In the distortion a figure emerged, then the distortion was gone but the figure remained—a man with a backpack, dim with fog and distance, standing on a window ledge a hundred feet above Thirty-fourth Street.

Sal stood staring, mute and amazed, as the man strolled casually along the ledge, looking in windows as he passed. He had traversed nearly half of the ledge when he paused, squatted on his heels, and took off his pack. He opened it, took out a small object like a tomato can, and began to paint the windowpane beside him. When the painting was done, the entire pane coated with a pearl-like substance, he replaced the can in the pack and took out a hammer. Methodically, he went from one side to another of the pane, tapping at its top and bottom, then swung a blow at the middle, and the entire pane collapsed inward, leaving a wide, slightly jagged opening.

The man on the ledge picked up his pack, stepped through the gaping window, and disappeared into the shadows beyond.

Just that quickly, it was done, and Sal wasn't quite sure what he had seen . . . or whether he had seen anything at all. He blinked, rubbed his eyes, and looked again.

The paneless window gaped darkly, the glass still gone, but otherwise the day was just as it had been. Out in front, the armored truck idled, its driver drumming his fingers on the steering wheel. Harvey was hovering under the Pirot's awning, lighting a cigarette. Down the street, the uniformed policemen still lurked in their sheltering doorways, and the few people hurrying past didn't seem to have noticed anything out of the ordinary.

"So now what? I'm having hal . . . hallu . . . imagining things?" Sal chided himself. "Got to be the weather."

He turned back to his crank, and abruptly the awning slammed down, full open, cascading a solid sheet of water onto the walk. A tall, athletic-looking man in a dark, close-fitted uniform rolled from its outer edge, clung for an instant, and dropped to the walk, landing in a nimble crouch. The stranger turned full around, as though memorizing the scene around him, then stood and brushed water from his jacket. "Sorry about that," he told Sal. "Bad landing. What time is it?"

Obediently, Sal pulled up his sleeve to look at his Gübelin watch. "Uh . . . it's ten to nine," he said.

The man glanced at an indescribable contrivance on his own wrist and nodded. "Well, that checks, anyway," he said. He looked at the striped awning and at its mountings. "No damage done, I guess."

Sal stared at the holster on the man's belt. "What's that thing?" he demanded. "You gonna perpetra . . . perp . . . you robbin' me, or what? There's cops right over there—"

"I see them," the man said. "I'm a cop, too. Different branch. Name's Logan."

"You here about the break-in across the street, maybe?"

Sal pointed upward, at the paneless window. It was about the eleventh or twelfth floor. "I can't tell you much. The guy was just there, all of a sudden, then he painted the window, then he busted it and went in."

When Sal, prompted by a few questions, had related what he thought he saw across the street, Logan pursed his lips thoughtfully. "I like that overcoat of yours," he said. "What'll you take for it?"

"My—my coat? Buddy, I sell pasta. Linguine, scalloppini, spaghetti, macaroni . . . pasta! You want coats, you go see Robert Hall, four doors down. He sells coats."

Logan pulled out a roll of crisp, new silver certificates. "How much pasta do I buy to get the coat thrown in, *right now?*"

"It's just got to be the weather," Sal told himself, watching as his alpaca overcoat crossed Thirty-fourth Street on the back of a tall, dark-haired young man who carried a gun, bounced off awnings, and looked like no flatfoot Sal had ever seen. "Meteorol . . . met . . . the screwy weather! Just got to be!"

Over at St. Francis, the bells were ringing. It was nine o'clock.

### The Empire State Building
### 9:00 A.M.

The north lobby of the world's tallest office building had one thing in common with most such structures of a century defined as the Age of the Edifice Complex. It was big, austere, and imposing.

It echoed hollowly as Logan strode across the embellished floor. On a normal weekday, there would be at least twenty thousand people in this building, and the lobby would teem with crowds. This was Saturday, though, and fewer than a fourth that number were here.

This was the kind of mission Logan detested—a ripple with no easily defined source. TEC's ThinkTank, probably the best team of analytic historians the world had ever

seen, with the awesome capacity and link resources of
ChronComp at their disposal, usually could pinpoint the
source of a ripple right down to what was done, when it
was done, and who did it. In those cases, the field agent's
job was simple—go to where and when it happened, before it happened, and stop it from happening.

But now he had no clear idea what he was looking for,
and even less how to find it. E-warp never gave clues as to
what caused a historic alteration. The liquid-stasis marvel
simply scanned the timestream, reflecting eventualities as
smooth, swirling patterns displayed in the huge monitor
called the Dome of History. The flow of unaltered history
swirled smoothly there, a weave of iridescent sweeps like
oil on water, and alterations showed as ripples in the
blend. The point of origin of a ripple was T-time, and
T-time on this mission was 9:41 A.M., eastern daylight
time, July 28, 1945. Today!

ChronComp, on the other hand, told too much. The big
dedicated computer with its worldwide web had two
tasks—to collect historical data and to display it on command. ChronComp's report for 9:41 A.M. today, at this
location, was that a lot of occurrences occurred exactly
then . . . followed by a major, unrelated occurrence four
minutes later.

It was a historian's puzzle, and a timecop's nightmare.

Still, he had a starting point, thanks to Salvatore Mancuso. That, and the luck of the Irish. At the nearest bank of
elevators, Logan stepped into a waiting car and smiled at
the girl operator—pinafore, pageboy hair, too much rouge
on a too-young face, and a name badge. "Eleven, please,
Pamela," he said.

"Yes, sir." She closed the cage, tilted the control, and
the lift clattered upward. She glanced at Logan, sizing him

up. Then she looked at him again, more carefully, haircut to boots. "Ah . . . if you wanted the other . . . I mean, the out-of-town gentleman from—well, like you, sir—he wanted to go on up to seventy-eight."

"He did?" Logan raised an eyebrow.

"Yes, sir. I took him down to first, to catch the high bank. Do you want to go to seventy-eight, too? I'll take you back down, if you do."

"Maybe he had the wrong floor. What's on eleven?"

"Oh, insurances and lawyers, mostly. There's a government requisition office there, but they're not open Saturdays. There isn't much of anything on seventy-eight."

"I'll stop on eleven," Logan said. "Then maybe I'll go to seventy-eight." He returned her curious gaze. "Is there anything wrong?"

"Oh! Oh, no, sir. I was just wondering where you get your hair cut. You and the other gentleman."

### 9:18 A.M.

It was no surprise to Logan to find the office door of Paine and Associates, U.S. Requisitions, open. The lock was broken. Thanks to speed-brief, it took only a few minutes to find what he was looking for—a declaration of loss of some $18 million worth of bearer bonds issued by the War Department to expedite several defense-plant contracts. The bonds—as negotiable as cash—were simply gone, and Paine and Associates was disavowing any knowledge of their whereabouts.

Logan's lips thinned in a derisive smile. Count on a war to bring out corruption, he thought. Big chunks of money floating around, and nobody really keeping track.

So somebody walks off with a piece of the pie, and who can find it? All the crook has to do is hide it for a while, and it's just lost money, never recovered.

And where do you hide lost money? Someplace nearby, someplace where nobody will look for it. The smile became a grin. The seventy-eighth floor, for example.

The same elevator took him back to the ground floor, where another car waited at the high banks. A girl who might have been Pamela's cousin smiled at him.

"Seventy-eight," he said.

As the car careened upward, Logan gritted his teeth, controlling his impulse to tell the girl—to tell all of them—to get the hell out of this building, to get as far away as they could. As a policeman, as a human being, every instinct he had screamed at him to evacuate this place, to get everyone out of harm's way.

But as a timecop, he lived by a special rule: Don't make tracks. TEC's mission was to preserve history, not clean it up.

When he stepped out on the seventy-eighth floor, he didn't look back.

When the sounds of the elevator had faded, he listened to the silence. This entire floor of the building was empty—just the elevator bays and a short hall leading to a double door. Beyond the door was the expanse of a big, open area not yet decorated for occupants. There were a few stud walls, but mostly it was just an acre of available floor space being used at the moment for storage.

Soundlessly, Logan moved from cover to cover, from stack to stack of stored maintenance materials, until he saw what he was looking for.

Over by the north wall, between fog-shrouded bare-pane windows, fifty-five-gallon drums marked ESB JANITORIAL were neatly stacked two deep in a double row eight drums wide . . . neatly except for one drum that had been pulled aside and opened. Drawing his weapon, Logan edged around a stud wall, heading for the drums.

Pure reflex noted the little dot of red light that danced across the plaster just beside him, and pure reflex threw him down and back as a bullet shattered the wall right where he had been.

## 9:31 A.M.

Little rain showers dappled a misty, gray world like patterns of white on white. Lieutenant Colonel William Smith squinted into the mist beyond his cabin, then leaned forward to tap his compass with a knuckle. The needle bobbed, shivered, and settled back on its peg. "Deader'n last Sunday's fried chicken," he muttered. "What have we got here, Chris? A fog bank?"

"Looks like it," Domitrovich said. "It comes and goes. I can still see the islands, all right, but I can't tell whether it's Jones Beach or Long Beach. The bay's fogged over, but there's land beyond it. I see terrain."

"Okay," Smith said. "We'll have to do this by the seat of our pants. Find New York Harbor, and we can step-stone from there."

"I don't know what New York Harbor looks like," Domitrovich confessed. "I never flew over it before."

"Look for the Statue of Liberty," Smith said. "Or maybe you can see the Empire State Building. That's the biggest thing around."

"We haven't got but about a mile visibility," Domitrovich cautioned. "Little clearer down under this stuff."

"Well, at least look for some wide water inland of the beach. I'm dropping to eight hundred feet, see if I can get us below these clouds."

"Wide water?" Domitrovich glanced around.

"More than a mile wide," Smith explained. "Let me know when you see it."

"Roger." Domitrovich studied his chart, comparing its ink lines to the dim, misty realities below the B-25's right wing. It was really hard to be certain of anything in sporadic fog like this.

He squinted, peering out across the leading edge of the big wing, trying to see through the haze beyond. "That may be it, Bill," he said. "Wide water at two o'clock. Looks like the shoreline turns north."

"Time's about right," Smith decided. "Keep an eye open for landmarks now, we're heading for Jersey."

Victor Baker Niner slanted its wings and swung right, coming north over the Grass Hassock Channel, heading for Howard Beach, Queens, and Manhattan Island. In the haze, with cloud ceiling lowering above and misting rain below, Atlantic Beach and Jamaica Bay *did* look a little like the contours of Coney Island and Lower New York Bay, from the cockpit of a B-25.

### 9:37 A.M.

Another gunshot sounded, and running feet echoed hollowly through the cavernous acre of the building's seventy-eighth floor. Logan dived across an open area, scuttled around the stacked drums, and crouched, listening. That was no 1940s weapon, firing at him. The distinctive ping of a blowback action said it was a weapon of his own time.

Scurrying along the row of drums, he found the opened one and glanced inside. It was empty. But he knew what it had held. Eighteen million dollars in stolen War Department bearer bonds, carefully embezzled by someone in the chain of politics, industry contracts, and wartime demand, had been hidden there. Lost money, never found. Now the treasure that was lost was truly gone.

Logan saw a shadow move fifty feet away, and aimed his gun. "You are in violation of Timelaw I!" he shouted. "Put down your gun and step out—"

The laser dot winked and he ducked as a shot punctured a floor-wax drum to his left. Logan rolled, came up two yards away, and fired as the shadow ducked behind a wall. Plaster rattled across the floor beyond, and footsteps echoed through the din. Logan raced across to a stud upright, pivoted, and fired again. Another miss, but for an instant he glimpsed the time traveler—a tall, lean man carrying a small suitcase.

The man disappeared from sight, and Logan ran to intercept him. He skidded around a wall section, his gun leveled . . . but there was no one there. The time jumper had doubled back. Logan heard an elevator door opening, as though forced.

He ran toward the nearest elevator tower and heard the door slam closed. Rounding the corner, he glanced upward at the floor indicators above the three shafts. One was at eighty-four, the others at ground level.

He turned and hit the floor as a shot from the south wall sang through the nearest elevator door. Rolling and aiming, he saw the man over by the south wall, silhouetted by the pale light of fog-shrouded windows. The suitcase he had carried was gone. The tall figure ducked behind stacked cases, then appeared again, zigzagging toward a plumbing chute.

Logan fired and a window dissolved into shards, letting in the mist. While his shot still echoed, he headed for the plumbing chute. The lazy mist rolled through the broken window, and suddenly there was a man there, firing point-blank. Logan felt the impact of the bullet, like a massive fist against his chest, and tumbled backward, sprawling.

## 9:40 A.M.

In the tower at La Guardia Airport, the radio came to life. "La Guardia Control," the voice said. "This is USAAF Victor Baker Niner, requesting weather to Newark."

Tim Canby bent to the mike, his eyes on the radar scan. "Victor Baker Niner, you have La Guardia Control," he said. "What is your position?"

"Victor Baker Niner," the squawk said, "La Guardia, I am estimated fifteen miles southeast of you, repeat, estimated fifteen southeast, on VFR with poor visibility. Request present weather Newark Airport."

"Roger, Victor Baker Niner," Canby droned. "Newark ceiling six hundred feet, visibility one to two miles. Suggest you land at La Guardia, repeat, Newark ceiling six-zero-zero, strongly urge you land La Guardia."

There was a pause, then "Negative, La Guardia. Victor Baker Niner proceeding to Newark, on flight plan. Can you confirm my position?"

"Negative . . . negative. We do not, repeat, *do not* have you in sight."

"La Guardia Tower, request you maintain scan, advise if you see us."

"Roger, Victor Baker Niner," Canby said. "Good luck."

### 9:41:30 A.M.

Stunned by the impact of the shot, Logan lay motionless, staring at the unfinished ceiling of the Empire State Building's seventy-eighth floor. His chest throbbed and his ears rang. Then a tall figure was standing over him, holding a laser-sighted pistol with a snub muffler like none Logan had ever seen.

"I knew there was someone after me," the man said casually. "Another time-tracker. What are you, a bounty hunter?"

Logan didn't move. Only his eyes showed life.

"Well, I have to admit," the man said, "you were good—finding me here like this. Very good! Or very lucky." Pale, cold eyes shadowed beneath a jutting brow bored into Logan, and the man smiled thinly, his gun steadying. "Or maybe you're after the same thing I am. You're not the first, but you got closest. But I guess you know, now. You bought into the wrong game, when you tracked me. Because now you're dead."

### 9:42 A.M.

"Victor Baker Niner!" Flight Controller Tim Canby said into his microphone. "La Guardia Tower to USAAF Victor Baker Niner! Do you read?"

"Victor Baker Niner," the squawk responded. "Loud and clear, La Guardia."

"Victor Baker Niner, we have you on triangulation. Your position is three to six miles east, repeat, three to six miles *east* of us. Your position is not, repeat, *not* as estimated, Victor Baker Niner. Strongly advise you come to course 270 for La Guardia landing pattern. You're almost on top of us right now!"

"Negative on that, La Guardia. Correcting for Newark. Thank you. This is Victor Baker Niner out."

I hope you've been living right, fellow, Canby thought as he flipped the mike off. Maybe you can see where you're going, but from here we can't even see the top of the Empire State.

### 9:42:15 A.M.

Logan lay unmoving as the laser-equipped pistol steadied for a killing shot. His vest had stopped the one that hit him, but it wouldn't stop the next one. At this range, barely an arm's length, the man would aim for the head.

He saw the laser wink on, saw the little glow of red brighten as it aligned, and saw the fingers tighten on the grip. As the beam crossed his eye, Logan seemed to explode. He twisted aside, felt the sting of shards as the bullet hit the floor next to his ear, and levered upward, doubling and uncoiling with both feet.

The force of the attack doubled the man over and flung him backward, staggering, toward the south windows. Before he could catch his balance, Logan hit him with a rolling body block at the knees, and the man thumped against a fog-white pane.

Logan sprang up, crouched, and caught the time jumper with his shoulder, just as the man rebounded. This time, when he hit the window, it shattered around him, and he teetered at the edge of the frame. Logan dived for him, but the man sidestepped—aside and out. Nine hundred feet above the pavement of Fifth Avenue, the time jumper toppled from the window. Around him, fog swirled and coalesced as a wormhole in time opened to receive him.

At the broken sill, Logan clenched his teeth. "Missed!" he muttered. Whenever the traveler came from—somewhere in the future, probably Logan's own time of 2007—he was back there now, out of TEC's reach. But he had gone back empty handed.

Logan got to his feet, glanced at the time, and scowled. There was less than a minute remaining. Somewhere in this building was a suitcase containing $18 million in bearer bonds—money lost in history. And in just a few seconds all hell was going to break loose.

### 9:44 A.M.

Lieutenant Colonel William Smith realized too late the mistake they had made. His turn to the north hadn't been over New York Harbor, but ten miles short of there. He was flying over the city, not the bay, and dropping to eight hundred feet for visibility was the worst thing he could have done.

The instant he saw buildings below him, he tried to correct—to climb and to turn. But it was too late. Just as the B-25 banked to turn, a monstrous silhouette loomed dead ahead in the fog. Smith hauled at the yoke, heard Domitrovich yell, "Oh, sweet Jesus!" and the bomber plunged directly into the south wall of the Empire State Building at its seventy-eighth and seventy-ninth floors.

Inside the building, Logan saw the aircraft loom out of the fog, almost dead-on, and triggered his retrieval bracelet. The air around him shimmered, seemed to flow, and was swept away by a rolling wall of flame and debris. The shock of impact, like an earthquake rippling across the city, was felt as far away as Wall Street and Central Park South.

## TEC Headquarters
## 2007

Between huge armatures at the far extreme of a half-mile tunnel housed in one of the world's most secret locations— the Time Enforcement Commission complex in Washington, D.C.—massive energies writhed and mingled, extending dimensions into other dimensions to create a momentary gate between reasoned reality and the fourth-dimensional continuity of the timestream. In Kleindastian theory, from which time travel had evolved, the gate had been there all along, an unfinished cycle now completed with retrieval of the original launch.

In the swirl of iridescence between the armatures a rocket sled sprang into existence, hurtling backward at more than 2,994 feet per second, decelerating from near Mach 12. The sled settled to a halt beside the launch bay ramps, and Jack Logan slid back its hatch and climbed out, stiffly.

He was scorched and smoke-smudged, singed and bruised, and he cursed quietly to himself as he straightened and turned toward the bay doors . . . and stopped.

Claire Hemmings stood there, blocking his path and

gazing up at him with disapproving eyes. She was flanked by two techs with test trays. "Logan, you look like hell," she said. "Get that armor off and make a fist. I need a blood sample."

Glaring at the systems analyst, Logan stripped off his overcoat and blast suit, removed his uniform jacket, and held out his left arm. One of the techs drew blood with a vibro syringe, while the other measured his pulse, body temperature, and blood pressure.

Claire examined his scorched blast suit and what was left of the overcoat. Her pretty nose wrinkled in disgust. "What did you do, wait till the last second to activate retrieve?" To the nearest tech, she said, "Operations note: Consider stress-activated retrieval backup . . . automated fail-safe for agents displaying impaired judgment."

*"Impaired judgment?"* Logan stared at her. "I had forty-five seconds to search for eighteen million dollars that was about to be blown to kingdom come! I used all forty-five seconds! You call that impaired judgment?"

"Did you find the eighteen million dollars?"

"No."

She arched a smug brow and changed the subject. "Respiration rate acceptable. Any symptoms of excessive stress?"

"Not till I got here," he growled.

She glanced again at the burned overcoat. "What was this? Alpaca?" Laying it aside, she prodded at the gaping puncture in his vest. "Nine millimeter or larger," she noted. She probed the puncture with her memcorder stylus and removed a flattened slug. "How does this feel?" she asked. Doubling her fist, she punched him in the chest, just where the bullet had hit. Logan winced and stepped back.

"Moderate trauma at point of impact," Claire noted.

"We'd better take a look at the rigidity of our flakwear." She handed Logan his blast suit and jacket and turned away. "They're waiting for you in debrief," she said. "Better get a move on."

"Fourteen people dead," Jack Logan repeated, drumming his fingers on the tabletop in the briefing room. "Fourteen!"

"Correct," Dale Easter confirmed. "The pilot and co-pilot, of course, and a sailor hitching a ride on the plane. The rest were civilians."

"One of the plane's engines went all the way through the building," Bob O'Donnelly noted. "It punched out the north wall and fell on top of a twelve-story building next door. The other engine went into an elevator shaft and wound up in the subbasement."

Amy Fuller glanced at the moody Logan. "No one named Pamela died," she said.

"No, but some others just like her did."

"The point is," Captain Eugene Matuzek said, "who was the jumper you tangled with? What was he there for?"

"I'll include a description of him in my file report," Logan said. "I have a hunch it was the same man I saw in Arizona, and this time I got a good look at him. He looks a little like the secretary of state. As to what he was after—obviously, eighteen million dollars in bearer bonds. That's 1945 dollars. God only knows what those bonds would be worth now."

"God and ChronComp," Dale Easter muttered. "Sixty-two years at a conservative average of 10 percent annual growth . . . that's approximately three-point-nine billion dollars. Triple that, for inflation, it's eleven-point-seven billion dollars. My own investments may be going to hell lately, but I can still do an economic equation."

Matuzek whistled. "Nearly twelve *billion* dollars . . . from eighteen million? God, no wonder the rich get richer."

"A billion here, a billion there," Bob O'Donnelly quipped, "and pretty soon you're talking about real money. Everett Dirksen said that, in the 1960s. At any rate, Logan, you stopped the perp. The ripple is gone. He didn't get what he was after."

"I didn't make my collar, either. And he mentioned 'others' who had tracked him." He nodded toward the bustling squad room beyond the glass partitions of the briefing room. "Do any of the AMITs connect with anything resembling this guy's MO? Or any deaths unaccounted for?"

All of them glanced at the somber AMIT display near the main eventuality banks. Agents missing in time. There were a lot of names on that list—too many for comfort. "Not so far," Matuzek said. "We've got techs running comparisons to see what they can find. AMITs are always open files, so it shouldn't take long. I'll send inquiries to the Europeans and Australians, too, to see if they're missing anybody."

Claire Hemmings had come in from the squad room, carrying her memcorder as usual. Since the blond woman's assignment to TEC Central from S and R, there had been numerous wagers as to whether the petite blonde slept with her memcorder. No one, so far, had claimed any winnings.

"Well, Logan, this one sounds better than your last launch," she offered now. "At least this time you didn't mention any ripples of your own. Last time out, you changed the boundary between the U.S. and Mexico."

Logan turned half-around in his chair, frowning. "Hemmings, do you go out of your way to be irritating, or does it just come naturally?"

"I'm serious," she said. "How do you know you didn't alter history this time? Have you done an anomaly scan? Maybe Montana is in Canada now, or something."

"Button it, you two!" Matuzek snapped. "What about your perp, Logan? You said he looked like the secretary of state?"

"Just a handy, random comparison." Logan stifled his temper to get back to the routine of debriefing. "The perp was tall, six one or two; indeterminate age, maybe thirty to thirty-five; spare build, not skinny but lean. Prominent nose and ears, heavy brow, deep-set eyes, pale . . . blue or gray. If you picture the secretary of state, this guy could be a cousin or something. I'm just exemplifying. He wasn't Walter Scofield."

Matuzek stared at him, mystified. Easter and O'Donnelly glanced at each other, both tapping notes into their consoles. "Scofield?" Amy blurted. "Who's Scofield? The secretary of state is a pudgy little man named George Ryland."

"You've done it again, Logan," Claire drawled. "You erased a ripple, and changed history in the process."

"He *did* describe the Beacon Hill Scofields, though," Easter noted. "Reclusive bunch, but I've seen snaps of a couple of them. Ninth wealthiest family in the world, according to September's *Midas Touch*. A modern 'golden dynasty.' I don't know any Walter, but he'd be third or fourth generation. And they do all look a little alike. The nose, ears, pale eyes . . . there's a look to the Scofields. A family resemblance."

"I want an anomaly scan, Jack," Matuzek ordered. "Current events, geography, recent history . . . the whole works. If that event changed one element of history, it probably changed others."

"That event *couldn't* have changed history," Logan stated. "I was there. The perp didn't get what he went for, and I didn't leave any tracks. The lost bonds were already lost before that event. And they're still lost. Nothing changed! So how could things be different now?"

"Maybe you're looking at the wrong event," Claire suggested.

Matuzek closed his notepad with a thump. "Anomaly scan, Jack. I want it by this time tomorrow. Hemmings can help you with it."

Bob O'Donnelly and Amy Fuller shot surprised glances at the captain of the Time Enforcement Commission, then worried glances at each other. Logan and Hemmings? Working together? The two were flint and steel. Sparks flew every time they met. The prevalent theory around the squad room was that Claire Hemmings—the ultimate scientist in addition to her obvious natural attributes—despised Jack Logan for his unscientific, intuitive approach to problems, and that Logan resented Hemmings because she reminded him too much of someone he had loved and lost.

Whatever the reasons, Logan and Hemmings—the field cop and the systems analyst—were about as likely to get along together as a mongoose and a cobra.

"Great!" Logan said to Matuzek now, cutting a glare toward Claire. "Well, lots of luck, Gene. My duty shift ended three hours ago. I'm going home."

Claire returned his glare for an instant, then put on a serene smile. "That will work out just fine," she said. "The primitive comforts of the home cave. We'll just work on this in your lair, Conan. Maybe you'll think better there."

"Seal visuals," Logan told his private car when he and Claire Hemmings were settled inside it. "Full autopilot. Destination, home."

"Confirm destination home," the car's electronic voice said sweetly. "ETA forty-six minutes. Sealing." Obediently, metal louvers slid into place over all the windows, and the car came to life, its main computer setting a course out of the garage and onto the ramp that led out of the TEC complex to the streets of D.C.

"You're a trusting soul, aren't you?" Claire said, indicating the sealed windows. "Are you afraid of snipers, or of somebody finding out where you live?"

"Old habit." Logan shrugged. "I don't want either of those to happen. Can we get on with the anomaly scan?"

"Right." She opened her memcorder and accessed the working files. "We just finished the Ops Center. Negative alterations. And I take it there's nothing different about your car. The logical next step is your observations of a familiar route of travel. How about you open your windows and look around, and I'll promise not to notice where we are?"

With a barely audible growl, Logan touched a stud and told the car, "Cancel seals. Full visibility."

The louvers slid away, revealing the panorama of the Eisenhower Expressway, flanked on the left by MacArthur Boulevard and on the right by the Potomac River. "Where do you live?" Claire asked, looking around, "Arlington?"

"Georgetown," he said. "What happened to promises

and privacy?" Before she could answer, though, he pointed. "Anomaly at one o'clock. The Jefferson Bridge has six lanes."

"Of course, it does." Claire nodded. "So?"

"So it had eight lanes, in the reality I remember."

She muttered a note into her memcorder. "Okay, keep looking."

"I'm looking," he sighed. "That skyline across the river—maybe it's a little different. Couple of towers there that I don't recall, and maybe there used to be more trees. I think there were."

*"Maybe,"* Claire sneered. "Two maybes and one 'I think'? How about some specifics, Logan?"

"You want specifics? Okay. All the transit buses are different now. They used to be pearly white with pink spots. They had tail fins, and they were pulled by teams of water buffalo—"

"Come on, Logan! You think this is a game? You may be enjoying it, but I'm not. I canceled twelve hours' worth of private plans, to come along and help you with this analysis!"

"I thought you just wanted to get into my private quarters."

"Don't hold your breath!" she snapped. "And don't get any wrong ideas about me going to your place with you, either. I'd as soon crawl into a cave with Og the Primate! This is strictly business."

He turned from the window to gaze at her. "Of course, it is. What brought that up?"

"You did, and you might as well understand one thing. I'm a scientist, Logan. First and foremost, I deal with temporal theory and timetravel subsystems. I'm also an expert in process systems and operations, and a TEC Academy graduate. What I do on my own time is my own business, Agent Logan. What I'm doing now is my job, and you're just part of it."

The sardonic expression on Logan's face was almost a smile . . . but not quite. "Good for you," he drawled. "I imagine it does wonders for your social life, giving that little speech to every guy you meet."

Her cheeks reddened slightly, and she turned away. "All right. I just don't want you to get any unrealistic ideas, and be let down. It might bruise that tender ego of yours."

"Let down . . ." Logan murmured the words, as though turning them this way and that for inspection. Then his eyes narrowed. "That's it! The elevator shaft!"

"What?" She blinked. "What elevator shaft?"

"In the Empire State Building! The time jumper *did* get what he went for. And he didn't lose it, he dropped it down an elevator shaft. He knew right where it was, and that it would be safe because a fallen elevator would be resting on it. He simply went back and got it later." He reached for the car's reprogram stud. "Forget the anomaly scan, Hemmings. We're going back to TEC." To the car he said, "Destination correction. Cancel home. Destination TEC."

Before the vehicle's computer voice could respond, Claire reached across Logan and hit the button. "Countermand!" she ordered. "Phase six override, code L-two-M-nine-dot-three-dot! Resume original destination! Confirm!"

"Override accepted," the car's cheerful voice announced. "Original destination resumed. ETA twenty-one minutes."

"How the hell did you do that?" Logan demanded. "This is my private car, programmed to me, personally!"

"Gen-Em Trace, model A-III, with a 2850 CT master

control. It's stock coded and I know the code. I already told you, I'm an expert." Her eyes taunted him, her stubborn little chin was high, and her tight smile smug. "You can transmit your inspiration to TEC by phone. Your day sheet says you've made three launches in two days, the last two back-to-back, and you probably haven't slept in four days. The blood tests I drew confirm borderline exhaustion. You're running on adrenaline, Logan. So we're going to your place, and you're going to complete this anomaly scan and get some sleep. Consider that an order."

"You don't give me orders!" Logan snapped. "I'm a senior agent and you're a systems analyst!"

"Precisely." Claire shrugged. "You want to verify my authority, Logan? My assignment is to maintain optimum performance in all TEC operating systems. As a field agent, you're just another operating system."

### The Mississippi River, above St. Louis
### August 19, 1856

Great side-wheels turned tirelessly in the evening light, churning muddy water as the steamboat *Delta Belle* made its way northward under smoking stacks. Far out to the east, little wooded islands lined a floodplain shore where little patches of farmland lay scattered here and there in darkening forest. On the west bank, somewhat nearer, high bluffs hid the setting sun. But Phil Nash wasn't interested in the scenery right now. He was interested in the crates stacked on the boat's open stern deck, and on anyone who approached them.

*Delta Belle*'s manifest had the crates listed as farm tools, shipped from New Orleans for the new settlers in Minnesota. But the watchful gang of toughs hanging around those crates suggested otherwise. Whatever was going to happen would happen soon.

Phil Nash—elegant in spat breeches, Prince Albert coat, ruffled shirt, and cravat—pushed back his wide, planter-style hat and set a booted foot on the whitewashed fender rail, pretending to gaze out across the rolling river. St. Louis was behind him, downstream and out of sight, and Hannibal was still fifty miles ahead. Along here, above the juncture with the Illinois, the great river was a wide highway through a wilderness barely touched by civilization.

Somewhere along here, probably within the next ten miles, was the last shoreline that would echo to the thrum of *Delta Belle*'s big wood-burning steam engines.

Phil Nash was no rookie. He was a two-year veteran with the Time Enforcement Commission. A former Texas Ranger, he had been one of five selected from a 2004 list of more than a hundred candidates—none of whom knew they were being evaluated—and recruited personally by Captain Eugene Matuzek into the ranks of the world's most secret agency, the time police.

On graduation from TEC Academy, Nash had joined the best of the best—a full-fledged timecop.

He had made more than a hundred time launches, with an 87 percent capture record. He had worked with both EuroTEC and AusTEC—the other two time-policing agencies, both precinct affiliates of TEC. Smaller than TEC, the European consortium directed by Jean-Luc Poulon and the Australian force led by Captain Dudley Wilkins were nonetheless highly professional agencies. Unlike TEC-US, they had no launch facilities of their own, but worked as adjuncts to temporal research agencies known as Timetrust and Pastime, which did. It was from Poulon himself—a former *Sûreté* official—that Nash learned the art of intuitive surveillance.

At the age of forty-two, Phil Nash was one of the top time policemen in the world. But this mission bothered him. It seemed to have no substance, beyond a small E-warp ripple. It was pure surveillance, any way you cut it, but ThinkTank had not been able to come up with anything more precise than an event—the explosion and sinking of the side-wheel steamer *Delta Belle*. The Dome of History showed a level 0.02 ripple centered at 8:09 P.M., August 19, 1856, and this was the only incident Chron-Comp had that matched it closely. The exact time of the *Belle*'s destruction wasn't known, but it was sometime shortly after eight in the evening. A tragic event, but hardly one worth altering history over . . . unless there was a lot more to it than that.

Thus Phil Nash became a passenger on an antebellum Mississippi riverboat, without the vaguest idea what to look for except that someone was doing something to jiggle the probability chain, and it would probably happen here.

He was sure it had something to do with those crates of tools on the stern deck. Thanks to the sublimator and its speed-brief capabilities, and to the training of Poulon, Nash had a hunch what was in those crates, besides farm tools. Almost a year ago—in late 1855—a consignment of U.S. Mint gold certificates had disappeared in transit to New Orleans. There was suspicion that the consignment had been diverted by French Arcadians in Louisiana to fund a coup in Montreal. But the currency had never been recovered and was written off as lost.

Nash had a hunch, watching the crates bound for Minnesota, that he knew where the gold certificates were.

Among Mississippi riverboats, *Belle* was only a small steamer. Her complement, Nash estimated, was about eighty people, including a crew of nine. In the past two days he had familiarized himself with all of them, from captain and pilot right down to the deckhands, from gentry strolling the promenade decks to the smattering of "penny passengers" who used the steamer as transit between St. Louis and Hannibal.

Now he simply watched the cargo, waiting for either a situation or an inspiration, whichever came first, and wondering just when the big boilers amidships would blow.

A string of laden keelboats floated past, far out toward the eastern shore. The commerce of the river, Nash mused. Grains, furs, lumber, and farm produce moved southward on keelboats that were, themselves, part of their own cargo. At St. Louis or Natchez or New Orleans the boats would be broken up for building materials, while tools, supplies, and cash traveled northward on steamers to go into new loads of grain, furs, and goods.

The keels were dwindling downstream in the dusk as a solitary flatboat hove into sight upstream, gliding downriver on the current—a small craft hardly more than a raft with a cabin. Nash watched as it neared. He could see only one figure on deck—a tall, ragged man at the tiller.

*Delta Belle*'s steam whistles shrilled, and the big boat lurched slightly as its side-wheel paddles hesitated. Bright plumes of fire gushed from its high stacks, and a deep rumbling began somewhere amidships. Nash gripped the promenade rail and braced himself.

The rumbling grew, became a roar, and people ran past him—panicky people shouting and scurrying along the decks, most of them heading for the high bow of the ship. The explosion, when it came, was a rending, grinding shrill that began amidships and rocked the ship violently, then literally tore it in half as huge clouds of steam and released vapor shot out through both sides of the hull, tearing away the planking and destroying the keel.

The stern section, where Nash clung to shadowed rails, bucked and slewed violently, then seemed to settle. Through the smoke and steam he saw the bow section drifting away, a broken, misshapen thing with people clinging to it everywhere. All around, the water teemed with debris, flotsam, and thrashing people trying to find something to cling to.

It was unbelievably quick. By the time Nash got his feet under him, it seemed, the litter of wreckage was floating away downstream, followed by *Belle*'s bow section. Just across from him, on the opposite side of the stern superstructure, a dozen or so men and two or three women hacked loose the cables of a slung lifeboat. It smacked into the flowing water below, and they jumped for it. Some made it to the boat and some didn't, but it didn't matter. Within seconds, the boat rolled, capsized, and sank, borne down by the weight of its davit tackle.

Alone on the sinking stern, Phil Nash fought clear of a tangle of debris and climbed, gasping, to the highest point he could reach—a shattered portion of the upper deck. He heard strange, scuffing sounds, and crawled to the rear edge of the bobbing platform. Just below, the man with the flatboat had slung grapples onto the steamer's rear deck and climbed aboard. He had an ax and was methodically taking apart crates of farm tools.

Two of the crates lay open, and as Nash saw him, the slatted sides of a third collapsed. The man stooped, peered at the implements inside, and hauled out a bulky carpetbag. He carried it to the rail and heaved it over, onto his flatboat.

Nash drew his gun and stood. "Hold it right there!" he shouted. "That's—"

The tall, ragged figure straightened and turned. Nash never saw where the man's gun came from, only the wink of a laser sight and the blossom of flame at its snout. He felt the instant of impact, like a sledgehammer, as the bullet smashed into his forehead, then he didn't feel anything anymore.

The tall man came up to the wreckage where the timecop lay. He looked the body over curiously, found the dead agent's gun and examined it, then dropped it into a pocket. He searched the corpse, finding no identification except a wristband fitted with a microminiature electronic device whose configurations he recognized. It was a temporal retrieval unit. He compared it to his own retrieve, then threw it into the river. Finally he turned, made his way back to the stern rail and from there to the flatboat.

As the last piece of *Delta Belle* settled into the great river that was its grave—and Phil Nash's—the flatboat floated on downstream. But now there was no one aboard. The man and everything he carried, including the bulging carpetbag, were gone.

# IV

## Georgetown
## 2007

"You don't like me very much, do you?" Claire Hemmings called, stooping to peer into Jack Logan's old-fashioned refrigerator. She wrinkled her nose in disgust at what she found there.

Logan's voice came from a closed door beyond a large packing box stamped—upside down—FURNITURE ... THIS END UP. "What?" It was a loud mumble. He was brushing his teeth.

Claire closed the refrigerator and looked into a couple of cabinets flanking the vent hood of an old cooking grill. "I said," she shouted, "who does your grocery shopping? Fred Flintstone?"

"Bacon and toast will be fine for me," he called. "Check the refrigerator."

Claire shook her head, looking around at the loft apartment that was Jack Logan's temporary home. "This is a disaster area," she muttered. The apartment looked more like a storage space than somebody's home. Most of the furniture and fixtures were in unopened packing boxes stacked here and there. A few mismatched dishes sat on a drainboard by the sink, and a table with one chair occupied the living space among the crates.

A bow-tension exerciser and a free-weight pressing bench shared floor space with a multicom console and an old-fashioned stereo system. Logan's "bedroom ensemble" consisted of a hard cot and a hanging rack. There was a closet in that room, but it was empty. The man apparently lived out of packing boxes.

Not a curtain or drape anywhere, not a picture on the wall, no personal touches of any kind except a few books strewn here and there. The only tidy area in the three-room flat was the couch where Claire had slept the night.

She knew from his file that this was only temporary quarters. The building where he had lived before had been destroyed by a bomb, and he would probably find a new place. Still, he had lived here for months. She sighed in disgust, wondering whether TEC's number one field agent didn't know how to decorate an apartment, or simply didn't care.

She opened the refrigerator again, looking for bacon and bread, and maybe some eggs. It wasn't an impoverished refrigerator. There was food there—frozen steaks, frozen ground beef, frozen bacon, canned biscuits, and six containers of freeze-dried potatoes in the vegetable bin— but the only eggs were powdered, and the only thing even slightly green was the mold on the stale bread.

There was real ground coffee, though, and a brewer. By the time Logan finished shaving and appeared in a clean, tailored TEC uniform, Claire was eating her breakfast. "There's yours." She pointed at the multiwave. "Bacon and biscuits. No toast. I don't need a penicillin reaction. How'd you sleep?"

He glanced at the couch. "Alone, apparently." He filled

a plate from the multiwave, found a fork, and sat on a packing box. "Thank you."

"I filed the anomaly scan with ChronComp," she said. "They don't have anything yet on your stashed-treasure theory, but ThinkTank is working on it."

"It's more than a theory," he said. "I know that's what happened. The guy went after a lost treasure. He found it, and stashed it where it would be safe. Then he went back and got it."

"When?"

"During the repairs on the Empire State, I'd guess. He picked his time, then went back to collect it. The same guy located the old Lost Dutchman mine, and I'd bet he went back later and cleaned it out. It's what he does. He's a treasure hunter. What I can't figure out is why the Dome isn't registering ripples. Here's somebody cruising around in history, looting legendary treasures, and E-warp doesn't seem to notice it."

"There were ripples," Claire corrected him. "You were there at both of those events. You launched because of ripples."

"Minor ripples," he pointed out. "History distorted by some slight thing he did, not by the money he took. That's the big question. *Why?*"

"Maybe," she suggested, "we're looking at the wrong events."

Logan gazed at the woman, his eyes narrowing. "That's the third time you've said that, Hemmings. What do you mean, 'wrong events'?"

"Well, I'm not sure," she said. "It gets into alternate probability theory, the idea of widely spaced cause and effect in a single historic modification . . ."

Somewhere in the cluttered apartment an alert chirped,

and Logan picked up a handset. TEC had its own directed-beam satellite band—a narrow range of dedicated channels on the National Science Agency black-ops system. The system was rarely used, except in times of urgency.

Logan keyed in, listened for a moment, and put the handset down. He crossed the room, set the apartment's master controls on standby, and collected his gun belt and jacket.

"Let's roll," he said. "That was Matuzek. Phil Nash isn't missing in time anymore. ChronComp has located his skull . . . in a museum at the University of Missouri. The bullet that killed him matches the one you took out of my flak vest."

## TEC Headquarters

The squad room was a hive of furious activity when Logan pushed through the scramble entrance, with Claire Hemmings scurrying behind him. The confirmed death of a TEC officer, in the line of duty, was an automatic full-alert situation. Every available agent, tech, and tanker was at the station and busy. Matuzek paced among them, directing operations.

Spotting the latest arrivals, the captain waved them toward the briefing room and followed them in. "You got the message," he said. "It's Phil Nash. You know the background?"

"I know he was sent on a surveillance and never came back," Logan said. "What happened?"

"Don't know, yet." Matuzek motioned them to chairs and clicked a remote. The main wall screen came to life. The image was slightly distorted, its colors not quite balanced, like an old-fashioned camcorder tape, but the picture was clear—a pudgy man with thick eyeglasses, holding a bleached-out human skull and talking to a camera. A credit in the lower right corner of the screen identified the speaker as James McGrath, a professor of history, and the date and place, Hull Auditorium, University of Missouri, December 4, 1996.

". . . found in a dig near New Madrid," the man was saying. "Associated artifacts suggest that he died between 1845 and the beginning of the war between the states in 1860. There is conjecture that he may have been aboard the *Delta Belle* when it exploded, yet the apparent cause of death—this hole above the left eye—is a bullet wound.

"The oddities are several," the speaker continued, as though lecturing to a class. "First, there is the bullet." The view panned to a tabletop beside him and zoomed in on a gray-green mushroom shape inside a little glass dome. "This was recovered from this skull. It is a hot-molded bullet of modern design, 0.3573 inch in diameter at the base, copper-cased lead. In short, a nine-millimeter projectile similar to those used today. No such bullet is known to have existed in the middle nineteenth century."

"The bullet matches the one Claire pulled out of your flak vest," Matuzek told Logan. "Same rifling pattern, same odd afterburn on the base. NSA's been testing a double-thrust magnum charge that does it, but it hasn't been marketed for handgun loads yet."

The camera panned back, for a shaky closeup of the skull and the speaker's hands. "Please notice the teeth," the voice said. "This gentleman was approximately thirty-five years of age—"

"Phil was forty-two," Logan muttered.

"—yet the teeth appear to be perfect. Examination has revealed that he had some dental work done, but the dentistry involved procedures unknown at the time of his death . . . or, for that matter, a hundred years later . . ."

Matuzek clicked off the screen. "It's Agent Nash," he said. "ChronComp came across this data in a routine scan of library sources, and matched it to Nash's dental records."

"ChronComp has had this since 1996?" Claire asked.

"No, only for a few months." Matuzek looked from one to the other of them. "ChronComp's data entry exactly matches the time of Nash's disappearance."

"Then we have a fix." Logan stood, glancing over his shoulder at the entrance to the launch bays, beyond the squad room. "I want to do the recon, Gene. Maybe I can—"

"Can what?" Matuzek's level gaze was a negation. "You can't undo this, Jack. It's too late. You know that. The anachronism has blended. It's part of the fabric of history."

A rumble of deep thunder grew and crescendoed, more felt than heard through the soundproofing of the huge complex. Beyond the launch bays, tachyon-drive boosters roared as the timesled hurtled down its track and into the oblivion of fourth-dimensional flow.

"Besides," the captain added, "I've already sent recon. Julie Price went. She never knew Phil Nash, so she won't relate to that time like someone who did. Minimum likelihood she'll jeopardize the normal timeline. Maybe she can get a line on what our scavenger was doing there, on the Mississippi."

Logan's shoulders sagged. "So what's the story? You called me on the NSA link."

"We have another ripple." Matuzek indicated the Dome of History overhead. "Level one this time, and the historians have a situation that matches it. April of 1982, Intracoastal Waterway at Key Largo, Florida. A ninety-foot offshore service boat exploded during a drug raid. At least five people killed, including a DEA undercover agent. And get this, the boat was supposed to be carrying money—a boatload of small-denomination currency bound for Bogotá and Medellín. Most of the money was never found, just enough bills to confirm the cargo. The rest went up in the fire. An estimated four million dollars, mostly twenty-dollar bills, untraceable if they were in circulation.

"Lost money, Logan. Another lost treasure, and a ripple to match it. Seven to five it's the Scavenger again. You ready for speed-brief?"

"Ready as I'll ever be." Logan nodded. He turned to Claire Hemmings. "If you want to do something useful while I'm gone," he rasped, "why don't you reprogram the damned sublimator, before speed-brief gets somebody killed. Most of us aren't machines or systems analysts. We're real, human people. Assimilating sublimator data is like trying to digest a brick."

"I've got a better idea, Logan," she snapped. "*I'll* speed-brief and take the launch. You can just stay here and complain about the equipment."

"Cut it out, both of you!" Matuzek ordered. In the momentary silence he glared at both of them for a moment, then said, "Suit up, Hemmings. For once, the two of you have come up with a good idea. We'll make this a team launch. Logan, you're senior in the field. Work out the speed-brief any way you like as long as *somebody* has it. You've got twenty minutes."

* * *

"You observe, you analyze, you record," Logan said as they strapped in. "You don't make field decisions."

"You just do your job!" Claire snapped. "I know mine!"

Behind inches-thick reinforced glass in the launch-control booth, Eugene Matuzek growled, "Don't they ever stop? God! It's like listening to a couple of squabbling kids!"

"It's chemistry, Captain." Dale Easter smiled. "Logan and Hemmings, they're like white phosphorus and water. They're both elementals, and in each other's presence they explode."

Countdown had begun. The sled looked small and lonely, sitting on its rails beyond the launch docks, its tachyon polarizers beginning to glow. A sleek, aerodynamic module, the timesled existed for one purpose—to streak down a half-mile shaft on reinforced railing at tremendous acceleration toward a solid, blank wall at the end of the launch corridor, and to reach Q-velocity— 2,994-plus feet per second—before reaching the wall.

At the far end of the shaft, just ahead of the wall, mighty armatures framed an aperture where enormous energies collided to open a wormhole into the fourth dimension—a door to the timestream. The armatures provided three of the energies required to achieve this phenomenon. The sled itself supplied the fourth, provided that it had reached Q-velocity by that point.

If not, no wormhole would occur. Only another stain where a timesled and its occupants had become part of the inseparable unity of the wall.

Countdown proceeded, its measures counted for all to hear, over a PA system linking all sections of the launch chamber. Control screens flashed and spun their patterns as Jack Logan, at the sled's controls, completed checkdown. Optical shielding now darkened the viewport, screening the blinding intensity of the sled's tachyon thrusters building toward polarization.

In launch control a tech indicated a bank of monitors. "Hemmings's vital signs are all over the board," he said. "Is this her first time-launch?"

"She's an Academy grad," Matuzek said. "She's done all the simulations."

"Well, simulation and actual launch aren't the same, and she knows it. She's wound tighter'n a cable spool."

In the sled, Logan saw the same readings and grinned. "Don't vomit in transit, Hemmings," he suggested, his voice a malevolent presence in Claire's headset. "It makes an awful mess."

"Will you just shut up and drive?" she hissed. "I'm doing fine! God, but you are an arrogant, bullheaded, aggravating son—"

"Tachyon polarity in three . . ." the calm countdown voice said. ". . . two . . . one . . . contact!"

Logan hit comply, and the massive power of tach-thrust hit the sled like a giant fist. The sled hurtled downtrack, piling on gravities—two Gs, four, eight, a streak at midshaft and a blur beyond that. In the momentary crush of massive acceleration Logan held to one thought: 2,994 fps! 2,994 . . . Q-velocity! In a heartbeat the great armatures towered over and around the shaft, with the wall just beyond. The space there seemed to swirl, to coalesce, and the sled entered the nothingness of extradimensional stasis.

### Florida Keys
### 1982

"—of a bitch!" Claire Hemmings's tirade became a shriek as dark waters rose to meet her and closed around her. She flailed at the murky bath, felt a soft surface beneath her feet, and kicked off, arrowing upward. Her head and shoulders erupted from the water just as Logan cannonballed into it two feet away. Water sheeted from him, engulfing the systems analyst again, turning her shriek to a burbling, spitting barrage of complaints.

Three yards away, a small boat rocked and bobbed on the waves. A man in a dripping, floppy hat and yellow raincoat hunkered there, gawking at the sudden commotion. As Logan surfaced and turned toward him, the man yelled, "Oh, Jesus! Aliens!" and flung himself backward, over the far side of the fishing craft.

Logan swam the few strokes to the boat, hoisted himself up, and looked around, as the echoes of the fisherman's splashing retreat died in the thickets of what seemed to be either a flooded forest or an overgrown lake. There was water everywhere, with cypress groves and tangled thickets scattered across it. A light, misty rain was falling, limiting visibility to thirty or forty yards.

"Sorry about dropping in this way!" Logan shouted. "I wonder if we could hitch a ride to the nearest dry land?"

Claire reached the boat and hauled up beside Logan. "Where . . . where'd he go?" she asked. "What is this place?"

"It's a mangrove swamp," Logan said. "It looks like we missed our target."

"But that man . . . where did he go? Did he drown?"

"Oh, he's all right." Logan braced himself on the boat's

rail, raised himself to arm's length, and flipped into the open vessel. He pointed. "He's over there, just past that thicket. He's hiding from us. He thinks we're aliens." He scanned the contents of the boat—a tackle box, a bait can, a paddle, a mismatched pair of fishing rods, an old blanket, a boater's flotation vest, a McDonald's sack, a thermos . . .

The boat was about fifteen feet in length, wide beamed and flat bottomed. On its stern brace, a little Johnson outboard motor was tipped inboard, its tiller resting on a fuel can.

"Come on back, sir!" Logan shouted through the mist. "We won't harm you! We just need a ride!"

"Go away!" a thin voice came from a misty thicket. "Leave me alone! What are you, Martians?"

"Sir, we aren't trying to hurt you. Look, I'll get this thing started, and we'll come pick you up!"

"Hell you will!" the man shrilled. "Just go away! You can have the damned boat! Go away! I know you're taking hostages! That's what you saucer people do!"

"He doesn't want to be rescued," Logan muttered, conversationally. He knelt to the motor, studying its controls. "Hemmings, you'd better get in here, unless you want to walk."

"Aren't you going to help me?"

Logan shrugged. Without looking around, he said, "Okay. You know, these marshes are just full of alligators, cottonmouth moccasins and man-of-war jellyfish, not to mention stingrays, spiny corals, poisonous puffer fish, and moray eels. And the shallows along here are the feeding grounds for about a dozen kinds of shark. Then there are barracuda, sea snakes, snapping turtles, a few transplanted crocodiles—"

Water cascaded, the boat rocked violently, and Claire rolled over the side and thumped into the bilge.

"There! I helped you." Logan grinned.

From beyond the thicket came the rustling, scrabbling sounds of a man climbing a tree.

Logan grasped the little motor's pull cord, then paused. "Listen!" Amidships, Claire stopped sputtering and raised her head. Through the mist they heard the distant, muted blare of a horn, answered by bells and another horn, lower pitched and farther away. Somewhere nearby, boats were making their way along a channel, signalling in the mist.

"I'd bet a week's pay that's the Intracoastal Canal," Logan said.

"Gulf Intracoastal Waterway, to be exact," Claire recited. "Maintained by the United States Army Corps of Engineers, it extends from Florida to Mexico, and is connected to Atlantic Shore waterways by the—" Turning to point, she lost her footing and thumped into the flat bottom of the little boat. The boat rocked precariously.

"The sublimator at work," Logan muttered. "Clumsy." He turned and shouted toward the misty thickets, "Sir, we have to be going now! Are you sure you don't want us to swing around and pick you up?"

"You stay away from me!" the man answered.

"Well, okay. Will you be all right, out here alone?"

"I'm not alone!" the man assured him. "My friend Tony is coming out to meet me. Tony has a gun!"

"All right, then!" Logan pushed the motor's primer bulb. "We'll leave your boat where you can recover it. Thank you!" He pulled the cord, pulled it again, and the little motor sputtered to life. Throttling up, Logan swung the tiller and headed for the ship channel. Claire, wet and embarrassed, clung to the side beam and looked straight ahead, ignoring him.

## U.S. Intracoastal Waterway near Key Largo, Florida
## April 21, 1982

Twin diesels thumped lazily as the offshore service vessel *Papa Joe* rounded the Barnes Sound bell buoy at a sedate five knots and entered the mile-wide forest of masts and flying decks of Dade Cove Yacht Club's anchorage. It was a foggy, bleak morning, and few boats were out today.

Here and there a few pleasure boats showed lazy signs of life—radio music, people coming and going on becalmed decks, a mist-muffled shout or two, a powerboat making its way through the jumble with a load of supplies from the stores ashore. But for the most part, the anchorage might have been a graveyard of expensive, abandoned toys.

*Papa Joe* carried a cargo of contraband today and had a complement of six men, though only three were visible. Captain Pancho Triste stood in the wheelhouse, steering his course, and two listless deckhands lounged against rails—one forward near the prow, the other astern. The rest of today's crewmen—three young Colombians with submachine guns, were out of sight, standing guard below.

Beyond the anchorage was the Intracoastal Canal, a buoyed channel arcing southwestward toward the causeway that connected mainland Florida to the Keys. Threading its way along narrow channels between ranks of yachts, sailboats, and other pleasure craft, *Papa Joe* made for that main channel, the Intracoastal Canal.

Captain Pancho, at the helm, was becoming nervous.

Somewhere overhead, a helicopter was circling the bay, and there was something spooky about all these boats around him. They were too quiet, mostly—as though someone had preceded him here, clearing away innocent bystanders. In the mists beyond the yacht anchorage he caught glimpses of movement, and up ahead—barely visible—a Coast Guard cutter lay across the anchorage channel like the gate of a trap.

"Sona'bitch," Triste muttered to himself. "I don' like this even a little bit." Carefully he eased *Papa Joe* along the fairway, keeping its speed down, trying to attract no attention. "Las' time I hire out to Colombians," he whispered. "Good money, but too dangerous."

The powerful craft negotiated a bend in the channel, then slewed and backed water as an obstruction appeared. Pancho Triste brought his vessel to a halt and peered ahead, through the mist, at the big boat blocking his way.

"A drifter," he muttered.

No one was visible aboard the yacht, but it lay there in the channel fairway, blocking his way. He keyed his intercom microphone. *"Cuidado, hombres,"* he cautioned those below. *"Hay una obstrucción."* He put down the mike, stepped out of the wheelhouse, and waved at his foredeck crewman. "What do you see, Chico?"

"Nobody visible," the man called. "Anchor line gone slack. Guess it threw its yoke."

"Damn!" Pancho muttered. "I can't stall aroun' here, attract attention." To the deckman he called, "Tend the fenders, Chico! I'll give her a nudge."

At dead slow, *Papa Joe* inched toward the drifting yacht and caressed its gleaming bow with his rubber-tire fenders. Carefully, gently, he eased it aside, herding it back away from the channel.

The deckhand on the afterdeck had his attention fixed ahead. An undercover agent of the DEA, he was trained and alert. But he didn't see the little boat that came up behind *Papa Joe*, or the man who came over the rail. He didn't see the hand that closed around his mouth, or the blade that sliced across his throat.

The muffled plips of a silenced gun below deck were drowned in the deep thrum of *Papa Joe*'s thudding diesels as Pancho Triste nudged the vagrant yacht aside to clear the channel.

The boarder moved swiftly, tying slings to the three big bundles of currency under the hatch. He unlatched the main sling cover and thrust his yoke through the crack. Then he reappeared on deck and strode forward.

Pancho Triste saw movement out of the corner of his eye as the stranger appeared at the starboard entry. A moment later the captain lay dead beside his wheel, and *Papa Joe*'s engines throttled down to idle. Coming from the foredeck, Chico gaped at the tall, raincoated figure standing in front of him, then fell as a bullet smashed through his heart.

Alone now on the work boat, the invader attached its winches to the cargo below deck. Crane booms hoisted the burlap-bundled currency, swung it clear of the hold, and dropped it onto the deck of the abandoned yacht alongside. That done, he checked the time and closed a tiny electromagnetic switch on his belt. Down in the hold, between drums of diesel fuel and contraband gasoline, an electronic timer began its countdown. The man turned full around, surveying his work, and smiled grimly. Back in the cabin, he geared-in *Papa Joe*'s twin screws, secured the throttle, and set the rudder downchannel. As the big work boat began to accelerate, unattended and aimed at the barricade on the Intracoastal, its visitor went over the side where his little boat waited.

Several hulls away, a sleek speedboat thrust its snout from between anchored yachts. Crouched in its cockpit, two people trained electronically amplified binoculars on the big work boat as it began to move.

"That's him," Jack Logan growled. "The man from the Empire State. The scavenger."

"We could have stopped that," Claire Hemmings said. "That old captain, and those sailors . . . he just . . . he just *killed* them. As though they were nothing."

"You're the theorist here," Logan purred. "What are the odds that we could have stopped that and not changed history? Those men died today, Hemmings. In real-time history, that's what happened. Some of them opened fire on a Coast Guard cutter, and the cutter returned fire. That boat there, the *Papa Joe*, exploded. Among other things, that captain was smuggling gasoline."

"Carter's fuel crisis," Claire recited. "Yes, 1977 . . . fuel lines . . . blackouts . . . Venus launches . . . Pele . . ." She shifted, her elbow slipped off the speedboat's rail, and she almost dropped her binoculars.

"The sublimator in action," Logan drawled. "I warned you about speed-brief. It makes you clumsy."

"All right!" she snapped. "I'll look into it! But those men on that boat . . . God!"

"History is messy." Logan nodded. "But we don't make tracks, do we?"

"Well, they're not going to shoot at any Coast Guard cutters now," the woman snapped. "They're dead."

"How is that a level-one ripple?" Logan muttered. "The only change here so far is that there's nobody to open fire on the Coast Guard. So Coast Guard return fire won't blow up their boat."

"But the boat *did* blow up," Claire said. "Has this guy stopped that?"

"I don't think he did," Logan said. "Hang on." Easing the speedboat's throttle, he backed it into the shadows between the deserted yachts, then turned and gunned it, circling around the anchorage, using the boats for cover. The deep thrum of *Papa Joe*'s engines helped to muffle the sound.

Logan brought the boat alongside the drifting yacht, gave Claire the wheel, and climbed over the port rail of the larger vessel. Claire held the speedboat in close as a large, heavy bundle thudded down from above. Then Logan rejoined her, took the controls, and jockeyed the speedboat back to a vantage point downchannel. *Papa Joe*, now deserted but under power, had just passed, heading down the fairway.

Claire trained glasses on the work boat. "Where did the killer go? I don't see him."

"I do." Logan pointed. A few hundred yards upstream, in the channel between anchorages, the abandoned yacht was moving again. But now there was a small boat alongside, and a man climbing over the yacht's rail. The man scurried into the yacht's cockpit, and engines came to life. Slowly, sedately, the boat edged into the channel, coming their way.

The man at the wheel was tall, lean-faced, and confident. As the yacht neared the speedboat, he lashed its wheel, stepped out on deck, and executed a formal, old-fashioned bow. Then he pointed south, where *Papa Joe* was chugging along toward the waiting Coast Guard cutter. He looked directly at Logan and Hemmings, and cupped his hands at his cheeks. "One minute, fifteen seconds!" he called. "Then good-bye!"

Logan stiffened. "A bomb!" he hissed. "He's planted a bomb!"

Downchannel, the cutter's siren sounded, and an amplified voice was raised. "Ahoy the service boat! Ahoy, *Papa Joe*! This is the United States Coast Guard! Come about and shut down! Repeat, shut down! Prepare to be boarded!"

"Hang on!" Logan ordered. He hit the speedboat's starters, shoved the throttle to full, and hauled the wheel over. The sleek racer slewed water, raised its nose, and shot out into the channel in a tight turn that sheeted spray for fifty yards to starboard. With Claire clinging to her webs, they raced toward the big work boat, skipping into and out of its wake as it loomed ahead of them.

"You can't stop that thing!" Claire shouted. "It's too big!"

"If it goes up alongside the cutter," Logan gritted, "the cutter'll go with it." Coming alongside *Papa Joe* he eased the speedboat over, directly into its bow fenders, and sideswiped the big vessel. Rubber tires and cables flew as the speedboat bounced off, almost capsizing.

With a growl, Logan brought the racer about and headed in again, from aflank. This time the impact was less. Using both throttle and wheel to skid the racer into an angle, he rammed its nose into the fouled cables of the fenders, tangling it there. He throttled forward and felt the little boat's thrust begin to overcome the inertia of the heavy vessel. Standing then, bracing himself in the roaring, rocking boat, he faced the Coast Guard vessel and shouted, "Bomb! Back off! Back off!"

"Time to go," he told Claire, grabbing her shoulders and lifting her from the seat. Before she could complain, he lifted her over his head and threw her out over the fantail of the struggling racer. "Swim!" he shouted, and followed, towing canvas bags.

They were fifty yards away when a rumble sounded and a shock wave sent them tumbling, rolling under the surface. Even seven feet down in murky water, they could see the firestorm that swept across the surface above them.

Long minutes later, sodden and exhausted, they climbed the ladder of an anchored sportfisher and sprawled on its little deck. Claire raised her head to look out across the misty waters. "The cutter's still there," she panted. "And some police boats. They're doing a search. For us, I guess." She turned, looking upchannel. "The yacht's gone," she said.

"So what did you expect?" Logan raised himself on his elbows, shaking his head. "Same pattern as before. Something lost stays lost, but now he has it. Or at least, he thought he did. A time raid with an overshadowing event, to mask the anomalies. And E-warp doesn't give us a reading to match the event."

"I think we're looking at the wrong event, again. I—" She blinked and stared at him. "What do you mean, 'thought he did'?"

Logan reached over the fishing boat's rail and lifted a rope from the water. He tugged on it and hauled its load aboard—a zippered nylon sleeping bag, bulging, lumpy, and heavy. "I got the money," he said. "When Mr. Scavenger opens his packs, he'll find a few blankets and a folded tarp."

## TEC Headquarters
## 2007

"He gave us a choice." Logan's fingers drummed the tabletop—a slow, implacable rhythm that matched his mood. "Cold as ice, and arrogant . . . the bastard saw us there, and he *dared* us to interfere. He gave us a choice. Keep that boat away from the cutter, or change history."

"He was playing with us!" Claire seethed. "He even bowed!"

"Well, at least he went away empty-handed this time," Dale Easter pointed out. "That bag you brought back contained roughly four million dollars in small bills. Do you know, that much money invested in 1982, in a good portfolio, would be around *forty* million now?"

"Still playing the stock market, Dale?"

"I may get out of it," Easter said. "It's been crazy lately."

"You're sure the man you saw was the same man?" Matuzek asked Logan.

Logan nodded. "Absolutely sure. The same man I encountered in the Empire State, the one who shot me. The same man who killed Phil Nash. And I'm convinced it was the same man I saw at the Dutchman's mine. I've given you a composite on each debriefing. What does Chron-Comp say?"

"That they're probably all the same man," Amy Fuller responded. "And by the way, he *does* resemble the Scofield family. But it's not Walter Scofield."

"You tracked down Walter Scofield?"

"Finally," Easter nodded, tapping up a likeness on the viewscreens. A poor-quality enlargement from some tabloid page, the picture was that of a lean, craggy-featured old man whose seamed face, beneath a thin tousle of white hair, reflected decades of bitterness. "ChronComp dug it out of the obituaries. Walter Restin Scofield—eccentric recluse, multimillionaire investor, and a sort of black-sheep cousin of the Scofield family dynasty. He died a little over two years ago, in a Washington, D.C., hospital, at the age of seventy-four. He left a personal estate valued at about twenty million dollars, most of it in real estate."

Logan studied the screen. "That's Walter Scofield," he said, finally. "He's older looking than I remember, but that's the man I remember as secretary of state, before the history alteration."

"Well, he never was secretary of state now," Easter said. "He was just a crazy old miser who kept to himself, hated his neighbors, and tried to build a fortress. Quite a place, too, his dream castle. But he didn't live in it very long. His health failed, and he was institutionalized his last few years."

The screens flickered to multiple views of an austere, fortresslike estate on the crest of a sheer, granite-faced wilderness peak. A rich man's hideaway, surrounded by a few square miles of private forest enclosed by high walls and electrified fence.

"It's west of here, in Virginia," Amy noted. "The Blue Ridge range. The story is, Walter Scofield backed the wrong politicians when he was young. He got burned, got out, then turned his back on it all and became a recluse. Secretive, solitary, and camera-shy. Nobody was sure whether he ever even had any close family, until after he died. The other Scofields—cousins and the like—wrote him off a long time ago. He was the family eccentric, the skeleton in the closet. There are some fairly sinister rumors about him, but they're only rumors.

"Anyway, he spent years—and millions—building this place on Baldrock Peak. All the contractors and workers were imported, and disappeared when their jobs were done. The locals around there avoid the place."

"Who has it now?" Claire Hemmings asked.

"An appointed executor. It turns out Walter Scofield did have family—a son, Felix Scofield. The kid was a genius or something. Kind of a prodigy, but we can't find much of a record about him except that he's the sole heir in Walter's will. The trouble is, Felix disappeared years ago. Vanished without a trace. He was an MIT grad, doing some kind of sociology program at UCLA. Maybe he got crossways with some wacko crowd out there, maybe he's a hophead, maybe he's dead, nobody knows. He just disappeared. People disappear all the time in Southern California. Even his school records are gone, lost in a freak spontaneous download. Along with everything else about him."

"You can erase most anything, for a price," Dale Easter muttered to himself.

Amy shrugged. "When Walter Scofield died, the court appointed one of his cousins, Raymond Scofield, as executor. He doesn't live at Walter's house, but there's an on-site custodian. A man named Cress. Apparently he stays up there, to look after things. ChronComp thinks he's using an assumed name, because there aren't any records of him."

"What if the heir never shows up?" Logan wondered.

"The executor's term is perpetual. Old Walter set up his will that way, to last forever."

"In legal reality, of course," Easter said, and shrugged, "*forever* is an unspecified time. In the case of trusts and estates, forever means until some lawyer finds a chink in the wall."

"Any data on Raymond Scofield, the executor?"

"Very little, that we can access," Amy said. "Even ChronComp has to abide by the Constitution. He lives within a hundred miles or so, gets a retainer to mind his own business, and hardly ever goes near the mountain house."

"It looks like your scavenger theory is right, Logan." The captain changed the subject, impatiently. "Our perp's modus operandi is consistent. He's a treasure hunter. So far he's had it all his own way. What worries me is that he knows somebody is after him now. He's seen you twice, at least. And he knew about Phil Nash. And now you've thwarted him. You did him out of four million dollars. What he does about it—how he reacts to interference— depends on what kind of man he is."

"He's a vulture," Claire muttered. "And a cold-blooded killer. He didn't know we were there when he killed those boatmen, or when he set the bomb on that work boat. He'd have killed that cutter's crew, too, just for the sake of an explosion."

At one corner of the conference table, Julie Price opened a file and thumbed through its pages. The youngest of Matuzek's squad of timecops, Julie was a legacy from the future. She had come as a courier from a later TEC, and found herself stuck in 2007. Unable to return to her own time because of the probability of anachronism, she had stayed on with TEC. Matuzek considered the willowy, auburn-haired young woman one of his best surveillance agents. The rest of the male contingent of TEC headquarters considered her the stuff of dreams.

"I poked around for a few days in pre–Civil War St. Louis," she said. "You all have my report. That steamboat that blew up on the Mississippi was carrying U.S. Mint gold certificates, a consignment stolen by Arcadians at New Orleans and sent north to Montreal. The certificates were—and still are—officially classified as lost."

"Lost treasure," Matuzek said. "That's the pattern. So far, we know that our vulture has located a lost gold mine, which remains officially lost; found a fortune in lost World War II bearer bonds, which never surfaced; collected a lost shipment of gold certificates, which are still lost; and come into momentary possession of four million dollars in lost drug money, which also will remain lost in public record. All in all, a lot of money. A *lot* of money! And every bit of it negotiable and untraceable. So what does he do with it? Where does all that treasure go?"

"Money leaves big tracks in history," Dale Easter said. "Especially that kind of money. We're looking at billions. Whole countries have been bought and sold for a lot less. Any contrahistoric transaction involving billions of dollars would show as a real granddaddy ripple on E-warp. But we haven't seen anything like it. Every event involving the scavenger has been only a minor ripple on the Dome."

"Every one we *know about*," Claire corrected him.

"This perp is no amateur, Dr. Easter. He's no basement jumper or one-time adventurer. He obviously has unlimited access to a working time device, and uses it like we'd use a car. He knows just what he can do and how to do it. And he doesn't hesitate at killing people while he's at it."

"Well, it's obvious he's in it for the money, but that's what I don't understand. This guy has accumulated billions of dollars! Believe me, E-warp would notice it if he spent it. Why hasn't that money caused more commotion?"

"Maybe you're looking at the wrong events," Claire said. "Lost money doesn't change history. *Found* money changes history. Maybe he hasn't used his money yet. When he does, *then* we'll see the effect."

"That doesn't make sense, either. Why would he just sit on some old millions when he could convert them to new billions?"

Logan had stopped drumming his fingers. Now he stood and walked to the glass partition. Beyond it, TEC headquarters bustled with activity. "I have a hunch," he said. "I don't think the scavenger is a treasure hunter. This creep is a showman. He's a game player, not a miser. I saw his eyes when he took his shot at me. The man's a fanatic. Maybe even a psycho. He won't just get rich and walk away."

"What are you suggesting, Logan?" Matuzek leaned on his elbows, studying the timecop. "You think he's doing this just for fun?"

"Oh, he's enjoying it, all right," Logan said. "But I think he has a purpose in mind. It isn't random acts, and it isn't for the money. The money's just a tool, for something else. Hemmings was right. That creep was laughing at us. He's laughing at everybody. I think he plans to change history, and he knows exactly what he's doing."

Beijing, China
1976

Screened sunlight, reflecting from the waters of Chung Hai, dappled the pristine segments of a framed ceiling and filtered across a half acre of carpet in the domain of Hung Chaio-lin, highlighting the center of the wide room where the minister of provincial affairs sat at his huge desk, reading reports. Periodically he glanced up, nervously, noting the closed doors along three shadowed walls and the alert, quiet scrutiny of the guards who patrolled there.

Beyond his windows, beyond the carefully tended floral arrangements lining the high balcony, Hung had a clear view of the tiled roofs of neighboring buildings and the old Imperial Wall beyond, bordered by parks. In the square at Tiananmen, the Gate of Heavenly Peace, banners waved and tanks rolled while thousands gathered along the fringes to witness the might of Chinese solidarity.

All was peaceful today within the inner city, and it was the wish of Minister Hung that it remain so. It would take more than parades to heal the wounds of the recent coup attempt by Madame Mao and her conspirators. It would be months before all the counterrevolutionaries were identified and dealt with, and a lot of scapegoats would fall with them, in the interests of restoring normalcy. The Gang of Four had done more than undermine the authority of Hua Kuo-feng and the party. The equanimity of the entire nation was disturbed, and there would be necessary sacrifices for months to come.

Worry lines creased Hung's brow as he read further into the recommendations of the Central Party. The symbols were ordinary symbols for ordinary words, couching their suggestions in the most respectful terms. But Hung had spent enough years in the front lines of Chinese Communism to read the intent behind the courteous phrasing. The placing of blame would be required, and the enumeration had begun. High-level heads would roll. Nowhere in the texts did he find assurance that he, himself, would not be one of the scapegoats.

He glanced up at a slight sound, and his breath caught in his throat. Halfway across the wide room, the empty air suddenly shimmered, a receding coalescence as though a chunk of reality were being sucked away—drawn swirling into the maw of some fantastic elsewhere.

Hung blinked, and a man appeared in that coalescing sphere. Tall, dark-clothed, and crouching, the man shimmered for an instant as a phantasm in a dream, then became real and solid as the air around him snapped back to normalcy.

The stranger held a weapon—a Russian-built AK-47 assault rifle with a stubby, muffled snout. He glanced at Hung, then raised the rifle and turned. Three shots sounded—shots that were no more than heavy thumps in the silence—and the three guards at the portal walls crumpled, falling soddenly to lie in welling pools of their own blood.

In the span of a heartbeat it was done, and Hung saw the rifle aimed at him. A shriek of protest rose in his throat, then froze there as the intruder smiled a cold smile and lowered his weapon.

"We will speak in English, Hung," he said. "No, don't reach for your alarm, or for that pistol under your desktop. Hear me out, first. I have just saved your life."

In English, Hung hissed, "Who are you? What is this about?"

The man started to answer, then turned abruptly. A yard

away, the coalescence had appeared again, the impression of immensities drawing away the reality of a sphere of empty air. This time the figure there was a stocky, red-haired man in a dark gray uniform. The coalescence steadied, the newcomer crouched, and the tall man shot him where he stood.

Kneeling over the gray-uniformed corpse, the killer mused, "Another of those, eh? Meddlers! It seems they respond to historic change. Interesting."

The dark figure inspected the fallen one, lifted a limp arm, and studied an instrument strapped to its wrist. "Ah, yes," he muttered. He did something with his fingers, then stepped back, quickly. Once again the eerie otherness filled the air, and the gray-uniformed body disappeared as though it had never been there, except for the pool of blood it left behind.

The dark stranger stood and turned back to Hung. "Now, shall we continue?" He smiled, an ugly smile on a face not made for smiling—a craggy, ascetic occidental face with the intense gaze of a fanatic. As he spoke, the man lowered his AK-47, butt down. He rested it on the carpet, removed the stubby silencer from its muzzle, and let the gun fall. He dropped the silencer into a pocket of his coat, then whipped out another gun—a handgun unlike anything Hung had ever seen. "Ah, yes. We were about to negotiate a deal."

## TEC Headquarters
## 2007

For a moment, a full level-one ripple appeared on the Dome in the Time Enforcement Commission's command center. It circled there, radiating outward, then dimmed and went to blue as E-warp responded to satellite signals from another part of the world.

"EuroTEC's handling that one," a tech noted. "They have an event fix that gives them jurisdiction."

In his beloved history library, Dr. Dale Easter noted the report from the tech and glanced curiously at E-warp's vectors on the ripple's source. It took only a moment for him to cross-link the data to ClironComp. "China, 1976." He grimaced. "Earthquakes . . . a typhoon . . . the Manchurian scare . . . Chairman Mao died and Premiere Hua took over . . . the Gang of Four Revolt . . . hot damn! Poulon's folks are welcome to that one!"

## Paris, France
## 2007

Jean-Luc Poulon was Director General of EuroTEC, the TEC affiliate located in the City of Lights. Right now, though, looking down into the cockpit of the returned timesled in the launch bays beneath the old Bastille, Jean-Luc wished that he were back with the *Sûreté*. The life of a chief inspector with the French police—even a chief inspector who was arguably the best policeman in all of Europe—had been a simple thing, compared to directing European operations for one of the most secret organizations in the world, the Time Enforcement Commission.

In real-time police work, where only three dimensions existed in any equation, a crime committed remained committed no matter how long it took to solve it. And the murder of a policeman in the line of duty demanded a clear course of action—find and arrest the murderer, wherever he was. In time enforcement, though, it was different. It was all now, then, and when.

There was no question that Ian Rafferty had been murdered by a time jumper. Who else would have sent the body back? It was a taunt and a challenge. It was an ultimatum. I know you're out there, it said. Don't send any more policemen or they will die, too.

From the open sled, the dead eyes of Rafferty stared up into the vaulted darkness of the timefield tunnel, and Jean-Luc Poulon felt as helpless as a kitten. They would do their best to find the Irish cop's killer, but there was little they could do. The minor ripple Rafferty had gone to investigate—thirty years in the past and two continents away—was no longer a ripple. It had passed into the timestream. Whatever changes were made in history at that moment in 1976 in the city of Beijing, were already made. The changes *were* history, now. They were no longer aberrations.

The ripple was part of general history, and with Rafferty dead there was no way to know what had been changed.

"Get him out of there," Poulon told his techs. "And treat him gently. He was a good man."

Turning his back, Poulon went to send the required reports to TEC-US.

## Heilungkiang Province, Manchuria
## June 1977

The train from Shin-kau to Dairen made a brief stop at Nen-ch'eng, just long enough for General Po Chang-hi to board. Then it headed southward again in the shadow of the Khingan Mountains. While General Po's aides attended to their luggage, the general paused to gaze out a window. The Cho-lo River lay just ahead, and beyond it the Manchurian highlands stepping down toward the Gulf of Liao-tung and the Yellow Sea.

Behind the general, a man in fine civilian dress waved Po's guards aside and stepped to the window beside him, balancing himself with one hand on the sill as the train rocked gently.

"Welcome to Manchuria, General," the man said. "I hope your tour of the provinces has been pleasant."

General Po glanced aside at him, expressionless. "Minister Hung," he said, and nodded. "Until this moment, it has been pleasant enough. Now I wonder, though, why my aides and I are confined to this one shabby car on the People's Train, and why there are so many Supreme Command troops visible on the other cars."

"It is permitted, to wonder," Hung said. "The transfer of materials and devices by the Ministry of Science always arouses curiosity. I, myself, do not understand the great technologies our People's Republic is developing, but I try to do my job and not ask too many questions."

Po stared at the minister of provincial affairs for a moment, then looked away. Beyond the window, the Khingans rose like a mighty wall—the wall of Mongolia, separating the People's Republic of China from Siberia and the Union of Soviet Socialist Republics.

General Po was a veteran, a career soldier who had remained aloof from the great purges that had so many times reshaped the Red Chinese Army at the whims of those in power. As a veteran, he knew how and when to hold his tongue. But his mind was its own, and it seethed at the hypocrisy of the man beside him.

Po recognized the hardware of nuclear weaponry when

he saw it, and he knew that this train carried a device withdrawn from the experimental ranges beyond Lupin. He also knew that minister Hung Chiao-lin had, in the past year, become one of the most powerful men in China. Hung had survived the chaotic last years of the Mao regime, escaped the Hua purges, had even become a Hero of the People. The story of his heroic encounter—how he had used an old AK-47 Russian rifle to defend himself against his own guards in his own office during the Madame Mao counterrevolution, had become legend.

Hung had become virtually untouchable. But privately, General Po suspected some truth to the rumors that Hung's power—at least in part—was based on personal wealth from unknown sources, accumulating in a Hong Kong bank.

Po had heard of the Lupin experiments. He knew that there were fearsome weapons being tested in northern Mongolia, partly to perfect the technologies of these things and partly as a reminder to the Russians across the border that China was not and would never be part of the CCCP—or, as it was called in the western world, the USSR.

And Po knew that the materials for these weapons were carried by rail. The Lupin region, almost on the Siberian border, had become a major proving ground for Chinese IRBMs and thermonuclear research. It was common to see railroad trains northbound, especially between Ch'i-ch'i-ha-erh and Nen-ch'eng, carrying components for sophisticated weapons.

But why would a missile train, with two ugly lead-shielded radiation cars, be in transit southward, out of Mongolia toward the seaports? And why did it happen that the minister of provincial affairs was aboard the same train?

And why, when General Po's own specialists examined Hung's office in Peking the past year—after the minister's heroic battle with his own guards—were there four pools of blood on the carpeting and only three bodies?

"You will be changing accommodations at Ch'ang-ch'un, General," the minister told him now. "This poor train is ill equipped for comfort. Your journey will be far more serene on the Sungari Limited."

Are you selling a bomb, Hung? General Po asked himself. Is that what this is about? But he held his tongue. Second only to Premier Hua himself these days, Hung Chiao-lin was not one to be questioned.


## Washington, D.C.
## 1993

It was Herbert Grove who finally closed the old file on the Manchurian Device—a file that had pestered the intelligence community for nearly seventeen years. Rumors and whispers, the stuff of nightmare and of fantasy, but time had passed and governments had changed. In the span of years from 1977 to 1993, the whole world had changed.

"The unresolved question of the Manchurian Device may be concluded to be nothing more than outdated scare propaganda," Grove told his oversight committee at a closed hearing. "The original tip, of a Chinese thermo-nuclear device similar to our own neutron bomb—a device capable of emitting lethal short-term neutron radiation with limited effect on real estate—came from Soviet sources in Siberia. The suggestion that a Chinese neutron bomb was being smuggled into the United States came eighteen months later, through CIA channels. The operative attributed the information to an aide of General Po Chang-hi, who was assassinated in 1977.

"The Brits provided us with some leads during 1978 and 1979, regarding smuggling operations out of the Port of Dairen by way of Hong Kong, and there were persistent rumors—unverifiable—of the transport of an experimental nuclear detonation device from Hong Kong to the United States.

"An operation of that magnitude, undertaken by any government in the world, would have raised flags throughout the intelligence community. It was therefore considered to be a hoax. Nonetheless, the file remained open—and has been open—all these years. And nothing has come of it. The Manchurian Device file has been inactive for the past ten years. We conclude that it had no substance, and propose to close it."

A hand went up across the conference table. "Mr. Grove, you said an operation of that size by any *government* would have alerted the intelligence community. How about a private transaction? Was that possibility considered?"

"Of course, it was." Grove smiled. "But I assure you, sir, the purchase and transportation of a neutron bomb— by *anyone*—would have involved major financial transactions. There are no such transactions of record."

"How long would such a device remain stable, in storage?" another committee member asked.

"As separate components, indefinitely." The head of Central Intelligence shrugged. "But we are convinced that no such weapon survives today. All neutron-release fission tests worldwide were abandoned in 1979, even in the USSR and China. No one—not even the most fanatic annihilationists—could condone the possible use of such a weapon."

With the closing of the Manchurian file by Central Intelligence, its sanitized contents became just another grain in the vast mountains of repository data generated daily by oversize governments—repository data available to the voracious harvesting of massive data-bank computers everywhere ... the primary interlinks of the system known as ChronComp.

### TEC Headquarters
### 2007

Eugene Matuzek hurried into the library, which Dr. Dale Easter considered his own domain, to find the chief historian half-hidden behind a jumble of open books, survey charts, and printouts. Easter had a book in one hand, a stack of transparencies in the other, and every screen in his monitor bank in operation.

Matuzek circled the mess to come up behind the historian, who barely glanced at him over his shoulder. "Easter!" the captain snapped. "Didn't you hear the alert? We have a brand new ripple. A strong point-two."

"O'Donnelly's on it," Easter said. "I'm just finishing up here." He peered into a screen—columns of codes and numbers. "I can't believe this! Amfram is up seven and a quarter! God, nothing makes sense anymore!"

"You sound like you're losing money," Matuzek said.

"No, as a matter of fact I made money on that one. I just can't figure out why! Oh, well . . ." With a sigh, the historian blacked the screen, arranged transparencies on a justi-fier plate, and thumbed the key. Above his monitor banks a topographical map of a mountainous region appeared, with multiple overlays.

"I'd like to know what's inside the Scofield place on Baldrock Peak," the historian mused, focusing on three history screens at once. "You don't suppose the FBI or somebody could check that out for us, do you, Captain?"

"Not without a search warrant," Matuzek snapped. "Why?"

"I've found some interesting geohistoric combinations here," Easter said. "Did you know that Baldrock Peak sits above an extensive subterranean cavern? It's deep—Cambrian substructure washed out during one of the ice ages—but there's a history on it. Some of the early settlers in the Blue Ridge entered an erosion shaft and saw part of the cave by torchlight. But they had their hands full of In-dian wars, and never explored further."

"There isn't a judge in this country who'd grant a search warrant based on the fact that somebody has a cave under his house," Matuzek said. "What brought this up?"

"Oh, just some background chatter in ChronComp's general logs. Did you know that the entire output of three Missouri lead mines was purchased by private funds in 1991? The fine lead was delivered to warehouses in the Blue Ridge Mountains. Somebody around there also was buying paraffin and graphite by the long ton."

"What is this, Easter? Trivial Pursuit? Does this relate in any way to temporal enforcement?"

Easter shook his head, concentrating on his screens. "Not that I know of," he said. "Some of this is stuff O'Donnelly pulled up in one of his random association exercises. Him and his mental gymnastics—I guess he's got me doing it, too. Like this note, for example. Did you know that the innards of an annihilation bomb disappeared from northern Mongolia in 1977? How much space do you suppose it would take to assemble and store a thing like that?"

"I haven't the vaguest idea," Matuzek admitted. "What's this all about, Easter?"

"Just curiosity." Easter grinned. "I keep thinking about what Logan said—about his time jumper having something big in mind, and about the Scofield resemblance. I guess I'd just like to know more about the Scofield place."

"You and a lot of other people," Matuzek growled. "Give me a reason for looking, and we'll get it looked at. Otherwise, forget it, Dale. We need you in ThinkTank. Somebody's changing some history in 1999."

# VI

Newport, Rhode Island
November 6, 1999

Just off Fairlawn, a mile east of the Louisquisset Pike, Tuck'n'Take Store No. 19 was a lonely island of light in a sea of residential slumber. Margie Crowell slid a late customer's credit card through the scanner, watched as he signed the receipt, and waved to him as he went out the door, his sheepskin collar pulled up around his ears.

"Have a nice evening, Joe," she called, then went back to her weekly inventory. As night clerk at the Fairlawn Tuck'n'Take, Margie knew most of her regulars and was on a first-name basis with half of them. But the young man who came in next was a stranger. By the odd haircut he displayed when he took off his stocking cap to shake the snow from it, Margie took him for a student at one of the colleges. But he looked as though he had been in a wreck. His coat was badly scorched, his hands were black with tar stain, and his face was smudged.

"Are you all right?" Margie asked. "Do you want me to call somebody?"

He stared at her for an instant, not understanding, then looked at his hands. "Oh," he muttered. "No, I'm okay.

85

Figured that ride would be some kind of wild, but I didn't know I'd wind up on top of a lamp pole. Ah . . . what day is this?"

"Saturday," Margie told him.

"I mean, *when*? What day, what year?"

Margie cocked her head, her eyes narrowing. Maybe he'd fallen and bumped his head. "Saturday, November sixth," she said. "Nineteen ninety-nine."

"Wow!" he muttered. He dug into a pocket of his coat and came out with some wadded bills. He looked at them carefully, as though they were strange to him. "Ah, how much do lottery tickets cost?"

"Lotto?" She shrugged. "Same as usual. A dollar. How many do you need?"

"Just one," he said.

"Quick-pick?"

"No, I want my own numbers." From another pocket he produced a slip of paper. "Four . . . nineteen . . . twenty-six . . . twenty-seven . . . forty-two."

"Got a hunch, eh?" Margie turned to key in the numbers, then gasped as the refrigerated display case just beyond the back counter seemed to become distorted. The solid, glass-front case dissolved into swirling segments of light and color, receding and spiraling, sinking backward into the wall behind it. The impression was gone in an instant, replaced by the unlikely sight of a man in a dark uniform, standing inside the cabinet while dairy cartons, frozen dinners, ice cream containers, and wire racks cascaded and rattled around him.

The display door slid open, and the man stepped out. "Hold it!" he ordered. "No sale!"

Margie gaped at him. Behind her, the smudged kid gasped, turned to run, and sprawled headlong over a bundle of lurid tabloids displaying bizarre photos of Sigrid Kris, the Ramsey Fair Glee Club, and President Clinton.

Before the kid could get to his feet, the man from the refrigerator was standing over him, snapping fragile-looking connected bracelets onto his wrists. "Bad move, Willy," he said in a policeman's voice. "You're under arrest, by authority of TEC. You have the right to immediate trial before Timecourt."

He hauled the kid to his feet and dusted him off. "How did you manage it, son? Where's your launch vehicle and the stasis field?"

"I . . . I used a roller-bearing plate and a tachyon harness," Willy said, hanging his head. "And the supercollider shaft at Brown University. I figured it might work, and it did."

The policeman shook his head in disbelief. "It's a wonder you didn't kill yourself," he said.

"I didn't hurt anybody, man!" Willy's voice broke and tears appeared in his eyes. "I mean, it's just a lottery, right? Four million dollars. Nobody else won it."

The man shook his head again, and for the first time Margie took a close look at the uniform he was wearing. It was nylon and vinyl or something similar—dark, reinforced-looking clothing, with a holstered *something* at his hip and a patch on his jacket that said TEC.

"That isn't how it works, Willy," he said. "You don't change history. Even if you had, the state would take half and the federal government half of the rest. About a dozen other kinds of taxes, too, and it comes out you risked your life for about six months' worth of honest wages, which you couldn't have collected anyway since you're not in the IRS files for 1999. But the repercussions would have changed a lot of people's lives. Not bright, Willy. Clever, but not bright."

With Willy in tow, the uniformed man turned to Margie. "Sorry about the display case," he said. "I'm Officer Logan. Special assignment for TEC. Would you mind looking at this for a moment?"

The thing he set on the counter was like a videotape container with a wire loop on top. But when Margie looked at it, it seemed to come alive. Images formed there in rapid succession, holographic flickers faster than her eyes could follow or her mind could grasp. For a moment, she stared at it, then he turned it off and put it away in his coat. "What do you know about the year 1974?" he asked.

Margie blinked. "Price and wage controls ended, Tex Ritter died, Edward Heath resigned as prime minister in England, the Celtics won the NBA, Patty Hearst joined the nutcakes, *The Godfather, Part II* was the best movie, Nixon and Watergate—my God, how do I know all that?"

"Just checking." Officer Logan smiled. "Those numbers the kid wanted to buy . . . what were they?"

"Uh . . ." Margie stared at him, in confusion. "I, ah . . . I don't remember."

Logan's smile became a grin. "I *knew* that damned sublimator would come in handy," he said, as though to himself. He stepped back, pulling the kid along with him, and touched something on his wrist. The space where they stood seemed to shimmer, to swirl, to flow away . . . and they were both gone.

Alone in Tuck'n'Take No. 19, Margie Crowell turned full around, dazed, staring at the wrecked refrigerator display, the little handful of bills on the counter, and finally at the falling snow outside the lighted window. "What *were* those numbers?" she asked herself. For the life of her, she couldn't remember.

### TEC Headquarters
### 2007

"You did *what*?" Claire Hemmings hissed, glaring at Logan with unbelieving eyes.

"I borrowed your speed-brief toy," he said, grinning. "The sublimator. I found a valid use for it."

"You—you *borrowed* the—Logan, I'm putting you on report to S and R for this! The sublimator is still experimental and classified! You don't have the authority to *touch* it, much less the training to use it!"

Captain Eugene Matuzek slapped the debrief table with his open palm. "Come off it, you two!" he roared. "If you have to fight, do it on your own time!" In the silence that followed, he sighed. "Good collar, Logan. Nice and clean. No tracks this time?"

"I don't think so." Logan shook his head. "Nothing broken that can't be fixed, and only one civilian involved. The clerk at the store."

"One Margie Crowell," Bob O'Donnelly filled in. "I ran a trace on her. No historic change that I could find."

"She might have won a winnerless lottery if it hadn't been for the sublimator," Logan said, shooting a victorious glance at the seething Claire Hemmings. "I confused her with speed-brief. That's the one thing it's good for."

"I'll make a note," Matuzek growled.

Amy Fuller looked up from her memcorder to ask, "What will become of the boy? Willy Carmichael? That was pretty clever, what he did—converting a physics lab particle collider into a timesled."

"I filed a clemency recommendation with Timecourt," Logan said. "On my own volition, as amicus curiae. I suggested he be remanded to TEC's Science and Research division, to serve his sentence as an apprentice. Who knows? He might be the one to invent another marvel like the sublimator."

It was more than Claire could stand. "Logan, I'll get you for this!" she hissed.

"Oh, for God's sake!" Matuzek growled.

ChronComp yielded Brown University security footage of the rig Willy Carmichael had used to launch himself back in time, and Claire Hemmings studied it, making notes. For a college sophomore, Willy had created quite a piece of engineering.

At the top of her screen, an E-mail message appeared: *Would you have believed it?*

She turned, wondering who else was logged into her access, and Jack Logan waved at her from across the squad room.

With an irritated frown, Claire turned back to her own keyboard. Accessing Logan, she typed: *Quantum physics 101 . . . dimensional transit . . . $T - pi > < S2994 = QV$ . . . $QVI - WH = timeshift$.* Figure that one out, bonehead, she thought.

But almost before she cleared the send window, another message appeared: *Not QVI . . . QVpiI . . . I went to school, too.*

Dale Easter paused behind her, his arms loaded with old books, and glanced over her shoulder. "Love notes, Hemmings? On company time? For shame!" He put down his books, adjusted his glasses, and peered at her screen. "Interesting," he said. "Could a thing like that really work?"

"It worked," she said. "A kid named Willy Carmichael used that apparatus to launch himself back in time. He swears he got the idea from some old Harvard Business School data downloaded to Brown University's business curriculum. It proves one of S and R's pet theories about dimensional transit. The configuration of a timestream insertion doesn't matter, as long as the elements of the equation are present. Willy couldn't have reached Q-velocity on a roller-bearing plate. He couldn't have gone more than about 800 fps. But by creating his timefield in a collider shaft—an electron vortex triggered by electromagnetic pulse—he got the field to come to him . . . at more than 2,500 fps."

"So time travel doesn't *have* to begin with a half mile of track and a timesled?"

"That's the way we do it. The Kleindast method—hurl a projectile at Q-velocity into a volatile dimensional matrix, and the matrix becomes a singularity, a wormhole in time. Every legitimate timefield works that way, and all the illicit ones we've uncovered so far. But it's only one of the possibilities." She swiveled around in her chair. "Hans Kleindast didn't invent time theory. That goes all the way back to Bergstrom and G.F.B. Riemann. It even goes back to Euclid in some respects. Heindl defined the dimensions, and Einstein explained their relativity. Kleindast just perfected the hardware. But the theory could apply to other hardware. The classic example is a centrifuge. Theoretically, you could snap to four dimensions in a circular acceleration chamber, if you could reach about Mach 9 and make your timefield pop into place at just the right instant."

"Or in a Cambrian layer cavern," Easter muttered, turning away. "By the way," he said, over his shoulder, "I don't suppose you have any theories on stock market variation? No, I guess you wouldn't . . ." As though he had forgotten she was there, he picked up his books and wandered off, deep in thought.

"Historians!" Claire told herself. "They're all weird!"

Logan was just leaving when Eugene Matuzek flagged him down at checkout. "I got the report on that agent EuroTEC lost," the captain said. "His name was Ian Rafferty. Irish national, age thirty-nine, a three-year man with Poulon's outfit. Good service record. He was on a mission to Beijing, China, 1976, tracking a ripple that originated there. Forensics says he was killed instantly—probably the moment he materialized at target. He never had a chance. Probably never knew what hit him."

"Murder?" Logan asked. "Or accident?"

"Definitely murder. His retrieve was activated, and his corpse went back to Paris Timetrust. Nothing missing, launch suit and equipment intact, and his sidearm was still in its sheath. Not the work of indigenous 1976 personnel. Poulon is satisfied his man was killed by a time jumper."

Logan's eyes narrowed. "The scavenger again?"

"Could be," Matuzek said. "But the weapon wasn't the same as the one that killed Nash and hit you. Rafferty was killed with a military rifle. A Russian-made AK-47, point-blank range. EuroTEC thinks it was the same rifle that a Chinese Communist official named Hung used that day, to kill three of his own guards. One thing the Paris team did get was a clean fingerprint from Rafferty's wrist retrieve."

"Hung's?"

"No, somebody else. ChronComp is still searching, but so far the print doesn't match anybody of record."

"The scavenger," Logan growled. "Obvious but invisible. It's him, Gene. I feel it."

The chamber was a rock-arched vault, deep and silent, the wide expanse of it broken at intervals by sturdy pillars capped by Gothic arches—support for the weight above. It was circular, a vast tunnel that curved around to meet itself, then veered away, a passage of shadowed stone. The veer receded into darkness, a huge, walled tunnel curving away.

At a room-size recession on the outside curve, bright lights illuminated solid walls of computer banks and electronic equipment, enclosing a wide desk where a tall, gaunt man sat, framed by stacks of paper and bound volumes of data. On a small computer console he made delicate adjustments, creating an image on the screen from bits and pieces—a composite likeness of Jack Logan, assembled from glimpses on the eight-millimeter tape of a belt-cam and filled in with selected bits from a mosaic assembly program.

As the image took shape, the man lowered heavy brows in a frown, muttering to himself. "Close," he mumbled. "Very close. He is a prototype for many, I think. The costume is a uniform, of course. Some kind of police. This is the one who interfered at Empire State, though, and the one who stole from us. We must watch for them, learn how they happen to be where we go. This one, especially, we must see again. They interfere with us, and they must be punished. He steals from us, and he must be punished."

A cold anger set itself into the craggy planes of the man's face. "We want to be left alone," he muttered.

"These . . . these police people must learn . . . not to inter-fere with us."

## Georgetown

It was nearly four A.M. when Logan's private line awak-ened him. The caller was a tired-sounding Dale Easter.

"Thought you'd like to know," the historian said, "we've got a match on that fingerprint from Ian Rafferty's retrieve. It matches prints found at the scene of a robbery eight months ago."

"Particulars?" Logan yawned, rubbing sleep from his eyes.

"ChronComp download from FBI," Easter recited. "Felony trespass, breaking and entering, theft of federal property . . . the usual rigmarole. What it amounts to is that somebody penetrated the CIA/SS small-munitions arsenal and walked off with some hardware. Specifical-ly, a pair of Springer Special Issue laser-equipped nine-millimeter parabellum handguns, a plasma gun, two cases of ammunition for the aforementioned devices, and a so-phisticated thermal-release detonator of the kind used with some old-style thermonuclear weapons."

"Are the prints identified?"

"Nope. No matching prints on any record. The Bureau ran a complete workup on this one. Whoever that finger belongs to has never been printed, by anybody. Which means he's never had a criminal arrest record—not to mention a driver's license, a bank box, a security clear-ance, a credit account, or any public service employment. He hasn't even been born, married, audited, enrolled, ex-pelled, recruited, or buried. But he's still out there. His right index finger came into contact with various surfaces in the CIA/SS arsenal and with Ian Rafferty's controller. And one of those same L9s killed Phil Nash and put a slug in your vest."

Logan sat up, ran fingers through his tousled hair, and glanced at his clock. "Okay, I got it," he said. "What do we have, an alert?"

"No, no alert," Easter said. "We have a ripple, but Jackson's already launched on it. I'm just filling you in on what we've found."

"At four in the morning? Look, Dale, this is all very interesting, but I could have used another hour's sleep."

"Hey, don't grouse at me," Easter snapped. "I'm just being helpful. Hemmings said to let you know as soon as there was any kind of a match on that print. Night or day, anytime, she said. Priority one."

"Hemmings," Logan muttered. "Dale, when did our little systems analyst burden you with this responsibility?"

"Right before she went home," Easter told him. "That was about nine last night. I told her we wouldn't have anything until the general downloads, after midnight."

Logan sighed. "I see," he said. "Did she happen to be looking at the sublimator when she said you should call me?"

"Matter of fact, she had it in her hand. She worked on it for hours, grumbling about 1999 feedback in the 1974 matrix. I guess she took it home. Anything else I can do for you, Logan? It's getting late—oh! Good lord, it *is* four in the morning, isn't it!"

"It sure is," Logan growled. "See you in a while, Dale."

"You're on deck at seven," Easter reminded him. "See you then."

Wide awake and having nothing better to do, Logan put on the coffee and showered while it brewed. In the hiss of the hot water, he could almost hear Claire laughing at him. But she probably wasn't. She was probably sound asleep—dreaming sweet, spiteful dreams.

"I'll bet she *does* sleep with her sublimator," Logan told himself.

He had discovered, to his surprise, that his thoughts these days turned often to Claire Hemmings. Contrary, he had decided. That word described the systems analyst from S and R as perfectly as any phrase he could think of. She was aggravating, irritating, persistent, combative, arrogant, and hostile. She was a nuisance, a pest, an irritant, and a constant distraction. She was *contrary*! She also happened to be small, blond, beautiful, and quite appealing.

And it was that, Logan realized, that set off his own combative nature more than anything else. Claire Hemmings reminded him of another little, blond angel who had gotten under his skin more thoroughly than anyone else ever had.

Hemmings had no right to affect him the way she did. She wasn't Harriet Blevins! She had no right to be so damned cute!

But even his unwanted thoughts of the systems analyst didn't seem to interrupt that separate, cold part of his mind that now wrestled with a far different question: What would anybody want with an old-fashioned thermal-release detonator? Why would the scavenger steal a device designed for only one purpose—to be the catalyst for a nuclear fission reaction?

Bucks Ridge, Virginia
September 2005

Walter Scofield's retreat on Baldrock Peak was a remarkable piece of architecture. Designed to blend into its surroundings, it had a timeless look about it, as though it was not so much a building as an extension of the mountain itself. The best of foreign craftsmen—architects from Greece, a structural team from Germany, and master stonemasons from Italy—had created on Walter Scofield's mountain an edifice to match the grandeur of any Old World castle, then camouflaged it so cunningly that many who saw it from a distance never knew it was there.

It was a mark of the old hermit's eccentricity that the sheer, massive elegance of his wilderness stronghold reflected itself entirely inward, where no one but himself could enjoy it.

The old man was dead now, but his legacy of solitude lived on. As estate executor, Raymond Scofield himself drove the limousine up the curving mountain road from the airport at Dustin. He sat bleak and silent at the wheel as the solitary miles receded behind, disappearing around the vertiginous shoulders of wooded slopes. He barely glanced at the weathered, bearded man beside him, and hardly spoke to him until the tall, iron gates of the estate appeared ahead.

He looked around, then, with a cold smile. "I hope you enjoy solitude, Mr. Cress," he said. "There is a lot of it up here. You'll be lucky if you see another person—even along here—once in three months."

"I don't mind being alone." The bearded man shrugged. "I prefer my own company to anyone else's."

Raymond pulled the limousine up to the gate's security

console and activated the scanners—palm, voice, and retina. The heavy gates swung open, and Cress noted the sensors in the pedestals as the limousine pulled through. The system would pass one vehicle, but would stop anyone trying to follow. "Last time I saw a security system like this was at . . . well, a long way from here," he mused. "Back in the nineties. The old man must have valued his privacy."

"He did," Raymond said. "It will be part of your job to maintain these systems, of course. Along with general care of the estate."

Three miles farther on, the climbing, switchback road rounded a stone cliff and widened, its narrow vista flaring out into a wide, overgrown meadow, above which loomed Scofield Manor. Forbidding and austere, the great walls rose sheer, blending with the stone formations around them. "It's like a vulture's roost," Cress muttered. "Just how big is this place, anyway?"

"It's quite large," Raymond told him. "But you'll concern yourself only with the summer wing and the grounds. You'll maintain the security system, keep the utilities in good repair, and tend the generators. Your quarters and all the estate controls are in the summer wing. All the rest of the house is sealed off, and is to remain that way."

"Fine with me." Cress nodded, leaning forward to look upward through the car's windshield. In the distance, a helicopter was rising from the top of the building. It hovered for a moment, then banked sharply and dipped away, out of sight. "What's that up there on top?" Cress asked. "A penthouse?"

"Observation suite with a heliport," Raymond said. "Walter lived there . . . until his illness. The computer maintenance people use it now. This estate houses a megaframe analog system, Mr. Cress. It is leased by a foundation, which sends in technical people to maintain it. They use that upper entry. I really don't know what else this mausoleum contains, nor do I care. Walter was a very private person, Mr. Cress. He didn't confide in me . . . or in anyone else so far as I know."

"But you're his executor?"

"Court-appointed executor. Of all his relatives, I was the only one living in the Commonwealth of Virginia. My compensation as executor is a modest retainer, Mr. Cress. Yours as custodian will be your monthly wage. I ask no questions beyond that, and I suggest that you follow suit."

Approaching the main grounds, in the shadow of the looming fortress, the limousine skirted around a big, low stone building with no windows. "The generators," Raymond said, nodding. "Your résumé indicated you are familiar with large-scale electrical generation."

Cress squinted at the stacked insulators atop the blockhouse, the banks of transformers visible from outside. "I am," he said. "Familiar enough to know that system would supply enough electrical power for a small city. What's all that power for?"

"I don't know, Mr. Cress. The megaframe computer, I suppose, and internal systems. This estate is a functioning, self-contained entity. It has a complete inventory of power, water, heating, and ventilation systems, all mechanized and controlled by computers within the main house. There is automated machinery there that runs the place. Your access to those systems is external. You simply monitor and maintain them."

Cress stared through the window, his eyes climbing the forbidding walls of the huge house. "Is there someone in there?" he asked.

"Not to my knowledge," Raymond cut him off with finality. "Just machines. You will be amply paid, Mr. Cress. Just do your job."

The limousine pulled up at a cozy bungalow a hundred yards from the forbidding stone of Scofield Manor's south wall. "These are your quarters," Raymond said. "There is a garage with some vehicles, a fuel-storage complex, some shops, and barns. You'll find adequate food supplies in the freezers, and there's a monthly delivery of staples and fresh produce that you will collect down at the gate. You'll have the run of the estate, and responsibility for its care. You will let no one, repeat, *no one,* enter these grounds unless they have my personal authorization. And, Mr. Cress, the big house is off limits. It is locked and has its own security system. You will have no reason to try to enter there."

Cress got out, opened the car's spacious trunk, and removed his luggage. Then he turned, slowly, surveying his new domain. The big, somber house held his attention. It reminded him of the old main gather at Ossining. "So who does get in there?" he asked. "Who maintains all that equipment? Computers, security systems . . . they don't just take care of themselves, Mr. Scofield."

"The foundation that leases the computer takes care of all that, I'm sure." Scofield frowned. "Do not concern yourself with such matters, Mr. Cress. They do not concern you, in the slightest."

In other words, Cress thought, curiosity is not a requirement for my job. He grinned, shrugged, and accepted the situation. Minding his own business was little enough to ask, for a job that promised good pay, modest demands, and all the seclusion a man could want.

The fact that those electrical power couplings he had

seen were a hundred times larger than anything a country estate with a megaframe computer would ever need was something he didn't need to be curious about.

If Raymond Scofield could pretend that this place was nothing more than an old, sealed-off mansion on a mountaintop, then so could he. For a while, anyway.

Claire Hemmings was putting on a show when Logan strode into the squad room. She had a monitor bay set up with a bank of six buffer computers, a headset and virtual reality mask, and a stack of segment wafers. In the midst of all this paraphernalia, the sublimator was almost unrecognizable. Its pickup base was fitted into a circuit-board cradle with at least a dozen coaxial cables looping, dipping, and diving into various feeder ports in the assembly.

At least a dozen people—techs, computer daticians, and process specialists—were gathered around, listening with various degrees of fascination to what seemed to be a lecture on subjective assimilation of subliminal data.

Logan, heading for the day board, slowed and veered aside at a gesture from Bob O'Donnelly. The young historian was nose-down in his littered cubicle, studying columns of trend data on a ChronComp screen. At O'Donnelly's portal Logan nodded, then pointed toward the gathering of techs. "What's that about?" he asked.

"It's about you, as much as anything," the young historian said distractedly. "Seems like your adaptation of the sublimator as a forgetfulness device has had repercussions clear up to NSA and Black Ops. I guess Hemmings has accepted it as a personal challenge that electronic sublimation has side effects. Right now she's got about half the techs in TEC working on ways to restructure Chron-Comp's subliminal menu. I'd help, but Dr. Easter has me boxed in on this other project. Not my choice. I'm a historian, not a banker."

Logan peered at the screen O'Donnelly was studying. The trend data seemed to be financial reports. It read like a page of *Wall Street Journal* market quotes. "What's all this? Something going on in the stock markets?"

"Yeah," O'Donnelly muttered, absorbed in what he was doing. "Remember the blip analysis the captain ordered? ChronComp found a pattern. It looks like every little bobble we've seen on E-warp lately has a corresponding blip in the stock exchanges. It's really odd."

"Time travel related?"

"If so, it isn't obvious. This isn't something being done in the past. It's current. These are stock market quotations for the present quarter to date. ChronComp flagged it because of the E-warp similarities, but I'm darned if I can see why the stock market would track probability blips from past times. I'm trying to trace some of the market shifts, to see if there's a significant point of origin."

"Why?"

O'Donnelly glanced around at him. "Better see Dr. Easter about that," he suggested. "They don't tell me anything, except to see what I can come up with on these sequences."

It must be a fascinating question, Logan thought, to so occupy Bob O'Donnelly's mercurial attention. With another glance at the shifting crowd around the blond systems analyst and her flock of techs, he crossed the squad room and logged in for the day, pausing to glance at the overhead E-warp screen as he passed the Dome of History. For the moment, it was clear. Just the usual static of microdistortions that rarely made it to the threshold level of historical alteration.

The duty sheet indicated one launch during the preceding night: Agent Will Jackson sent to check a level-one ripple originating just six days ago right here in Washington. The corresponding event—the only corresponding event ThinkTank had found—was a traffic tie-up on the Southwest Freeway, involving a pair of tankers.

Jackson hadn't yet returned, but the ripple had winked out. Only tiny blips showed on the Dome.

Nobody had ever figured out why E-warp showed that sparse "snow" of little anachronisms. Theoretically, history was a fixed continuum unless it was intentionally altered through time travel. Yet there were always the little adjustments, appearing and fading. They showed up on the Dome as tiny blips, and those that persisted—or that grew to levels higher than 0.01—were tracked.

At his desk, he screened his reports and messages. One stood out, noted as urgent. It was a memo from Dale Easter. "Logan, see me," it said.

Was Easter still here? Logan glanced across at the closed door of the library. Didn't the chief historian ever sleep? Scanning the rest of his morning mail, Logan set it aside and crossed to the library.

Dr. Dale Easter's domain, usually pristine and organized, was a mess this morning. Printouts and obscure reference volumes were stacked everywhere. Easter had obviously worked all night on some project, and now

Logan followed the sound of snoring to locate the chief historian, who was sound asleep in a swivel chair in front of the reference banks.

"Well, what suits the goose is fit for the gander," Logan muttered. "This makes us even." Without hesitation, he crossed to the senior historian and shook him awake.

Easter looked up at his tormentor, bleary-eyed. "What time is it?"

"Seven-oh-five," Logan said. "What's up?"

"What?"

"You left me a memo. What's it about?"

"Oh." Easter rubbed his eyes, yawned, and put on his glasses. He peered at the clock. "What it's about, Logan, is your perp. Your scavenger. Somebody's playing games with stock markets, and I have a hunch it's him."

"What have you got?"

"An anomaly scan. Something ChronComp picked up from Securities and Exchange central data. The SEC has a joint inquiry going with the Federal Reserve Board. The international monetary picture is out of sync. Stock share trading is doing some bizarre things, and the economists are trying to figure out why."

"That's what O'Donnelly is working on," Logan noted.

"Right. ChronComp alerted us, because the pattern of oddities in the stock markets matches up with a whole series of borderline blips on E-warp." Easter yawned again, stifled it, and gazed intently at the timecop. "All that money your scavenger has been accumulating . . . we've wondered where it went. Well, this is a possibility. If he's investing it, a little at a time, it would only show as a lot of small distortions, all fading out as they blend into the history mainstream. But the stock markets would feel the effect—a cumulative distortion in world finances that would grow like a snowball."

"Who knows about this so far?"

"Just us." Easter shrugged. "Remember, all those other agencies—SEC and the rest—don't even know about time travel, much less about TEC. So we can know what they know, but not the other way around. Captain Matuzek's been in touch with Black Ops about it, though." He glanced at the clock. "I expect we'll be hearing from Charles Graham this morning. My guess is, there'll be a high-level situation conference, very shortly. Pure speculation, Logan, but you might want to climb into your dress-parade behavior. Whatever happens, I expect you'll be on standby."

### The White House
### Third Floor, West

The big, solemn room was the only place the Black Ops oversight committee ever assembled. Intense security and architectural placement made it the ideal location for discussion of subjects so secret that even the slightest leak might be catastrophic.

"Nothing leaves this room," the president of the United States stressed, his words a ritual that everyone now present had heard before. "What you see here is for your eyes only. What you hear is for your ears only. The oath of secrecy you took upon entering—that each of us took—is absolutely binding. From the moment we leave this room, this meeting will have never happened."

That done, the president put on his famous we're-all-friends-here smile and took a seat at the head of the long table. "Bring us up to speed, Charlie," he said.

Of the nine people in the room, the one who stood now would have been the least noticeable in any crowd. Average height, average build, a quiet, somewhat balding man of indeterminate middle years, Charles Graham blended into whatever background was around him . . . at first glance. But only at first glance. In those rarified circles where he was known at all, Charles Graham was a legend.

To the vast majority of people, even in the highest of places, the name Charles Graham meant nothing. But to those few who knew of him, the name was all that was necessary. Where Charles Graham went, things happened. If Graham had an official title, it was never mentioned. As chief of NSA's black-ops branch, no title was required.

Graham nodded at those around the oak table. "What we are facing here—" He smiled faintly. "—is the worst nightmare of any bureaucrat—a cross-jurisdictional situation impacting taxable resources." He gestured and, in a darkened corner, patterns of light appeared, coalescing into recognizable forms. It was a display screen, but more than a screen. It was a hologram—a dimensional viewer, an exercise in virtual reality. The pattern that emerged was a complex, three-dimensional chart with its axis planes labeled *capital resources*, *goods/services output*, *capital earnings*.

"What you're looking at is called econometrics," Graham explained. "The science—or art—of tracking and measuring economic activity in any market system. This model is dramatically simplified, but our economists tell us this chart fairly represents a current model of the United States economy, which for the past decade has been the bellwether for world markets. Each of you has received documentation explaining—in far greater detail than any reasonable person is likely to require—exactly what each point in this model means. In overview, though, we are looking at a critical malfunction of a financial system that—despite its myriad peculiarities—has been a fairly reliable self-regulating mechanism for more than seventy-five years. We call it the stock market."

He touched a control, and the holographic display began to revolve slowly. "Equilibrium, continuity, and efficiency," he said. "These, with a slight nudge now and then from overseers such as the Federal Reserve Board and world banking interests, are the substance of economic stability. The entire system is, of course, delicate, highly volatile, and virtually undisciplined, but it does a remarkable job of correcting itself as it goes along . . . unless it is tampered with."

"Tampered with?" the president prompted. "In what way, Charlie?"

"Intentional tampering," Graham stated. "It has been attempted many times, for various reasons. The so-called communist utopia, for instance, was a sixty-five-year assault on economic principle. It failed, naturally, but its political repercussions in history are profound. The myth of socialism has caused more human grief than the Roman conquests, the European invasion of the Americas, and Hitler's Third Reich, combined. Another example, quite common down through history, is stock manipulation for purposes of cornering a specific market, or to establish a cartel. These are generally obvious ploys and usually self-curtailing. Then there have been at least three attempts to disrupt the economy of the nation by infusion of counterfeit currency, usually as a strategy of war. These efforts have been troublesome but traceable, since counterfeit currency has no basis in real wealth.

"But we are faced now with an assault of a different order—a systematic infusion of actual capital into various stock issues, triggering a massive disruption in the balance of the capital base." The holographic pattern swirled and reassembled itself into a scrolling display of economic data.

"These continued infusions may or may not have mortally wounded the entire system. Their effect on the measuring techniques has been so disruptive that we cannot tell. But they most certainly have caused investor panic and driven a great many publicly capitalized companies to the verge of bankruptcy."

"We estimate several hundred to date," the chairman of the SEC offered. "We have every investigator at our disposal busy on this, but all we're getting is questions." He leaned forward, narrowed eyes fixed on Graham. "I suspect you have an answer, Mr. Graham. We wouldn't be here, otherwise."

Several others around the table cast curious glances at the sturdy, solemn man seated at Graham's right hand. Most of the people in this room knew one another, but only a few had ever seen Eugene Matuzek, and only two of them—the president and Graham—knew who and what he was.

As though reading their minds, Graham lowered his head and smiled slightly. "Not an answer, Mr. Webb," he said. "But a likely scenario. The gentleman beside me is Captain Matuzek, chief administrative officer of an agency we call TEC. I really don't want to elaborate on that—and believe me, most of you really don't want to know about TEC—except to say that his organization is a highly classified federal agency known to the president, myself, and five members of the United States Senate, and has a working relationship with NSA. Captain Matuzek is here today because TEC has uncovered evidence bearing on the matter at hand."

"What kind of evidence?" the chairman of the Joint Chiefs of Staff demanded. "What do we have here? An act of war, a criminal conspiracy, or what?"

"It's a criminal venture," Matuzek said. "And we believe we know the source of the money that's been messing up the stock markets. We're investigating the source, but the market tampering—as Mr. Graham puts it—is outside our jurisdiction."

At the far end of the table the attorney general raised his hand. "And just what *is* your jurisdiction, Captain?"

Matuzek glanced at Graham, who nodded.

"TEC's jurisdiction is history, sir," Matuzek said.

"History?" The chairman of Joint Chiefs frowned. "What the hell does that mean?"

"Tell them, Charlie," the president ordered.

"It means time," Graham explained, grudgingly. "It means the past. The infusions that have disrupted American finance these past few months—and global economics, too—are moneys recovered from the past by a time traveler. The market tampering began small—widespread, but as small, scattered investments. Thus its historic significance wasn't obvious at first. But now it is snowballing. What was a few millions of dollars circulating through the market system has become many, many billions. The market is no longer serving its own interests, gentlemen. It is now serving the interests of a single person—a man we call the Scavenger."

They stared at him, muttering among themselves, and the attorney general dropped his glasses. *"Time?"* he demanded. "Are you suggesting . . . time travel, Mr. Graham? And that there are . . . ah . . . *time police*?"

"Exactly." Graham nodded. "TEC is the Time Enforcement Commission. Time police. Captain Matuzek is its chief officer."

The chairman of Joint Chiefs gaped, blinked, and appealed to the president, "Sir, this is unthinkable! Even if it's true, the consequences are—Sir, there is absolutely no precedent for such a thing! How are we to accept that people . . . people *move about in time*? What authority do we have? . . ."

"Sit down, General," the president said. "Yes, time travel does exist, and we have time police. Accept it or not, it is a fact. People do go back into history, and some of them don't have the best of motives. As to our authority . . . well, who's going to police the activities of time travelers if we don't?"

"What—what do you want from us?" the attorney general asked.

"Cooperation." Eugene Matuzek shrugged. "TEC's jurisdiction is the past. We need some present assistance in this case."

Outside the private tunnel entrance to the White House, Matuzek held the hatch of Jack Logan's car while Charles Graham climbed in, then followed the black-ops chief into the machine and closed it behind them.

At the controls, Logan thumbed the automode and said, "Seal visuals. Destination TEC."

"Destination confirmed," the car's sweet voice assured him. The louvers closed all around, and the car moved out, driving itself.

"Nice vehicle," Charles Graham noted. "Gen-Em Trace,

eh? I've looked at these, but never owned one. Isn't cardinal red a rather dramatic color, though, for a person in a . . . ah . . . covert profession?"

"It has its uses," Logan said. "You still think we'll be followed, sir?"

"I'd bet on it." Graham grinned. "Those are good people back there. Probably the first really honorable administration the United States has had in a hundred years. But they'll have to test us . . . and test themselves. The captain and I probably had a tail before we ever left the third floor."

"Secret Service?" Matuzek asked.

"More likely FBI. The director's a friend of mine. He wouldn't miss a chance to play Gotcha at my expense."

"Well, let's give them a show," Logan said. To the car he said, "Revised destination. Destination Glen Echo."

"Destination confirmed," the car's electronic voice said. On the monitor, the vehicle's trace turned left on Ninth Street, then right again on Constitution. Logan watched the electronic navigation display, and when they edged to the right on Virginia Avenue, he activated his pursuit sensors. Blips began to appear and disappear on the screen as the car took the Rock Creek ramp toward Whitehurst Freeway.

When they looped over onto MacArthur Boulevard, he opened the viewscreens and took manual control. On his tracking console, the computer was still sifting blips, color-coding those that evidenced pursuit behavior.

"We'll have to get a little rowdy up here," Logan warned.

Matuzek glanced around at Graham. "Do you mind, sir?"

Graham snugged his seat restraints and laced his fingers

across the fabric of his coat. "Wouldn't miss it for the world," he said. "Have fun, Agent Logan. Just don't hurt anybody."

Logan eased his bright red car out of the autocom lanes and into the flowing traffic of the speedway at the same time setting his controls for avoidance maneuvers. At eighty miles per hour the powerful car headed northwest along the Potomac shoreline, and the computer settled on three following vehicles as likely pursuit.

The Georgetown exit flicked past, and the Bethesda exit loomed ahead. At the last moment, Logan eased the wheel to the right. The Gen-Em leapt across eight lanes of traffic, a bullet through a shifting tunnel, and veered onto the exit ramp as two of the pursuit blips flashed past behind it. At the bottom of the ramp he cut back sharply, looped through the entry port of Mount Vernon College, and slewed around a service island to emerge once again on the same road he had just left, but going the other way.

At sedate, street-limit speed the Gen-Em headed back toward the freeway. A long, black car full of intense men zipped past, going the other way, and on the Gen-Em's tracking console the third and last pursuit blip disappeared.

"FBI," Logan mused. "Those boys might as well wear uniforms and carry flags. You can spot them a mile away."

"That was fascinating." Charles Graham grinned. "Three of our nation's best survcillance teams, and it took you only about a minute to lose them. What I don't understand, though . . . why didn't that last car see us? They went right past."

"They were following a *red* Gen-Em Trace," Logan explained.

Graham leaned to his window and looked out at the

gleaming side panels of the car carrying him. It was teal blue with copper trim.

"I like this car," Logan mused. "I'll be paying for it for another two years, but it's worth the price." Once again on the freeway, he told the car, "Resume autocontrol. Destination TEC."

Eastbound on Constitution, they had just passed the Federal Reserve building when Logan leaned forward, peering ahead and to the right. A half mile away, metro copters circled, like moths over a light, around the tall spire of the Washington Monument. "Scan," he told the car. "Long view, two o'clock."

A viewscreen on the main panel cleared and zoomed in on the top of the white spire. "My God," Charles Graham muttered.

Atop the tall monolith, a dead man hung head down from the pinnacle of the 120-year-old monument. Suspended from a length of chain attached to both ankles, the body sprawled in slanting sunlight, dead eyes staring out at an upside-down horizon they would never see. The car's scanner zoomed, focused, and held, its electronic eye so steady and so clear that even the red-rimmed blue and white patch on the dead man's blast suit was legible—a circular patch bearing a stylized hourglass symbol and the letters *TEC*.

The emblem of the Time Enforcement Commission.

"Jackson," Matuzek whispered. "That's Will Jackson. He's the senior agent on duty this morning at TEC."

## TEC Headquarters

"It was an ambush," Jack Logan growled, pacing Eugene Matuzek's office the way a tiger paces a circus cage. "Deliberate, premeditated murder of a time policeman! Jackson never had a chance!"

"I can't find any fault with procedure," Matuzek said. "They had a full level-one ripple, right on top of them. Less than a week in the past. The lieutenant was absolutely correct in authorizing the launch. A ripple that size, that close, it could have been anything! He couldn't chance letting it pass."

"I concur," Charles Graham said, and nodded. "There was no choice. But how did the ambusher arrange such a target?"

"It was ridiculously easy," Dale Easter explained. "Anybody could have done it, time travel or not. The Southwest Freeway is a normal artery for tank trucks carrying fertilizer from New Carrollton down to the Roanoke. Those tankers travel along there every day. And every day they pass other tankers going the other way, hauling fuels up to Baltimore. Standard, everyday traffic.

Not even particularly hazardous cargo, just loads of oil and agricultural fertilizer.

"But picture this: a passenger car with its auto controls locked jumps the median at the Tenth Street Loop. It sideswipes the oil tanker, which plows into the fertilizer truck, and voilà! A double-substance spill—ammonium nitrate and fuel oil, all mixed up together. Enough plain, simple, combustible ANFO to wipe out ten city blocks!"

"ANFO!" Matuzek growled.

"The easiest high-explosive there is to produce," Easter said. "Every farm in the country has the components. But don't underestimate the stuff. It wiped out a refinery complex in Texas in 1947 and a federal building in Oklahoma City in 1995."

"So the freeway spill was a staged accident," Graham said. "But the jumper went back in time to do what he could have done by simply driving to south D.C. Why did he go to all that trouble?"

"To set a trap," Jack Logan said, pausing to stare bleakly out at the subdued, hushed squad room. Another officer had died in the line of duty. That somber fact hung like a pall over the entire headquarters complex. "By jumping back, changing history, he created a ripple, and Jackson drew the short straw. It was an ambush and a message!"

"I agree." Easter took off his glasses and cleaned them. "He knew he'd attract a cop. That's what he wanted. Obviously he doesn't know where we are, and I doubt he knows who we are. But he knows how to get our attention. I believe it was an act of retaliation. We've got an angry man out there. He thought he'd have it all his own way, and we've ruffled his feathers. Now he's striking back.

He's telling us to stay out of his way—to leave him alone, or else!"

"You think it's that same man?" Graham asked. "Your Scavenger?"

"I *know* it is," Easter said. "Jackson's specific launch target was one of the things that happened during that traffic incident—a robbery, just two blocks away. An armored car, making daily pickups, went down. A lone bandit, armed with a plasma gun. No survivors, no witnesses. The take was approximately four million dollars."

"Four million?" Matuzek turned. "That's the amount Logan and Hemmings recovered from the Scavenger, on that Florida jump!"

"Exactly." Easter put his glasses on and nodded. "See what I mean? It was take-back and payback time."

"It should have been me," Logan muttered. "If I'd been here, I'd have made that launch."

"You were doing your job, elsewhere. Does S and R have the ME's report on Jackson, yet?"

"They'll call," Matuzek muttered. "They'll call, but I already know what they'll say. Agent Jackson has been dead for six days. Cause of death, a bullet to the head, nine-millimeter parabellum with blowback marks. A match for the bullet that killed Agent Nash." The captain's narrowed eyes glittered like a burning fuse. "Nash . . . Rafferty . . . Jackson . . . *I want* this creep, Mr. Graham. Whatever it takes, I want him. What can we expect?"

"Cooperation," Graham said. "A joining of forces, if that's what is needed. The FBI in the present, TEC in the past. Whatever we need from the SEC and Treasury. And from Interpol, too, for that matter. My suggestion is a liaison person, to be assigned here. Are you ready to call the shots?"

Before Matuzek could respond, Dale Easter asked, "Do we have reason enough now, Captain, to take a look at that Scofield place in Virginia? Because if we do, I can give you probable cause for a warrant. Those investments I've been tracking with ChronComp—it's the same game the SEC is looking into. The name of the game is manipulation."

"Explain, please," Graham said.

"Sure." Easter took off his glasses and sat back. "In corporate finance, there are two reliable driving forces. Call them opportunity and uncertainty, if you like them, or greed and ignorance if you don't. Either way, it's invested capital that makes commerce possible, but most investment has very little to do with commerce. Some studies say that the trading prices of capital stocks are based about 15 percent on corporate productivity and 85 percent on follow-the-leader behavior. It's that eighty-five percent of the market that makes corporate raiding possible. Anybody with enough money can make a stock's floor price skyrocket. You just pick a stock and buy a lot of it— enough to generate market excitement. Then to cash in, you sell abruptly and let those who followed your lead take the loss. Remember, it's appearance that counts most. Real values—even blue chips if the stakes are high enough—have relatively little to do with it. The sheep lead the sheep, and periodically some wolf harvests the flock. That's how fortunes are multiplied in the world of finance."

He shrugged, put on his glasses, and added, "There are laws, of course. But piracy is nothing new . . . except the way our Scavenger is going about it. His raids on the past have done more than just collect treasure. One of the people who died in the Empire State collision, for example, might—*just might*—not have been there that Saturday if a broken window hadn't set off an alarm. That young man's grandson *just might* have been the Senate staffer who added a variational-limits clause to the SEC codes in 1994. But, of course, that didn't ever happen. ChronComp has tracked two probability curves like that so far, and there may be others. As it stands, ChronComp figures the raider—our Scavenger—is just about this far from throwing half the world into a financial crisis."

"And that's where the lost treasures are going?" Matuzek growled. "Into the stock market?"

"In spades. An aggregate investment of more than twenty billion dollars infused into selected stocks in a matter of weeks. Big buys in little companies, but in separate amounts too small individually to make more than blips on the Dome.

"That's why we never saw a ripple from the lost treasures surfacing. Thirty-seven thousand separate stock purchases, in amounts always less than a million dollars! But they add up. Four hundred and nineteen separate companies have been impacted, as of ten days ago—all suddenly overcapitalized and inflated, then liquidated on the exchange at an average seven-day profit of 130 percent. That's three hundred and sixty billion dollars rolling over to set up a new cash crop of losers."

"But those companies, what happened to them?"

"Belly-up. Happens all the time. It isn't what an enterprise sells that keeps it going, nowadays. It's how it's capitalized. Those gutted companies all have one thing in common. They've all been recently bought and sold—51 percent or better—by a quiet little trust fund set up nearly forty years ago by ... guess who! The late Walter Scofield."

Logan squinted. "How could anybody do that? I mean, just the mechanics of handling that many transactions . . ."

Easter smiled, sadly. "Look around, Jack. The actual transactions are just donkey work. That's what computers are for. Buy/sell is simple software. Anybody can do it."

"We need a profile of this guy," Matuzek decided. "Everything we know about him, fact and conjecture. And get me that FBI liaison, Mr. Graham. Somebody with the balls to act in a crisis and the whiskers to recognize when that is."

"Poppin' Johnny," Graham muttered. "Special Agent John Davis Deere. The attorney general has already mentioned him."

"Get him." Matuzek nodded. "And brief him about TEC."

"I've got a real bad feeling about this one," Jack Logan muttered, moodily. "This Scavenger is a stone-cold fanatic. He has something big in mind, and he's only begun."

Logan's dark mood was a catalyst to Eugene Matuzek. "Logan, snap out of it!" he barked. "We've got work to do. Get Hemmings and O'Donnelly in here—" He glanced around. "—no, in the briefing room. Tell Hemmings to stop fiddling with that damned sublimator. If it doesn't work, send it over to S and R, for God's sake! As of now, she's a cop, not a damned scientist." He punched the recording intercom on his desk. "I want the case tapes on X ray one-one-seven, the *Scavenger* file," he snapped. "Get Amy Fuller on that MIA report, the Manchurian Device. I want every detail and every hunch ChronComp can come up with. Get me a safe line to Wilkins at AusTEC and Poulon at EuroTEC and keep it open. Clear Charles Graham and one FBI special agent—John Davis Deere—

for full TEC access. Notify Lieutenant Skinner that he's to take over routine operations as of now, until further notice. Top-priority alert status beginning now, and somebody put on the coffee!"

A slow grin spread across Charles Graham's face as TEC came to life and jumped to attention, from the squad room to the launch bays, from ThinkTank to the tech pool.

"Gloves off," the chief of Black Ops said to himself. "Ready on the right, ready on the left, ready on the firing line . . ."

From the outside—the streets and ways around the old railyards district—TEC headquarters was invisible. A drab, run-down complex of old office buildings, warehouses, and abandoned assembly shops, the complex had become a unit—a solid cluster of patchwork exteriors covering eleven city blocks. From the outside, only those exteriors could be seen, and the exteriors were all camouflage.

Within this encircling facade of fabric lofts, relief shelters, pawn shops, tattoo parlors, surplus outlets, and lawyers' offices—behind the sheltering skin of urban decay and marginal enterprise, a mile or so from the United States Capitol, lay one of the most secret installations in the world—the Time Enforcement Commission.

Outside TEC itself, only a select few people knew—or might even have guessed—that time travel was a reality and that a sophisticated policing agency existed in the United States, with precinct branches in Europe and Australia, and technology not only for launching agents into the past but also for tracking the timestream of history for anachronisms that created ripples of historic alteration.

The theoretical grounding for four-dimensional transit—or time travel—had, of course, been known and readily available since the time of Albert Einstein. But the theories were like extrasonic resonance. They were music only to those who could hear them. It had taken the genius of Josef Heindl and the persistence of Dr. Hans Kleindast to bridge the gap between theory and reality.

The first of these two men, in the 1940s, had developed working theses for two remarkable breakthroughs—the Eventuality-Wave Resonance Projector, or E-warp, that translated the timestream of sequential events to an image on an observation device, and the dimensional energy convergence phenomenon, or the so-called timefield, that allowed a projectile moving at a speed greater than 2,994 fps to shift from three to four existential dimensions by in fact becoming the fourth of the dimensional components.

Heindl's nephew and heir, Dr. Hans Kleindast, possibly influenced by his childhood exposure to the theorist, had independently invented the technology for both the timesled and the Dome of History, making practical time travel a reality.

And like Pandora's box, time-travel technology—once discovered—could never be absolutely contained. Thus, TEC—the time police—was created, as humanity's frontline defense against historical tampering.

TEC was the best-kept secret in the modern world, a secret known to its participants and a hundred or so others.

Now the latest initiate into this exclusive club—FBI Special Agent John Davis Deere, sometimes and seldom fondly referred to as Poppin' Johnny—stood in the command center and beating heart of the Time Enforcement Commission, TEC's sprawling squad room, and gawked at the wonders around him.

"I never . . . never in my whole life . . . saw anything like this," he muttered for maybe the tenth time, as Charles

Graham and a kid named O'Donnelly guided him through the vast complex.

Deere was no stranger to technology, or to innovation. At fifty-nine years of age, only slightly younger than Graham himself, Poppin' Johnny had seen everything from the development of modern rocketry to the replacement of vacuum tubes by transistors. He had seen computers progress from spinning tapes and keypunch cards to the compact laser-and-liquid marvels of the twenty-first century. He had heard the first radio broadcast from the moon and flown a Piper J-3. With degrees in law, accounting, and criminology, he knew not only the tools of his world but also their most intricate uses.

But he had never seen—or even imagined—a time-travel operation.

"Twenty-nine-ninety-four fps?" he demanded as Bob O'Donnelly tried to explain timefield insertion to him. "Hell, son, that's nearly the muzzle velocity of a Weatherby .300. How do you get a sled to go that fast?"

"Tachyon drive," O'Donnelly said. "The first sleds were powered by solid-fuel rockets, but that's pretty primitive. T-drive is standard now."

Then he had to explain the principles of the tachyon drive, which could be compared in some respects to plasma weaponry, and the mysteries of dimensional wormholes and E-warp eventuality monitoring, which couldn't be compared to anything.

Five minutes with O'Donnelly left the FBI veteran feeling confused and dinosaurish. But then he found solid ground as he was introduced to Matuzek and some of his people. Historians and scientists aside, these were law officers. Deere understood cops. He had been one for nearly forty years.

"How big is that Scofield place, and what do you expect to find there?" he asked Eugene Matuzek as they reviewed strategy in the briefing room.

Matuzek tapped in coordinates, and an aerial map appeared on the briefing monitors—a composite photo of an area of the Blue Ridge Mountains, overlaid with coded delineations, contour lines, projected boundaries, and surrounding terrain detail. In the center of the map, a large section lay almost unmarked, with a rugged peak at its center. The peak was capped with the stone fascia and surrounding grounds of a large, complex building.

"Judge for yourself," the captain said. "The place is a fortress."

"What's it look like, inside?"

Matuzek brought up new images—ChronComp's compilation of all available structural data, condensed into scale-justified displays like three-dimensional working drawings.

"This is all we have," he said. "County records, based on building permit applications filed in the late sixties. They're pretty sketchy, but as you can see, the place is a sort of grand manor in neo-Gothic, complete with winding stairways and arched ceilings. But behind the stone facades are all the modern conveniences, including two banks of elevators. One goes from the ground floor to the penthouse, five stories up. The other, a service elevator, goes down to the basement. There's a big computer there—a megaframe, linked into some conservancy trust that leases time and space on it."

"What trust is that?"

"It's called Farsight Trust. Apparently Walter Scofield set it up, back in the fifties. It's big. County records indicate the computer-time lease from that one trust is what pays taxes and maintenance on the estate."

Poppin' Johnny's seamed brow furrowed deeper. "You don't have a damned thing here," he growled. "This is just blueprints. If there's something going on in that place, I'll have to get inside to see it. Do we have a search warrant, or some kind of probable cause?"

"We have enough," Charles Graham said, as another screen came to life. "We have a subpoena for financial records on Farsight Trust, and an affidavit from an SEC investigator that Farsight failed to provide accountancy data on grounds of computer malfunction."

"But that's a New York subpoena," Deere pointed out. "This is Virginia."

"This is where the computer is physically located," Graham said. "SEC has issued a trace order, to that computer. That's your warrant."

Deere snorted. "Games," he said. "A trace order doesn't empower a search of premises. Just of data."

"So don't make any observations on your way in." Graham grinned.

Somewhere a signal sounded, and TEC officer Jack Logan appeared in the doorway. "We've got a ripple, Captain," the timecop snapped. "Level two."

"Come on, Johnny," Graham said. "You'll find this interesting."

"It's 1987, October 19 . . . Black Monday!" Dale Easter intoned, gazing up at the Dome. In the slowly swirling, coalescing patterns displayed there, an ugly asymmetry intruded, seeming to grow and spread as it crept outward from its source, chewing away at the normal sequences of events in the timestream. "The worst stock market crash in history." The historian spread his arms dramatically. "It made the stock exchange collapse of 1929 look like pocket change. The Dow Jones Industrials fell six hundred points! Almost half its face value!"

"Where?" Matuzek asked, interrupting the dissertation.

Easter blinked at him. "Where? *Everywhere!* Black Monday was a price crash in stock market shares . . . all over the world! Millions of people lost fortunes, in one day!"

"The ripple!" Matuzek snapped. "Where does the ripple originate?"

"Oh, that. Uh, the New York Stock Exchange. Wall Street, New York City. We're working on it."

"Here's something," Amy Fuller said, pulling up data on her ChronComp screen. "I've found the source of that idea about time travel, that Willy Carmichael claimed came from Harvard Business School's banks." The screen cleared and steadied. "It's part of somebody's spreadsheet calculations, and it has the same date—October 19, 1987. It's a hard-copy reproduction on microfilm—like a grocery list of stocks, with beginning and closing prices, and there's some doodling in the margin. A diagram and some equations."

Looking over her shoulder, Claire Hemmings drew a whistling breath. "That's a centrifuge equation! That, and a power diagram for a timefield. Can you get a mathematical analysis on that, Amy?"

"Got it." The historian nodded, snapping to another screen. "It *is* a timefield! See, these dimensional symbols are vectors and control data. But how? . . ."

"Willy Carmichael saw this," Claire said. "He found it in old university files, and put two and six together. This is where he got the idea for his roller-plate. Somebody left it scribbled here, and Willy figured it out. The kid's a genius! A stupid, lucky genius!"

"What's that got to do with our ripple?" Matuzek cut in, pointing at the growing pattern of intrusion in the Dome. It was the sort of pattern they all dreaded—a deepening, converging alteration in the serene coalescence around it. A full level-two ripple, and growing!

Amy Fuller pointed at her screen. "The date," she said. "The date on the spreadsheet. It's October 19, 1987."

"Fortunes lost, fortunes found," a harsh voice said, behind them. Matuzek turned and found Jack Logan already in his blast suit and field gear. "It's the Scavenger," the timecop said. "This one's mine, Gene."

A launch bay tech rushed in, carrying an old-fashioned clipboard, which he handed to Easter. Easter scanned it, nodded, and handed it over to Matuzek. "We have coordinates, Captain. The field is energized. Single insertion?"

"No!" Claire Hemmings called, from her own cubicle. A moment later she was there, looking up at Matuzek. "Logan was right, sir. There *are* side effects from the sublimator. The tests indicate at least a slight disorientation factor that could be cumulative. Let me go along, sir. I'm already speed-briefed on the coordinates."

Matuzek scowled, then made up his mind. "Suit up, Hemmings. You can be Logan's eyes and ears for '87, but he calls the shots." To Easter he said, "Team launch. Go in ten. Allow one hour for orientation and intervention."

Nine minutes later, FBI Special Agent John Davis Deere found himself at the launch bay viewport—a thick, reinforced glass window to the launch bays—with Charles Graham beside him.

"In one minute," Graham explained, "you're going to see something very few people have ever seen. I know you've been briefed in how this works, but briefing and seeing are two different things. That thing out there, at the dock, is a timesled. The people strapping in are timecops. Countdown is already started, and in a few moments that tachyon torch is going to fling that timesled down that track, which dead-ends just past those big generator arms you see down there. The sled will be traveling at Q-velocity when it hits the field between those armatures. An instant later, those field agents will be in the year 1987, trying to stop a historical alteration that we'll never know about if they don't succeed because then it will be just part of history."

"What if it doesn't work?" Deere rumbled.

"If the launch doesn't work, the sled and everything in it will become part of that wall out there, just past the armatures . . . so thoroughly fused into it that it would take spectrum analysis to find their remains." Graham shrugged. "It has happened. It's possible. What it amounts to is, if the sled fails, those two people will never know it. If their mission fails, they might be the only people on earth who do."

Countdown wound down and the tachyon drive came to life. With a roar that even the massive shielding of the launch bays couldn't muffle, the timesled shot downtrack like a bullet. Two hundred yards away, it was only a blur. Then at the far end of the launch tunnel the great armatures arced across and the distant wall dissolved into a momentary swirl of indescribable dimensions.

On the PA, the droning countdown voice said, "Launch complete, insertion achieved one-five-three-three-point-one-six hours. Received mode activated."

"How . . . how long will they be gone?" Poppin' Johnny asked.

"As long as it takes," Graham told him. "Time-in on location equals time-out here. Duration remains constant. A timecop doesn't terminate a temporal insertion until he's either completed his assignment or run out of options. Those people's only task now is to find what changed history at that time on that day in that place, and stop it from happening. They only get one shot at it."

"If you're ready, Agent Deere," Eugene Matuzek said when they returned to the squad room, "we'll get you and your partner started on your own mission."

"My partner?" Poppin' Johnny turned. "I don't have a—"

"You do now. When you get to the Blue Ridge, you'll need a computer wizard. Bob O'Donnelly's going with you."

# IX

## New York City
## October 19, 1987

Logan tumbled from a reeking, arched ceiling and sprawled across thundering railway tracks. Everywhere was stench, noise, and confusion, all interlaced by the sounds of hundreds of plaintive, angry voices. For an instant he squinted around him, half convinced that he had died and gone to hell. Then realization struck him—this wasn't hell, only the New York subway system. Hell was still an instant away, in the form of big, iron bumpers hurtling at him out of the darkness.

With a gasp, he flipped himself over and rolled aside just as a train thundered past—a dizzying blur of big wheels, lighted windows, and vortex currents that almost dragged him under. The deafening roar seemed to go on and on, then as suddenly as it had begun, it was gone. Logan stood in the railbed, staring at a crowded station platform three tracks away. Hundreds of people lined the platform, most of them staring back. Some jeered, a few screamed, and others applauded as he made his way carefully across the intervening space, turning this way and that, afraid of what he might find.

Claire Hemmings should have been right beside him when he materialized, but she was nowhere in sight. Avoiding the electrified rails, he searched the railbed for her—or any part of her—then sprinted for the platform. He made it barely ahead of another train, slowing as it approached from the other direction.

As he vaulted and rolled, clearing the lip, people scattered around him, and a pair of uniformed policemen pushed through. At the sight of the holster on Logan's hip, their hands went to their guns. "Don't make a move, sir!" the nearest one commanded. "Not a twitch! Now get your hands up where I can see them . . . please."

The one behind him had his service revolver half-drawn, his thumb on the hammer.

"Easy . . . easy!" Logan urged, raising his hands shoulder-high. "I'm a cop! Officer Jack Logan, TEC. My partner's down there, someplace."

The two relaxed slightly. "You're a cop?" The nearest one squinted. "What kind of uniform is that? What are you, SWAT?"

"Not exactly." Logan eased his arms down. "Look. My partner was right beside me when that engine went by. Now I can't find her."

*"Her?"* The second cop blinked. "Christ, they got women in SWAT now?" What's the world coming to, his tone asked.

"Well, if your partner was on that main track, whatever's left of her's pulling into Battery Station about now," the first one said. "Look, man, I'm sorry, but there's no way anybody could—"

A few yards away, herds of people milled at the entries of the train, and shouts erupted from there. A small, dark-uniformed figure—like a blond ninja with a bad attitude—

was clambering down from the half-hidden top of the subway car.

"Is that her?" The second policeman pointed. "How the hell did she get up there?"

For a moment, Claire was hidden by the throngs of people—people by the thousands swarming everywhere in contained spaces that seemed barely adequate for dozens. Then she emerged, disheveled and bristling. "I'm going to fry that launch tech!" she snarled. "He promised insertion within five hundred yards, but he never mentioned a damned subway!" Glancing at the bemused policemen standing there, she added, "Hi. Which way to the Stock Exchange?"

"It's right up there." One of them gestured. "This is Wall Street Station. Are you all right?"

"If you call landing on top of a subway car going the wrong direction, then having to jump to another one going the other way, all right, then I guess I'm all right. Come on, Logan. We've got things to do, and the clock's ticking."

Claire headed for the nearest exit stairway, and Logan grinned, shrugged, and followed, into the flowing ranks of inbound commuters and sundry other humanity. Behind them the two cops glanced at each other. "We should have checked IDs, I guess," the first one said.

"For what?" The second frowned. "Reports? Maybe a SWAT inquiry, in triplicate? Look, Mac . . . on subway detail, if nobody's bleeding, nothing happened. Forget it."

From the crowded subway, Logan and Hemmings emerged onto an even more crowded street. Morning foot traffic was at its peak, and a solid, seething mass of humanity flowed and eddied along battered sidewalks flanking streets that were like creeping parking lots.

Logan stepped up onto a lamppost pedestal to look around, and Claire tugged at his boot. "Come on!" she said. "I know the way."

He followed her, a zigzag path across a crowded street and through the crowds to a once-elegant entryway. Just inside, an X-ray scanner buzzed its alarm, and Claire flipped out a small wallet. She flashed a gold shield toward the guards and said, "Metro Unit, security inspection."

The guards backed off, and Logan followed her across a wide, marble-tiled lobby. "You *do* know your way around," he commented, as they strode up a wide stairway. "How did you know about that Metro Unit business?"

"The same way I know that Bernhard Goetz is being sentenced today, uptown," she said. "And that there's an antigenocide picket line outside the UN building, and that *Alien Nation* is the top-earning movie right now. The sublimator, Logan. It may have its peculiarities, but it *does* work."

"Touché, pussycat," Logan muttered. "Okay, where to now?"

"The ripple's source is here," she said. "ChronComp gives it a ninety-two that it has to do with transfer of stock shares, which means there are two possibilities: the trading floor and the quotation boards, which are upstairs. Now it's your turn. Exactly what are we looking for?"

"The Scavenger," Logan said. "We've both seen him. Now we have to find him."

"God!" she sighed. "In these crowds? Okay, which do you want, the floor or the boards?"

"I'll take the floor," he decided. "Keep in touch. Uh . . . where is the trading floor?"

She pointed to the right. "Follow the crowd. You can't miss it. Only members and pages are allowed on the floor, but you can observe from the clerks' stations along the sides."

As Claire headed up the next flight of stairs, Logan pushed his way into the tide of stock traders heading for the arena. Outside, it had been easy to blend with the crowd. In lower Manhattan, *anybody* could blend with the crowd. Here, though, his blast suit was painfully conspicuous among the gray suits, white shirts, and dark ties that were the protective coloration of the Wall Street wolf pack.

"Gray little men with their gray little suits and gray little minds," Logan muttered, recalling words that had defined the great MBA tide of the egocentric eighties.

Nearing the great double doors of the trading floor, Logan hesitated as a stir erupted just ahead of him. Pushing through the inbound crowd, an angry, outbound trader jostled and bumped those around him—a gray little man with fury in his eyes, going against the flow. Those around him did no more than glance at him and crowd aside—withdrawn, disinterested cogs in the wheels of commerce—and their very remoteness seemed to fuel his anger. "Clones!" he spat. "Count on it, you're next!" Turning, he bumped into Logan and almost fell before Logan caught him and steadied him on his feet.

"Well, by God," the man grumped, "a real, live person." He blinked at the rigid uniform, the holstered weapon, and looked upward, meeting Logan's eyes. "What planet are you from?"

"This one." Logan shrugged. "I'm Logan."

"Eldon Fister." The man nodded, straightening his tie. "Uh, have a nice day." He started on, cursing under his breath.

Logan caught his arm. "Wait a minute," he said. "Are you leaving? Why?"

"I'm out of it," Fister growled. "My clients dropped me and six others, before the bell. Nineteen years on that lousy floor and all of a sudden everything's buy/sell software and my broker's credentials don't rate in Standard and Poor's? What am I supposed to do now? Young Turks an' *Hahvahd* pip-squeaks! Yuppies! Only asset I have is my seat on the Exchange, an' the computer sharks have devalued that to ten cents on the dollar. Sons of bitches can all go take a flyin'—"

"How about showing me around in there?" Logan cut in. "I'm looking for a man."

"If you think I believe a story like that, you're crazy," Fister said as he led Logan around the perimeter of the New York Stock Exchange trading floor. "Criminal from the future . . . ha! That's a good one. Why not just tell me you're after an inside trader? That's what it amounts to, isn't it?"

"This guy *does* know what happens next," Logan admitted. "I guess it's the same thing. He's here today because there's a record plunge, and he knows it, and he's capitalizing on it. With stolen money."

"He'll be selling short, then." Fister shrugged. "Any particular stock?"

Logan gazed out across the room—a sea of bustling, frantic humanity seething and swirling around a forest of U-shaped posts where crowds of traders gathered, ready for the opening bell. "Probably small companies, but it could be anything. The market's going down like a rock today. It'll be the worst panic since '29."

"You're certain of that?" The trader turned, squinting up at him. "*Absolutely* certain?"

"I'm certain." Logan nodded. "Now, where do I start looking?"

A bell sounded, echoing through the vaulted enclosure of the world's primary trading arena, and the massive, crowded confusion of the place became a frenzied, elaborate dance as trading began. There were crowds everywhere, pushing and shoving, hurrying and shouting, waving lettered signs, thronging around the peripheries, and crowding around the myriad posts where stock deals were finalized.

"This is right out of medieval times," Logan muttered. "A freehand commodity market."

"That's what makes it work," Fister told him, shouting above the noise of countless, simultaneous offers and bids. "Computers can handle a thousand stock offers and orders a second, a million paper transfers can be made, but nothing actually happens until this seller's offer and that buyer's bid meet eyeball to eyeball on this floor and execute a deal. This is where the electronics stop and the people start. Machines don't run the open market. All the trading takes place right out there. Clerks take the orders around the perimeter, and flash their member codes on the big boards up there. Then an Exchange member hand-carries the order onto the floor. Every post out there is an auction in progress, and the members are the participants. As deals are made, the pages carry them to the posts and transmit upstairs to the big boards.

"It's a whole 'nother world in here, Logan, with rules and ceremonies all its own. The Exchange is a private club that prospers because it has exclusive trading rights in a three-trillion-dollar market and nobody but its members can participate."

The broker paused, looked thoughtfully around the big room, and pointed. "If your insider is here, my bet is he'd be somewhere in those galleries behind the phone banks, where he can see the action on the floor. But if he's doing what you said, he won't be flagging spot trades. First he'll be dumping his stock at bargain offer to drive the prices down. On a normal trading day, even a sell-off of ten or eleven billion dollars might not generate the kind of panic necessary to drive the whole market down. But if there's a big, across-the-board drop anyway, your man might be able to start a snowball.

"At any rate, he'll start a sell-off, then try to buy up the sound stuff—the issues that will regain price levels because of intrinsic value—at bargain-basement rates. He'll be issuing what's called 'limited orders' for purchase way below the current quotes. Maybe 15 to 20 percent below offer, on blocks of a thousand shares. That means his action will go to the specialists, as limited orders."

"So he'd sell his stocks low, then buy some of them back even lower. Then what?"

"What else?" Fister shrugged. "Give the market a month or so to adjust, then sell again at a huge profit. He might double or triple his money. Maybe it will work, but only once. The Exchange has ways to protect itself against repeat pirates. My bet is, he'd take his winnings and run. Maybe put the money in something else, not handled on this exchange. Like grain futures or pork bellies. If you'd like, I can nose around the floor and see how busy the specialists are with junk orders, maybe talk to some two-dollar brokers and get a line on what the bears are doing."

"I'd like," Logan decided. "See if you can point me to the buyer."

"But I need a client," Fister said, squinting up at him. "I've got to be in the market to get on the floor."

"Oh," Logan said, understanding. Fister was saying, Make it worth my while. Logan hesitated a moment, then retrieved a plastic card from his belt pouch. It was a Visa credit card, dated 1987, a memento procured by Charles Graham from FBI wares. "Okay, buy something." He handed the card to the broker. "The limit on this is five thousand dollars."

"A dabbler," Fister sneered, then grinned. "Okay, Logan. You're in the game. First time I ever had a client wandering around the Exchange with a gun on his hip."

On a higher floor in the same building, Claire Hemmings had already found something. Opening quotations across the board were tumbling, and there was a sense of panic in the air. In a big, fluorescent-lit room, clerks sat before a long bank of entry consoles, typing in quotations relayed by pages at the posts on the trading floor. Exchange executives gathered there, watching closely, and a chief clerk hovered over a master-board control. As the quotations were typed in, they appeared on scrolling screens all around the room—small duplicates of the big boards over the trading floor: *L&R 19³/4 +¹/2 . . . MLS 40⁷/8 +⁵/8 . . . CTY 37 +¹/2 . . .*

"Somebody's dumping a lot of shares," a harried Executive Committee member told her when she flashed her badge at him. "Starting at the bell, a hell of a lot of odd-lot stuff—little companies mostly—hit the floor at offers 10 to 15 percent below quotation, and it's still happening. Now the big stocks are following suit, even the blue chips. It's like a campaign to collapse the markets. Millions of dollars of loss-taking, heading for billions, and it's starting to snowball."

"Who?" Claire demanded. "Who's doing it?"

"It started with a couple of numbered accounts," the man said. "Somebody's computer running on buy/sell software. Happens all the time nowadays, but it's little investments—a few hundred shares here and there. This is millions of shares!"

The phenomenon was causing a stir on the trading floor as harried brokers reacted to the continuing slump—first buying frantically, then having second thoughts as prices continued to plunge. The trend had reversed itself within minutes. Now prices all over the board were plunging as traders responded to their clients and began to bail out in panic.

And there was something else, that Claire uncovered in a glean of specialist notations filed before the bell, in accordance with Exchange rules. The day's advance orders for basement bids, recorded and filed by member brokers, was nearly six times the normal junk traffic generated by speculators fishing for bargains. There were a dozen named accounts listed on the buyout orders, but Claire would have bet that most of them tracked back to a single trader, and in her sublimator-stimulated memories something clicked into place.

"Have you got a line to the Commodities Exchange in Chicago?" she asked a clerk.

"No direct line after the bell," the girl said. "Just cellular. But we get the opening reports. You want to see them?"

"Just pull up their silver futures." Claire leaned over the clerk's console to glance at the monitor. "I'd like to see the advance orders for dated purchase. What quantity and who's buying."

Fifteen minutes later, Claire put down her notes and expelled a low, whistling breath. "My God," she breathed. "What's this joker trying to do, corner the world?"

From the control gallery she could see the floor of the Stock Exchange. The great arena was alive with activity, Exchange members and their staff people scurrying from pillar to post as the big boards on the walls ticked off the decline of stock prices. Black Monday was in full swing. High on the walls of the Exchange floor, green-on-black sequence signs scrolled mindlessly, tracking the downward path of a thousand corporate stocks in the universal symbols of finance: *GM 49 +$\frac{1}{8}$ . . . ATL 17 +$\frac{3}{4}$ . . . C&B 31$\frac{1}{2}$ +$\frac{1}{2}$ . . .*

It took a while—there were so many people scurrying around down there—but finally she caught a glimpse of Jack Logan. He was over by the far wall, in earnest conversation with a little, balding man who wore the uniform of an Exchange broker—white shirt, dark tie, and gray pants that matched the coat slung over his shoulder.

There was no way for her to signal Logan, no way to reach him . . . no way to warn him that just above him, behind the glass of another observation gallery, a tall, thin man with the distinctive, craggy face and beak nose of the Scofields was also scanning the Exchange floor, watching the frantic, ritual dance of the brokers and traders. Even at this distance, Claire recognized the face of the man she had seen in another time and place, the man who had so disinterestedly murdered all those people on the Florida boat. The same man who had already killed three experienced timecops, who had displayed one of them atop the Washington Monument as an ultimatum . . . the Scavenger.

Fifty feet apart, Logan and the time jumper both watched Black Monday proceed on the trading floor of the New York Stock Exchange. They hadn't seen each other yet. Just above the gallery window where the jumper stood, the ubiquitous numbers and letters scrolled: $C\&B$ $28^{1}/_{4} +^{1}/_{4}$ . . . $GM\ 46 +^{7}/_{8}$ . . . $ATL\ 12^{5}/_{8} +^{1}/_{8}$ . . .

Claire glanced around. The only exits from the board compound were several hundred feet away, all leading to outer corridors. There was no quick path from here to the great arena of the trading floor.

Across the way, the balding little man had disappeared into the crowds on the floor, and Logan was prowling the perimeter. He looked like a big, dark stalking cat among scurrying mice. And above him, in the observers' gallery, the Scavenger saw him, too. Even at this distance, Claire saw the jumper's laser-sighted handgun appear from beneath his coat. He pressed for a moment at the enclosing glass, twenty feet above Logan's unsuspecting head, then turned and hurried toward the rear of the gallery.

Directly behind the clerks' cubicles, behind the perimeter ring where Logan prowled, a double door with an exit sign loomed like the jaws of a trap. "Get out of there, Logan," Claire breathed. "For God's sake, turn around. Watch that door behind you!"

"An hour into the day and the Dow's down eighty-eight points!" Someone over by the board banks swore. "God, this is going to be a bloodbath!"

Every telephone in the place was ringing or in use, and people were rushing everywhere. Claire focused on the far side of the trading floor, and saw the door behind the cubicles shiver as its lock was broken. An instant later it swung open, and a tall, lean silhouette appeared there, searching.

With an oath, Claire sprinted across to the board banks, shouldered the chief clerk aside, and hit the override key on the master control. All around the room——and on the big boards above the trading floor—scrolling symbols blinked out and were replaced with three words: *Behind you Logan . . .*

On the trading floor, the killer's beam aligned and the muffled spit of his Springer-9 was drowned in the tumult of the place. But Jack Logan wasn't where the bullet went. The agent had dived, rolled, and come up three yards away with his own weapon at the ready. He spotted the open door and the man standing there, and leveled his gun to shoot. But a hurrying page crossed his beam, and Logan hesitated. When his view was clear again, the doorway was empty. He sprinted toward it, vaulting over the desk of a surprised clerk, and disappeared into the corridor beyond.

In the quotations gallery, Claire made a decision. People were thronging around her, demanding her attention, reaching for her console's controls, and she pulled her Metro Unit shield and backed them away.

Taking advantage of the moment's confusion, she pulled out her list of specialist orders and handed it to the same clerk who had produced it for her. "Change these," she ordered. "Make them market orders at present offer."

The clerk stared at her, wide-eyed. "Just do it!" Claire snapped. "We're after a thief!"

The clerk looked at the chief clerk, who looked at the board executive, who took a deep breath. "Okay," he said. "Do it."

The clerk's fingers danced on the console, and all the scroll boards came to life again. On the floor there was turmoil as buy orders went to a dozen posts, and execution symbols flowed up the screens.

With each execution, the Scavenger's accounts bought back the stocks they had sold, and others . . . all at a stunning loss.

Jack Logan raced along the exit corridor, then dodged aside as a jacketed nine-millimeter bullet grazed his thigh and gouged the glazed tiles behind him. Its banshee wail as it ricocheted along the corridor drowned the little plips of two more shots, bracketing him as he caromed off a wall and reversed his dodge.

Thirty yards ahead, a phantom of shadow flickered at a corner, and Logan put a shot there. Tile shards and grout exploded as the shadow disappeared. "This guy is good," he muttered, sprinting toward the turn. "Where did he learn this?"

At the lighted corner he hesitated, then swung around the tiles, his gun leveled. Only an empty stairwell faced him, but somewhere above were faint footfalls and the hiss of an oiled door-closer. Logan headed up the stairs three at a time, his gun at the ready.

Two flights up a slow-closing fire door clicked into place just as he reached it. He kicked the stop-lock, wrenched the door open, and stepped out into a wide, carpeted hall where only one person was in sight—a man in a UPS uniform, down on his knees.

Logan squatted beside him, noting the welling blood from a fresh wound just above his eye. "Are you all right?"

"I—I guess so," the deliveryman mumbled. "Bastard hit me."

Logan looked at the man's eyes, felt his pulse, then helped him to his unsteady feet. "You'll be okay," he said, nodding.

At the end of an adjoining hall, an elevator door was closing just as Logan rounded the corner. He ran toward the elevator bank, then threw himself to one side as a tall figure emerged from a doorway, shooting.

Logan felt his left arm go numb, and returned the fire. The Scavenger ducked out of sight, then reappeared, snapping a shot as he dashed across the hall and through a door beyond.

Logan felt a moment's disorientation, and saw the blood dripping from his fingers, below the cuff of his blast suit. The Scavenger wasn't shooting at center target. He knew about vests and was placing his shots to score, not trying for a sure kill.

He found he could move his fingers, and the effort brought feeling flooding back into his stunned arm. His left shoulder suddenly hurt like hell, but everything seemed to be working.

Scuttling across the hall, his eyes and his gun trained on the door where the Scavenger had gone, Logan came up to the door frame and hesitated for an instant, then lunged and hit the door, hard, falling forward and down as it crashed open.

He expected bullets, but instead there was a scream of sheer, outraged anger. Logan rolled, came up, and pointed his gun . . . at a swirling, dissolving vortex of collapsing dimensions where the Scavenger's raging figure lingered for a blink, then disappeared.

"Damn!" Logan growled. Then, through the wall-wide

glass of a private gallery high above the trading floor of the New York Stock Exchange, he saw what the Scavenger had seen. On the big boards beyond, trades were being recorded, purchases executed on vast quantities of odd-lot shares. Intuitively, Logan knew what had occurred. The Scavenger's collapse-and-buy plan had been thwarted. The wheels of commerce were rolling and grinding the pirate's profits into economic fodder.

## TEC Headquarters
## 2007

"Well, you stopped the ripple," Eugene Matuzek admitted, gazing across his desk at Logan and Hemmings. "I can't say I like the way you did it, but you did it. Black Monday could have led to a world market collapse, if the Scavenger's ploy had worked. But it didn't. I only wish you could have brought that creep in. I have the feeling we may have a loose cannon on our hands, now that he's really angry."

"We left tracks." Claire Hemmings scowled. "Pretty big tracks, I'm afraid. Interfering with market orders, the way I did, that was sloppy. I just didn't know what else to do."

"Apparently it wasn't too bad." Dale Easter shrugged. "The Dow Jones Industrials fell five hundred and eight points that day, but it recovered. ChronComp's best scenario suggests a thousand-point crash if you hadn't stopped it. So how much damage did you do?"

"We changed history," Logan said. "In original history, the Black Monday plunge was more than six hundred points, and one of the repercussions was a change in market rules, for an automatic moratorium on world exchanges anytime share prices dropped more than three hundred points in one day."

"If that had been in place," Claire added, "we wouldn't have seen crashes in 1997 and 2005."

"Not to mention Eldon Fister becoming an overnight millionaire." Logan grinned ironically. "And doing it on our money."

"Your Visa card?" Matuzek blinked. "He reimbursed his charges on that. It's clear."

"Yeah," Logan said. "He 'borrowed' five thousand dollars and paid back five thousand dollars . . . out of total earnings of nearly forty thousand dollars, which he parlayed into more than a million in the following year. The little opportunist saw what was happening and played every card I'd dealt him."

Matuzek shook his head. "Well, it can't be helped now. History is history. But the Scavenger is still out there, and I dread what he'll do next." He gazed at Logan. "How are the wounds?"

"Just scratches. I was lucky."

"I think I know what the Scavenger'll do next," Claire said bleakly. "I saw his game plan. Dale, I'd like to see everything you and ThinkTank can come up with on silver futures."

"While you're at it," Logan added, "how about giving ChronComp everything we have on this guy, especially his description. Try for a deep check against Special Forces files—CIA, M-1, SEALs, Rangers, the whole smear. Our Scavenger handles himself like a pro in shoot-and-hide situations. Maybe he learned it somewhere."

## The Blue Ridge Mountains
## 2007

Clouds lay low in the valleys around Bucks Ridge, shrouding the uplands in thick, gray mist. Halfway up from Dustin, the haze was thick enough for headlights and wipers as the rental car squealed and fishtailed up a narrow, slippery blacktop between pine-clad slopes.

Baldrock Peak, the mountain retreat of Walter Scofield, was somewhere ahead, and Poppin' Johnny Deere growled and squinted as he manipulated the wheel, cursing the blinding fog while he slewed the machine around curve after curve of the treacherous road. Wet gravel flew from narrow shoulders at each bend, sometimes spraying forested slopes, sometimes showering outward over precipitous cliffs. Bob O'Donnelly sat in the passenger seat, pale and looking like a seasick teenager on his first roller-coaster ride. He was beginning to wonder if what had made John Davis Deere a legend among FBI special agents was a simple death wish.

Clinging to his electronics kit and his computer equipment, all of which was piled up in his lap, TEC's analog wizard squeezed his eyes closed as the rented car accelerated around a cliff-top hairpin curve, then suggested, "We aren't really in all that much of a hurry, you know."

The big man at the wheel barely glanced at him, then put on a new burst of speed as the car shot through a narrow, winding tunnel of forest with blind fog ahead. "Counting day-rental, mileage, and add-on insurance charges," he growled, "this automobile is costing the taxpayers approximately forty cents a minute, any way you cut it. Might as well get our money's worth."

Just as it seemed to O'Donnelly that this wild ride would never end, the road widened to a turnaround, and tall, iron gates loomed ahead in the fog. The gates were closed, and a limousine stood beyond them. As the newcomers approached, a man got out of the limousine and stood by the gates. Beyond, dim in the fog, a covered utility van sat waiting.

Deere brought his car to a halt, climbed out, and approached. "Raymond Scofield?" he inquired. "I'm Special Agent Deere, FBI. Thank you for coming up to meet us."

"I hope there's a good reason for all this," the executor said. "I was told you have a warrant."

"Yes, sir. Trace warrant from the SEC, to access the information banks of a computer system used by the Farsight Trust."

"Farsight Trust leases that equipment," Scofield pointed out. "It has nothing to do with this estate. You should be talking to the Trust people."

"Yes, sir, I understand." Deere nodded. "But the data system *is* located here, and we have a warrant to view it. Farsight has an independent contractor to maintain their computer. But we haven't been able to locate that individual. So we contacted you."

"Very well." Scofield shrugged. "I'll admit you. Please follow Mr. Cress over there. He's the caretaker, he'll lead you up to the house. I suppose I'll have to go inside with you, but I can't show you much. I hardly ever come here. My relative, Walter Scofield, was an eccentric, Mr. Deere. I didn't care for him when he was alive, and I still don't."

"Just show us where to access the computers," Deere said.

"I can do that, I suppose. It's all under the house, in a basement. There's an elevator."

Deere looked at him curiously. "Have you *ever* been in that house, sir?"

"Only once," Raymond admitted. "When Walter died and I was appointed executor, I came here. But I didn't stay. I didn't go past the entry hall. I don't like this place, Mr. Deere. I don't like to go in there."

"Why?"

Scofield hesitated, then lowered his head. "Sounds. Just sounds. The house is—alive, Mr. Deere. It maintains itself. It contains machinery for that purpose, and I know that's all it is, but I don't like the sounds. So I don't go in there. Nobody does, except the computer maintenance person who enters from the roof when he's here."

"Sounds," Deere muttered.

Scofield stepped aside and opened the gate—voice, palm, and retina security scans—and Deere climbed back into the rented car. "Do you have acoustical analysis equipment in all that stuff?"

"I can rig something up," O'Donnelly said. "Why?"

"We might hear sounds," Deere explained.

"Sounds?"

"Sounds."

Inside the gate, Cress the caretaker led off in the utility van while Deere and O'Donnelly followed. Scofield's unchauffeured limousine completed the caravan. The "driveway" was three miles long, a tended road winding around the fog-shrouded cap of Baldrock Peak. It emerged, finally, into a wide, high meadow where the forbidding heights of Walter Scofield's private castle overlooked its remote domain of gardens, outbuildings, and seclusion.

At a wide, paved courtyard, the vehicles pulled up and the men got out. Cress, the caretaker, stood aside and silent as Scofield headed for the massive entryway of the main house, followed by O'Donnelly. Poppin' Johnny started after them, then hesitated, glancing at the bearded man by the van. "You're Cress?" he asked. "My name is Deere. Do I know you from somewhere?"

"Don't think so." Cress shrugged.

"Seems like I've seen you, somewhere."

"Not likely," Cress said. "I don't go there anymore."

With a frown, Deere turned and tagged after the others. Just as Raymond Scofield reached the secured door, a deep, resonating rumble seemed to hang in the air, coming from everywhere and nowhere. Deere thought of earthquakes and distant thunderstorms, but realized that he wasn't actually hearing anything. The sound wasn't really a sound at all, just a deep resonance that he *felt* but didn't actually hear. The sound . . . the feeling . . . seemed to be inside him, an intense almost-emotional awareness like sudden dread.

Just ahead of him, Bob O'Donnelly had stopped, gazing around in wonder. "What *is* that?" the young historian grunted. At the door of Scofield Manor, Raymond had paused, looking around. In the paved courtyard, Cress shook his head and opened the door of the utility van.

Overhead, masked in the fog, a flock of geese honked in panic, scattered on flapping wings, then regrouped to flee, heading east.

As quickly as it had begun, the vibration ended, and the silent fog rolled lazily, touched by errant mountain breezes.

"Told you this place is alive," Scofield said. "Now you know. It's Walter's ghost, far as I'm concerned."

Behind Poppin' Johnny, Cress chuckled. Deere turned.

"Old fart's crazy as a loon." The caretaker grinned. "I guess it runs in the family."

"You know what that was?" Deere demanded.

"Sure." Cress pointed upward. Atop the penthouse of Scofield Manor, a single aircraft rotor protruded, barely visible. "It's him. The computer man. I hear that noise now and then when he's here. I guess he's runnin' machines of some kind, in there."

At the doorway, Raymond was working his way through an elaborate security system. "Subsonics," Bob O'Donnelly muttered. "That's no computer, doing that. That's pure acceleration-deceleration subsonics."

The door was just opening when rotors bit the air high above, and a sleek helicopter lifted from the penthouse pad to bank away into the shrouding mist.

"Well, you missed your chance to talk to Farsight's computer technician," Scofield said. "He just left."

"What's his name?" O'Donnelly asked.

"I don't know," Scofield told him. "I never met him. He's just a man the Trust sends to attend to the computer. Farsight leases time and data-bank capacity on the Scofield megaframe. They maintain the equipment as part of their fee."

"Marlow," Poppin' Johnny remembered. "I guess that's

the fellow the SEC wanted to talk to, to access the Farsight files, but they couldn't locate him or something. His name was Felix Marlow."

Raymond Scofield, just stepping through the open doorway, turned and stared at the FBI agent. "Marlow? Felix Marlow? Are you sure?"

"Yeah, why? What's the matter?"

Scofield collected himself. "Probably just a coincidence," he decided. "My cousin Walter had a son. He disappeared a long time ago. Nobody knows what became of him. But that was his name. Felix Marlow."

"Marlow?" Deere blinked. "Not Scofield?"

"Oh, Felix hardly ever used his father's name." Raymond shrugged. "He may have been listed as Scofield in school records and such, but he didn't call himself that. He preferred to use his mother's family name. Marlow. He always went by Felix Marlow."

As formidable as Scofield Manor appeared from outside, the interior was lavish. "A Gothic manse," Bob O'Donnelly mused as Raymond Scofield led them across the ornate grand salon. Elaborate lighting systems, unused since Walter Scofield's death, turned themselves on obediently as electronic sensors reacted to the presence of people. The panorama they displayed was a rich, ornate great room painstakingly decorated with vivid tapestries, fine paintings, crystal chandeliers, and lustrous woodwork, and furnished in lavish style.

Raymond Scofield turned this way and that, staring in unconcealable amazement as he led his guests across acres of magnificent carpet toward the service area beyond. But Deere and O'Donnelly did more than glance. They gaped. Everywhere they looked were priceless works of art, antiques, and gilt trim. Just the contents of this room, Deere thought, would fund fortunes several times over.

"Lordy," Bob O'Donnelly muttered. "It's no wonder this place has security like the U.S. Mint."

At Raymond Scofield's shoulder, Deere said, "You didn't know all this was here, did you?"

"I had no idea," Scofield admitted. "I don't remember any of this being—" He caught himself, clenched his jaws, and scowled at the FBI man. "It's none of my business," he said, "or of yours, either. Your warrant is only for the information in the Farsight Trust data bank. That's in the computer area, down below."

"Of course." Deere shrugged. "Just curious. How did your cousin come to build this place, anyway?"

"My cousin was a wealthy eccentric," Raymond said. "They tell me he never wanted to share anything with anyone. He refused visitors and was fanatic about trespassers. I understand he offered himself for public office once, and was rejected. He retaliated by rejecting the world. They tell me that the only person Walter ever confided in was his son, and after Felix disappeared, the old skinflint locked himself away here and never surfaced again until shortly before he died."

"How did he get to the hospital where he died?" Poppin' Johnny asked. "Walter Reed Medical Center is a long way from here. Who took him there?"

Raymond shrugged. "Airborne Ambulance, the hospital said."

"From way out here?"

"Well, no, actually. The ambulance picked him up at a private nursing home near Arlington. I have no idea how he got there, or how long he had been there."

A faint hum of circuitry and idle servomotors gave texture to the silence of the place, and everything in sight was meticulously clean, perfectly placed, and spotless. It was as though a cleaning crew had just gone through, tidying the household for its residents. But there were no residents. Nobody lived here.

"Weird," O'Donnelly said. "This place—it's like the whole house exists just for its own amusement."

"Ten'll get you fifty," Poppin' Johnny whispered, "the old man never lived here at all. And I'll bet he never saw any of this stuff in here, either."

At the rear of the grand salon, a wide hallway was lined with solid, closed doors, each leading to one of the manor's automated service and utility areas. In the middle was a trio of automatic elevators, one for going up to higher floors, one for access to the basements, and the third—secured by remote-control bolts—going to the penthouse atop the central tower.

"That penthouse lift is part of the Trust's lease," Raymond Scofield said. "The penthouse is theirs."

"Let's go see that computer," Bob O'Donnelly suggested.

At a slight sound behind them, Deere turned. The caretaker, Cress, had followed them into the house and was wandering around, looking at the artworks displayed in the salon.

Scofield noticed him then, too, and barked, "I didn't ask you to come in here, Mr. Cress!"

"You didn't say not to." Cress grinned. "Mercy, look at all this stuff. Where did it all come from?" He paused in front of a framed oil painting, looked it up and down, and stepped closer to peer at the daubed inscription in a lower corner. "Matisse," he muttered.

"Let Mr. Cress come along with us, sir," Deere instructed Scofield. "I *do* know him from somewhere."

Miles away, a slick turborotor wended its way through the shrouded mountains, with an angry man at its controls. He had seen the cars below, on the paved drive, when he lifted from the pad atop the mountain house—the caretaker's van, old Raymond's sedan, and a third, nondescript vehicle that he didn't recognize.

More property inspectors, Ice supposed. More glitter-eyed, curious little people hoping to learn secrets they had no business knowing.

He wasn't concerned about the intrusion. Raymond wasn't likely to let anyone inside the house. And even if he did, what harm could it do? They wouldn't find the base chamber, even if they searched the place. Let them satisfy themselves, and look at the baubles, and be amazed. Let them puzzle over the strangeness of the great house on the mountaintop, the madness of the old man who built it, the care that had gone into its security systems. Let them labor at their curiosity and discover the treasures hidden within, and make legends about what they have found.

Bread and circuses, Ice thought. Let them eat cake. Let them amuse themselves and when they're sated they will leave.

What better place to hide a puzzle than in a house of puzzles?

His anger arose from something else, entirely. Someone was meddling with his plans. Why had that policeman been at the Stock Exchange? The same man who had interfered before, at the Empire State and on the Florida coast. Different times, different places, but the same man. And there were more than one. He had killed some of them, but they kept coming. And each time *that one* showed up, he interfered with the great plan!

It was all so neat, so simple, and methodical—the great plan. Control time, and you control fortunes. Control fortunes, and you control commerce. Control commerce, and you control the world.

Ice had known it—known his destiny—from the day Einstein blew up the remote base with his stupid centrifuge experiment. Einstein . . . outside name Amos Wheeler, known and wanted stateside as the Beale Street Butcher. Einstein was always the dabbler, always the schemer. No one ever seemed to know how Einstein had made it from a Louisiana prison to Special Force WSL in Serbia, but the man was a genius at circuitry and obviously couldn't go home.

There was nothing unusual in that. A lot of WSL people couldn't, or wouldn't, go home. That was why they were "Weasels," doing the dirty work that no official source would admit ordering done. Some were in it for the money, some because they enjoyed the killing, and some simply had no place else to go. And very few Weasels ever used their real names.

To those who controlled WSL, that didn't matter. They were a nonaligned mercenary force, selling to the highest bidder, and it was what a man could do, not who he had been, that they cared about.

But Einstein always had wild ideas, and his last one was the wildest—to convert centrifugal force to selective gravity, with ideas of creating a new kind of power for space probes. At a covert installation at Seragova, he had bragged on what might be done with a device that could be focused on any large object—like an orbiting planet or even a distant star—and "fall" toward it.

Einstein was a genius, all right. He was also a fool. In a secluded armaments laboratory in the Transylvanian Alps, using notes gleaned from Roth's trajectory tables and Riemann's dimensional studies, Einstein had built a covert centrifuge and applied a trilateral force field at a critical speed.

The resulting explosion had destroyed nearly a third of Seragova.

It had also provided inspiration for Einstein's assigned flank man, a Weasel assassin known generally as Ice. Even among the Weasels, nobody talked much about Ice. He kept to himself, did what he did best—cold-blooded assassination—and amused himself by collecting treasures on the side. He was a devoted scavenger. He was also a dealer, specializing in heavy ordnance, an enterprise he pursued in his off-duty hours. But Ice had a Harvard and MIT background that he kept to himself, and unlike most of those around them, he had understood what Einstein was talking about . . . and more. Ice suspected all along that what the Beale Street lunatic had found was not gravity but time warp, and when Einstein's death was reported, he knew what errors he had made.

From there, it had been simply a matter of technological development. The centrifuge was too small to withstand dimensional stress. He needed a larger one. The force fields were erratic and underpowered. He needed a true wormhole matrix.

Einstein had lacked the resources to do it right. He needed a secure, isolated place and adequate financing. Ice had no such limitations. He knew where to get all these things. A month later he disappeared from Bosnia and returned to the States.

He had known the first time he used timespin that it

would work, and he had known something else, as well. He had known that it was his right and his destiny to rule the world, and to re-create it by his own standards.

He alone had time travel.

But now there were others, and it enraged him that they were there. They had no right to intrude!

Yet they did intrude—those people with the strange uniforms, like police uniforms, with the label TEC. They insisted on meddling in his great plan, and they were becoming a real nuisance.

That same man, who had interfered before and then interfered again, what was he doing there? And how had he stopped those stock transactions?

It wasn't just a few million in found currency that this latest meddling had cost. It was billions. Billions of dollars, and effective control of a fourth of the world's financial system! The loss could be recovered—Ice already had a plan in motion to regain the lost ground—but the sheer arrogance of it, of people interfering with his plans, was intolerable.

As the turbocopter swept around a slope and headed eastward into the populated areas east of the Blue Ridge, the man at its controls felt a growing rage—the pure, simple rage of a feral animal diverted from its path, disrupted in its orderly pursuit of what it wanted.

The same cold, killing rage that always came when anyone got in his way . . . and sometimes just for no reason at all.

They will pay for this, Ice told himself. He pictured in his mind the tall, dark-haired man in the TEC uniform. They'll all have to pay. They don't know what they're dealing with here!

Twice now, Ice had pulled a trigger on that timecop, and

he was still out there. Maybe, he thought, another trap might draw him out. Maybe I can hang him from the Washington Monument or dump him in the Mississippi, like I did those others.

The thought was a warm, sensual vision that fell short of dispersing the rage. I'll get the timecop, he thought, but right now let's just play a little game.

Shrouded foothills receded on both sides, and the helicopter came out of the mountain mist. At nine hundred feet it cruised eastward, over thinning forests and ribbons of highway. With his rage driving him, he scanned the rolling countryside like a hunter seeking prey, and his eyes fixed on a curving strip of roadway between strung-out little towns, a place where a two-lane wound upward onto the slope of a knob hill, clinging precariously to its side over a steep drop-off to a stony ravine far below.

Only a few vehicles, widely spaced, were in sight. The largest was a commuter bus, making its twice-daily run between a quaint little tourist town and the remote wilderness resorts in the valley beyond the knob.

Acting on familiar impulse, Ice the Scavenger banked his chopper to the right, crossing high above the road to disappear beyond the crest of the hill. He turned and hovered there for a moment, surveying the landscape around. The nearest domicile was half a mile away, and the nearest vehicle traveling the road was still at the foot of the slope, a mile or more.

Satisfied, the flier applied power and shoved his control yoke forward. Like an arrow from a bow, the helicopter dipped its nose and shot forward, over the crest of the hill, then down, down toward the winding, cliffside highway.

The commuter bus was just coming around an outward curve when the flying machine flashed into view, directly ahead, skids almost skimming the pavement as it bore down on the bus.

It was over in a moment. The bus driver, caught completely off guard, hauled his wheel to the right and realized his mistake too late. Big wheels crunched gravel, skidding and going over. With a sickening lurch, the bus wavered for an instant on the edge of the precipice, then rolled to the right. It went over the edge upside down and nose first, tumbling, bouncing, and rolling. What finally settled in the rocky ravine below was a demolished skeleton of a bus, crushed and bent, its wheels still spinning as wreckage, gravel, vegetation, and the mangled bodies of passengers rained down around it.

The helicopter settled on the pavement, its blades idly spinning. Ice climbed out, looked down at the wreckage, then got out a power router and used it on the stone of the ledge.

By the time another vehicle came along, there was no sign of the helicopter—no trace of what had caused the bus to go over the edge. It would be hours before they discovered the numbers scratched into the stone on the ledge where the bus went over—numbers that meant nothing to anyone until a computer system called ChronComp matched them up with the number code of a 1987 trading account on the New York Stock Exchange.

The basement of Scofield Manor was like no basement Bob O'Donnelly had ever seen. It was not a rectangular room, or series of rooms, but instead it resembled a big, vaulted archway fifty feet across and curving away beyond sight in each direction.

"This is a damned tunnel!" Poppin' Johnny Deere exclaimed, looking this way and that. "Where does it go?"

"It just circles around the central foundation," Raymond Scofield said. "It goes all the way around, and comes back here. Full circle." He turned left and signaled them to follow. "The computer vault is right over here, beyond these arches," he said.

The vault was a wide, well-lit room opening off the outer wall of the circular corridor. It housed banks of storage, several relay systems, and a main workstation, all tied in to the ceiling-high consoles of a megaframe computer in a glass-walled closet. O'Donnelly paced once around the area, activated the main keyboard, and toyed with codes and menus. It was no ChronComp, but it *was* a big computer system, very sophisticated, and—from what O'Donnelly could see of its banks and storage—hopelessly underutilized.

He sat at the main console, familiarized himself with the access and execution systems, and scrolled through a menu of available files. "Is this it?" he asked, not looking up. "Is this all this system's programmed to do?"

"So far as I know." Raymond shrugged. "Everything on the estate is controlled from here. Utilities, cleaning and security systems, lighting, even the plumbing. Everything. I believe it also keeps automatic accounts of estate fees and taxes, several escrow funds, and the general bookkeeping of the estate trust that pays the bills."

"I see all that." O'Donnelly nodded. "There is also a periodic inventory, an insurance modification program, and an expense account for external maintenance, which includes the caretaker's upkeep. Everything here could be handled on a PC."

"Go to Menu/FST," Raymond said. "The FST is Farsight Trust."

O'Donnelly keyed it in. The new menu was a twenty-code composite, which O'Donnelly recognized as a simple business maintenance program—assets and liabilities, a cash flow sequence, inventory of investments and expenditures, capital growth tracking, all the predictable things.

"That's it." Raymond shrugged. "That's what your warrant authorizes you to search, so search. Those are all password files, though, and I don't know the passwords."

"No sweat." O'Donnelly grinned. "Piece a cake."

With the skill of an accomplished technician and the zeal of a hacker, TEC's computer wizard went to work while Raymond Scofield relaxed on a leather sofa nearby. From the right, down the curving archway, they could hear the voices of Agent Deere and the caretaker, Cress.

The voices were coming from the other direction when O'Donnelly finished accessing, displaying, and copying all the data in the Farsight files. He ran through the big computer's main menu once more, thoughtfully, copied that, as well, then switched off the console. "I guess that's all I can do," he said.

Moments later Deere and Cress joined them, strolling into view from the left. "You're right—" Deere nodded to Raymond Scofield. "—this thing is just a big circle."

Scofield got to his feet, sourly. "If you gentlemen have finished, then, I'll show you out."

"Fine," Deere said. "Lead the way."

As Scofield and Cress went on ahead, Deere raised a rugged brow at O'Donnelly. "Anything?"

"Nothing I could reach. I copied everything. But I did find something odd. This computer is hardly being used at all. Less than 10 percent of capacity. But the available space in the data bank doesn't match that. I ran diagnostics and a tree trace. This may be the main box here, but it isn't the whole shebang. There is another whole section of memory that can't be reached, or even cross-indexed. It doesn't even exist, so far as this part of the ROM system knows."

"What does all that mean?" Deere looked at him blankly.

"My guess is, there's another terminal—a slave port—located somewhere else, hardwired to these terminals, that can access a whole different part of this computer."

"Where?"

"Dunno." O'Donnelly shrugged. "Nearby, though. It would have to have its own dedicated trunk cable. It must be within a few hundred feet of right here, but I sure don't see any hiding places."

"Interesting," Deere mused. "Well, I found out something, too. I had a visit with the caretaker while the whiz kid here was crashing numbers—"

"Crunching," O'Donnelly interrupted. "I think you mean *crunching* numbers, though I haven't heard that expression since I was about twelve."

"Whatever." Poppin' Johnny scowled. "Anyhow, there are some family portraits among the paintings hanging along that tunnel—and by the way, they're right, the Scofields *do* all look alike—but Cress recognized a face he knew."

"Who?"

"Turns out Cress is ex-military. Or ex-mercenary. Served a stint with a semiprivate covert outfit called WSL, long enough to hire lawyers to clear him of some charges against him a few years ago. One of the people he remembers from his Weasel days is an assassin called Ice. Well, we just saw a picture of Ice, around there on the other side of this center column. Only in the picture, he's identified by his own name.

"So I think we know who our Scavenger is, now. He's old Walter Scofield's long-lost son, Felix Marlow."

# XI

## TEC Headquarters

The Black Monday market plunge of 1987 was still history, but 30 percent less severe than in the original history version, and 70 percent less than it would have been had the Scavenger's raid succeeded. A team of economists tracking scenarios for TEC—they were under the impression that their task was a what-if exercise for the Corn Exchange Bank—found that world markets could not have survived the latter possibility and that a worldwide depression would have ensued.

"The Commerce Department's prophets tracked the effects of the actual five-hundred-point plunge for ten years," Charles Graham told the little group assembled in the briefing room. "Its residues lasted that long, then just sort of disappeared in another plunge in 1997. I'd say history adjusted itself, since price-value comparisons came out about the same a few years later, by either scenario."

"Well, the '87 ripple disappeared when Hemmings and Logan stopped the Scavenger at Wall Street," Eugene Matuzek said, and nodded. "So we caught that one. Sloppy, but at least we stopped it."

"But not *him*." Dale Easter frowned. "The Scavenger is

165

still out there, and now he's really mad." The historian indicated the packet of faxed photos and data just received from Brooks Knoll, Virginia. "He wrecked that bus, killed all those people, and left us a message, just to tell us that he's—forgive the aphorism—pissed!"

"I'd have said that was out of character, except for Agent Jackson." Matuzek sighed. He looked around the briefing table. TEC's entire first-string ThinkTank—Chief Historian Dale Easter, Amy Fuller, and Bob O'Donnelly—was present, along with field agents Jack Logan and Julie Price, and the systems analyst Claire Hemmings. In addition, Black Ops Chief Charles Graham was there with Special Agent John Davis Deere of the FBI. "What we have here is a cold-blooded, methodical criminal who goes berserk when he's thwarted," the TEC captain said. "He's a loose cannon with a time machine, and he might do anything. So let's see what we have."

"How about a mug shot?" Deere suggested. He fed microfilm into the briefing console, tapped a button, and viewscreens around the room displayed an image. "Felix Marlow," Deere said. "Thumb-camera likeness from a photo-oil in the Scofield place."

"That's him!" Jack Logan jerked upright in his chair. "That's the *Scavenger*!"

"It's him," Claire Hemmings agreed.

"Then we have a positive ID." Matuzek nodded. "Now what do we know about this subject?"

Dale Easter fiddled with his memcorder and tapped keys on his ChronComp link. "Felix Marlow Scofield," he said. "Age forty-four, about six foot two and one hundred eighty, sole offspring of Walter R. Scofield and the late Margaret Marlow Scofield. May have attended Harvard University and MIT but no transcripts are available and no record of graduation. No fingerprint or retina pattern record, no licenses, passports, medical transcripts, liaisons or aliases of record, no tax record beyond 1988, no records of any kind except that he was born, he existed, and he disappeared without a trace in the summer of 1997. He simply dropped out of sight."

"Probably when he went overseas," Deere cut in. "He may have been involved in some arms trading in eastern Europe, maybe some theft of valuables in transit, and my guess is that he got crossways with somebody and went to ground. Anyhow, he hooked up with a covert paramilitary force—the WSL, better known in the soldiers-of-fortune world as 'Weasels.' Mercenaries, but on a major scale. You don't hire a warrior with the Weasels, you contract a brigade.

"The Weasels may have originated in Northern Ireland, but they became international—selling their services as special forces units to anybody willing to pay the price. Demolitions, infiltration, assassination, covert engagements, you name it and the Weasels have got it.

"Felix Marlow's Weasel designation was Ice. His speciality was assassinations, but he was also highly qualified in infiltration and logistics. May have been a weapons broker on the side. A very methodical man, apparently, but unpredictable and given to sudden rage. My source— Cress—describes Ice as a berserker when things didn't go his way. His WSL buddies were leery of him. They didn't trust him much. A scary guy, Cress says.

"He also seemed to know a lot about history, particularly contemporary Chinese history. And he had an odd penchant for theatrics."

"It all matches what we know of our Scavenger," Easter

agreed. "But it doesn't tell us where he is now, or what he'll do next."

"Or how he came into possession of a time-travel device," Amy Fuller added.

"Yeah." Easter frowned, suddenly thinking about the semilegendary Manchurian Device, the missing bomb that had never been found. A EuroTEC agent had died in that investigation, and nothing had surfaced since that connected to it. "Makes you wonder what else he's got that we don't know about," he said.

"It sounds as though we're talking about three different people, doesn't it?" Amy Fuller suggested. "A cold-blooded, methodical killer named Ice, a treasure hunter we've been calling Scavenger, and someone else—a megalomaniac who has tried at least once to take over the world, and may try again."

"Different names, different proclivities, but all the same person," Charles Graham mused. "What's the story on his father?"

"Walter Scofield?" O'Donnelly keyed an inquiry to ChronComp. "In present history, there's nothing much to know. A rich man from a rich family, but an oddball. He ran for public office once, about 1985, and was creamed . . ."

"Why?"

O'Donnelly keyed in further codes. "A scandal," he said. "Something involving his son. It was all hushed up with Scofield money, but it cost old Walter his election to the U.S. Senate, and the career that would have followed. His wife died about then, apparently a suicide. Walter shut down his home in Georgetown and moved to the Blue Ridge. Became a hermit."

"Was that when Felix changed his name from Scofield to Marlow?"

"Might have been. This is real sketchy. Enough money erases a lot of things."

"Felix Marlow . . ." Graham mused. "Ice the Weasel . . . treasure hunter, scavenger . . . stock market raider . . . megalomaniac?"

"Crazy as a loon," Matuzek surmised. "But very dangerous. I'd like to know more about this guy's background. Dale, can we target a surveillance insertion, to gather data on what happened back then?"

"That should be simple enough, but we'll want to avoid making any tracks on that path—*any at all!* If we change any perimeter history, and this guy is still around, we could lose all the leads we have. We'd leave him wide open to do just whatever he takes a notion to do."

"I'll make the jump," Julie Price volunteered.

Jack Logan swung around, facing the red-haired young woman. "This creep's a shooter, Julie. He's a psycho. You're not ready for that kind of mission. You need experience—"

"And how is experience acquired?" She pinned him with determined eyes, then appealed to Matuzek, "I'm the logical choice, Captain. You've said, yourself, that I look more like a cheerleader than a cop. The Scavenger's never seen me, but I've studied his MO . . . that business with the gold certificates at antebellum St. Louis. I might notice things that another agent wouldn't."

"Okay, you've got it." Matuzek nodded. "Just be very careful, Julie. No tracks. No tracks whatever. No matter what you learn, you just observe, then report back. Understand?"

"Yes, sir." She grinned.

"Well, I have a hunch what the Scavenger's going after next," Claire Hemmings said. "A fortune in silver."

"Whatever it is, he has a use in mind for it, and it will have to do with getting even."

"Silver?" Amy Fuller looked at Claire. "The metal or the commodity?"

"The commodity. What do you have?"

"We'll have to research this a little," Amy said. "But wasn't there a big market scare back in the late seventies . . . like somebody trying to corner the world market on silver?"

## Georgetown Heights
## 1985

Milton Hale was shaving when the young woman stepped out of his shower. As chief Washington lobbyist for the Arkansas Feeders and Growers combine, Hale had an image to maintain on the Hill. Thus it was a daily after-lunch ritual for him to stop off at his private suite in Georgetown to shower, shave, and don fresh attire before the afternoon round of appointments.

The bathroom was steamy, the mirrors fogged, and Milton Hale—clad in a towel—was busy. He cleared a head-high section of mirror with a wet cloth, leaned close, and managed two strokes with his razor before it clouded over again. Between the fog on the mirror, the fog on his glasses, and the runnels of sweat in his eyes, shaving sometimes became a battle for him.

He was in midfog when the mist behind him swirled and a pretty young woman in a dark garment appeared abruptly in his shower stall. He didn't see her arrival, but he saw movement in the mirror's foggy surface and glanced around just as she opened the stall door and stepped out.

"Hello," she said sweetly. "Uh . . . is this 1301?" He blinked at her through fogged glasses, clenched the towel wrapped around his middle, and dropped his razor. She was a *doll*—trim, long-legged, auburn-haired, and certainly young enough to be his daughter. The garment she wore looked like a reinforced jumpsuit, with some sort of emblem, and she wore a gun that looked almost as big as she was. She also carried a small pack on a shoulder sling. "This house?" He goggled at her. "Uh, it's number 1303; 1301 is next door. Where did you—"

"Sorry about that," she said. "I must have taken a wrong turn somewhere. Please excuse the interruption. I'll find my own way out."

With a smile that would have fogged his glasses even without the help of steam, she stepped past him and out the door. Milton Hale took off his glasses, peered around the foggy bathroom, then stepped to the shower stall and looked in, carefully. When he was satisfied that there were no more where that one came from, he put on his robe, opened the bathroom door, and peered up and down the second-floor hall. There was no one in sight.

Worried and perplexed, he went to his bedroom, found a directory, and looked up the number of the Scofield residence, next door. The young woman had been looking for 1301. Maybe somebody there could explain how an auburn-haired little dumpling happened to have emerged from his shower stall. He dialed the number, and a male voice answered, "Scofield residence."

"Who's speaking?" Milton asked.

"This is Detective Lieutenant Mark Chrisman," the voice said. "Who's this?"

Milton hung up. Whatever was going on next door, it involved the police and smelled like bad publicity. He wanted no part of it.

In the downstairs foyer of Milton Hale's house, Julie paused, listening. There seemed to be no one else in the house, and she knew the man in the bathroom would remain upstairs for at least a few minutes.

From wide bay windows in a large, sparsely furnished room just off the foyer, she surveyed the neighborhood to get her bearings. Then from her "bag of tricks," assembled with Amy Fuller's help, Julie produced a Compacket and released its catch. One of the marvels of the international age, she thought as the packet, no larger than a thick paperback novel, unfolded to reveal two complete changes of wardrobe, air-sole slippers and all.

She changed quickly, paused to reflect at a hall mirror, and packed her launch garb and equipment into a roomy strap purse, which, folded, had been the size of a deck of cards.

The girl who stepped out onto the lawn of number 1303 then might have been a coed on her way to an afternoon lecture. Even her auburn hair was changed, pulled back to a jaunty ponytail held by a bright ribbon. The wide, tinted glasses she wore gave no hint of being more than glasses. Chameleonlike, she blended into the sparse crowd of gawkers hanging around outside the wrought-iron gates of 1301, where a police car blocked the entrance. "What is it?" she asked a business-suited woman standing beside a maroon Riviera.

"They're arresting somebody, or something." The woman shrugged. "All I heard is, some guy's been booking hunting trips into D.C."

"Hunting trips?"

"Yeah." The woman's smile was enigmatic. "In the projects. Isn't that something?"

"The projects? You mean the government housing units? What would anybody hunt there?"

"Whatever those places have the most of, I suppose. And I don't mean rats and roaches, either, if you catch my drift. Don't you watch the news? The Lincoln Heights killings?"

Julie hesitated, keeping her expression blank. "You mean, people? They hunt *people*?"

"Yes, dear." The woman glanced at her, pityingly. You poor, innocent little thing, the glance said, wake up and smell the eighties. "Urban safaris, they call it. It's considered a real sport. Been going on in New York for quite a while, and in Chicago. I guess D.C.'s just a natural, with places like Lincoln Heights and Barry Farms. Federal-fund ghettos, that's all they are."

Beyond the gates, a wide lawn swept back toward a large, secluded house surrounded by expensive landscaping. Two more police cruisers and a couple of unmarked cars sat on the brick drive in front. Julie moved to the fence and powered up her glasses.

People were coming from the house. A big man in a bulging sport coat led the way, followed by two uniforms guiding a tall, unkempt young man whose face was obscured by a jacket pulled high. Politely but firmly, they loaded him into one of the cruisers. Julie scanned the group with her enhanced-view lenses, then focused on the open front door. A tall, graying man had appeared there in earnest conversation with another plainclothes policeman and a smooth-faced man who had the cookie-cutter appearance of a lawyer or political aide.

Julie knew the gray-haired man from an obscure old photograph Dale Easter had found. It was Walter Scofield.

The crowd that had formed outside the gate was small—just a few nosy neighbors and curious passersby. Near the fence where Julie stood, a man and two women in jogging attire paused, nodding at some of the people already there. "What's going on?" the man asked. "Somebody hurt?"

"I think it's the Scofield boy," another man said, and shrugged. "They're arresting him. Somebody said he's maybe tied up in those murders around Lincoln Heights."

"What murders?"

"Hell, it's been on the news. There's been some killings over there lately. Devil-worship stuff, maybe. People killed with swords, axes, even crossbows. Nobody much, just homeless types, street gangs and welfare hypes. I don't know. Maybe Scofield's kid did do it."

"Urban safaris," the woman with the maroon Riviera enlightened the group. "Regular hunting trips, like in big game preserves, only they go out and hunt people."

One of the jogger women giggled. "I wonder if they take trophies," she chirped.

"Sure as hell do," a man said. "That's the thing, they're all missing body parts."

The other woman jogger grinned. "What part of a crackhead does one hang on one's wall, Lucy?"

"Whatever tickles your fancy," the Riviera woman suggested.

Inside the estate, two squad cars were moving. They came down the drive, waited while the officer opened the gate for them, then turned right and went down the street. The prisoner in the back of the first car had his head down, allowing not even a glimpse of his features.

"Was that him?" The jogger pointed. "The Scofield boy, what's-'is-name?"

"That was him," the Riviera woman asserted. "That was Felix."

Someone else asked, "Isn't Walter Scofield running for office?"

"Probably not anymore," a bystander said. "Whatever this was about, I bet it'll get him off the Democratic ticket."

A striking, severe-looking auburn-haired woman in stern business attire walked into the Fourth Precinct station, flashed a badge, and was forwarded to Detective Lieutenant Mark Chrisman. At his cubicle she flashed her badge again and said, "Julie Smith. Indigent affairs. I understand you have a suspect in custody in the Lincoln Heights snipings?"

Chrisman was a cop who had been a cop too long. The anger, the frustration, and the sadness no longer hid behind his eyes. He didn't stand. He leaned back in his chair, looked her up and down, and said, "I already bought Girl Scout cookies."

She frowned. "What?"

"If you're a cop, then I'm Dick Tracy. By God, why don't they keep you kids in school till you're grown?" He sighed, shook his head, and leaned forward. "Okay, what do you need?"

"Details," she said. "Who is he and what are you holding him for?"

"Felix Marlow Scofield, white male, age twenty-two. And we're not. His old man's lawyers had him out of here less than an hour after he was brought in."

"So he was booked and bailed?"

Chrisman glared at her. "You don't know much about high-dollar politics, do you, girl? He isn't out on bail, just out. We never even booked him. Officially, his arrest never happened. We didn't arrest a suspect. We simply provided a well-connected citizen with a free ride downtown, courtesy of the taxpayers, and gave him a guided tour of our magnificent facilities."

"But you arrested him!"

"No report will ever say that." Chrisman sighed "Look, Miss . . . Smith, is it? A deal has been cut and neither you nor I can do a damned thing about it. There was no arrest, no custody, no suspect, no *nothing*. Mr. Felix Scofield is as free as a bird in the sky, and the political big spenders own enough of that sky to get away with it."

"Then that's all you're going to do? Just let him go?" Julie knew the answer to that already. It was obviously what had happened, twenty years before her own time—a year before she was even born. But something in her demanded an answer.

"If he's smart," Chrisman said, "and I'm sure he is, he won't hang around here very long. No matter what the record says, some of the cops who were there to bring him in had personal knowledge of the killings in Lincoln Heights. One of the victims of those . . . those *trophy hunters* was a thirteen-year-old girl. Would you like to see the crime-scene photos? Would you like to see what some son of a bitch took as a trophy?"

"No, thanks," Julie whispered, turning away. "I've heard all I need to." Over her shoulder, she asked, "This Felix Scofield . . . as I understand it, he didn't actually *do* all those killings?"

"No. Not all of them, anyway. He just arranged them. For money. He planned the . . . the excursions, like a damned tour guide. 'The Ultimate Adventure for the Man Who's Done Everything.' The hunt, the pursuit, the stalk, the kill. Exotic weapons, the whole works! Felix is a game player. He laid out each hunt like a game, then probably even went along to watch. He's a vulture, you know . . . a scavenger. He'd want to watch.

"But we can't touch him. And without him, I doubt if we have a case against any of his clients. Just hearsay evidence. They'll walk away, just like Felix has. They'll sit in their trophy rooms and remember the greatest hunt of all." The detective shook his head, slowly. "But then, it's all money and politics, isn't it? Does anything else matter anymore?

"You asked what I'm going to do? I'm going to coast for another year, then retire. When I retire, I'll travel. Maybe I can get far enough away to not remember any more."

Outside, in the 1985 street, Julie Price put away her glasses, her recorder, and some of her innocence. In the privacy of a McDonald's rest room she changed back to her blast suit and touched the retrieval device on her wrist, hesitating as she did.

Don't make tracks, Captain Matuzek had said. Don't do anything to change history.

It would have been easy for Julie to locate Felix Marlow Scofield right then. Her sublimator briefing had been detailed on events of record in and around the District of Columbia on this date in 1985. A half mile east of the Anacostia River, in an old, abandoned fabric loft, someone was at this moment assembling a bomb that at 5:18 would destroy a half block of structures and kill fourteen people. Julie knew now who was planting that bomb. It was young

Felix Marlow/Scofield's parting gift to the city that had interrupted his fun.

It was the pattern the Scavenger would follow later in life—retribution for interruption.

It would be easy, Julie knew, to get to that old building in time to find Felix, stop the explosion, and mete out justice with a laser-guided .38 slug. It would have been easy. But it would have changed history, and it would have been raw justice, not law. And it would be murder. *This* Felix Marlow, the Felix Marlow of 1985, wasn't the Scavenger. He would be, but he wasn't yet, and even the classified legal code applying to time criminals did not allow for peremptory execution before the fact.

She had what she had come to 1985 for. She had a fix on the behavior patterns of the Scavenger. Maybe the TEC ThinkTank could surmise from it what he might do next.

When Julie activated the retrieve on her wrist and disappeared into the dimensional wormhole that was her return to 2007, she knew she had come of age as a cop.

## Washington, D.C.
## October 1977

The Manchurian Device arrived on U.S. soil in the hold of a vessel carrying routine cargo from Sudan. Disassembled and carefully shielded in its several crates, the device passed through customs as soil-test equipment, consigned to a fictitious construction company in Maryland. By dated orders, it was transferred on an October Friday to a public works site in Washington, half a mile from the U.S. Capitol, and off-loaded to a waiting flatbed.

On a frosty Saturday morning, as workmen fired up their machinery to complete the task of excavating for new piers at the south end of the Third Street tunnel, the air swirled and coalesced beneath the boom of an idle power dredge. Dimensions shifted and a man materialized there. For a moment he flailed for balance, then he grasped the boom, clung there while he looked around, and swung to the ground. He straightened his tie and his long topcoat, put on a white hard hat with a DCPW insignia, and retrieved a sheaf of official-looking blueprints from inside his coat. Carrying these and a clipboard, and with a large

179

valise slung from his shoulder, he strode to the edge of a fresh pit and tapped a job foreman on the shoulder.

When the man turned, the newcomer pointed at the pit. "That isn't deep enough," he said. "It's supposed to shaft down fourteen feet. That's no more than eight."

The foreman frowned. "What the hell you talkin' about? That's seven-nine from grade. Just what the specs call for."

"That was before the change order," the DCPW man said, tapping his roll of prints. "This *is* pier eleven, isn't it?"

"Yeah. Pier eleven, east berm, south entry ramp. Why?"

"Because this is where the soil-test monitor goes," the man said. "Look, I've got work orders from the National Park Service and the EPA to bury a soil monitor under pier eleven. It takes six feet of additional depth to do that. So this hole has to be fourteen feet deep. Start at the bottom of your pier shaft and give me a five-foot diameter bore going down another six feet. Bottom it with that lead base on the flatbed, then set that cylinder in it . . . yeah, that thing over there marked D-1. Get a crane on it. It's solid lead, four inches thick. I'll be back in two hours with a mechanism crew, so have it ready. Okay? Thanks."

Without waiting for comment, the tall man strode away, toward the traffic barricades across the south entry ramp to the Washington Mall tunnel. Behind him, the foreman shook his head and cursed under his breath. "Friggin' bureaucrats!" he muttered. Then he hauled a four-man team off the retaining wall berm and set them to digging a hole.

Felix Marlow helped himself to a city car at the south ramp blockoff, crossed the Mall on Seventh Street, and turned east on D Street. He left the vehicle in a no-parking zone in front of the U.S. District Court and walked across to the Department of Labor. Inside that building he passed easily through security, checked the time, and headed for a supply room off the south lobby. Six minutes later he emerged on the roof of the building, carrying a striped flasher base and a six-foot length of steel conduit. At the south lip of the roof he set the barricade in place, secured the conduit to its top ridge with tape, aligning it with shims of shingling from the supply room, and extended a mini-cam scanner—an electronic device that wouldn't be perfected for another twenty-six years—to clamp to the pipe. That easily, he had a ranging telescope, which he focused southward, on the pier excavation at the south entry of the Third Street tunnel.

He opened his view to cover an area of about a hundred yards around the work site, checked the time, then watched and waited. There would be a timecop, he knew. Somehow they seemed to know each time he jumped to the past, and when and where he would be. But observation had proved that they didn't know *exactly* where. The TEC meddler at Empire State had appeared within thirty minutes after Marlow's own arrival there. The one he had ambushed—that he had used a chopper to hang atop the Washington Monument—had taken twenty-four minutes to arrive. The two in Florida had shown up an hour and a half after Marlow's materialization, but they obviously had been there a while when he noticed them. So he estimated the meddler's response time at twenty to thirty minutes, their materialization at within five hundred yards of his own.

He didn't miss it by much. Within a few minutes, through his long-range scanner, he saw the telltale swirling of refracted light in an area just beyond where the workmen were digging, and a moment later a tall, dark-haired man in a blast suit materialized between a fork lift and a hydraulic tamper. Marlow refined his focus, and a cold smile tugged at his gaunt cheeks. It was the same man! The cop who had dogged his tracks all along the way, in at least four leaps into past times—the one who had stolen his found treasure from a yacht in south Florida, who had cost him billions by interfering with his stock market plan in 1987, who had become a serious nuisance in many ways.

Now Felix Marlow, the Scavenger, sighted his scanner on Jack Logan and made a reflexive hand gesture, like cocking a gun and squeezing the trigger. At a distance of half a mile, he activated the scanner's ID mode and triggered it, locking Logan's imprint in the little device's electronic memory, marking him for tracking.

Across the Mall, Logan peered around at the activity in the public works site and began a systematic search of the area. Marlow knew exactly what the timecop was looking for. He was looking for *him*.

Leaving his crude mountings on the Labor Department roof, the Scavenger collapsed and stowed the scanner, and descended to the bowels of the quiet building. On a Saturday morning there were few people in the place, beyond custodial crews and a few bored security guards.

In the building's communication and computer center, Marlow went to work on programs and circuits. It took him only a few minutes to access the department's central files, create a new, encrypted command file in the main bank, and cross connect it to the building's intercom circuits with its own pass-protect code.

This done, he traced the circuit to a central electronics port, locked it in, and followed the building's telephone-TV-fax clusters to an unassigned terminal in the subbasement maintenance complex. With his blueprints, he verified the exact location. The terminal was within twelve feet of the reinforced roof of the Third Street traffic tunnel, which ran directly beneath the building. Through a fuse relay in the building's main electrical circuit, he planted a tiny, almost invisible electronic impulse device into the wiring conduit. The electrical cables were unaffected, but the encasing conduit itself thus became a conductor. It was as though he had dropped hardwires directly into a cluster panel above the tunnel's northbound lanes.

Leaving the Labor Department building through an underground parking complex, he bypassed a dozen or more private vehicles—mostly Mercedes-Benzes, BMWs, Jaguars, Ferraris, and Corvettes, the little personal indulgences of people whose livelihood was as secure as federal taxes—to select a plush Lincoln Town Car from the Justice Department motor pool. He chose it because it reminded him of his uncle Raymond Scofield's limousine.

Breeching the antithefts on this or any pre-1990 vehicle was as easy for a man from 2007 as overriding the ignition. It took no more than thirty seconds. He drove south a few blocks on First, past the Capitol, then left the car a block south of the Botanic Garden and strolled up the incline of Washington Avenue. From a viaduct rail there he had a clear view of the tunnel ramp project. The scanner required no supports now to locate its target. Its little memory knew what to look for.

The TEC agent was still exploring the site, looking at the area from different angles, seeking a clue to why a time jumper had materialized there. When Marlow spotted him, Jack Logan was standing no more than ten feet from the flatbed truck holding the crated Manchurian Device—that close, and he had no idea what he was looking for. Beyond the site was busy Maryland Avenue, with its stream of weekend tourist traffic.

Acting on impulse, Felix Marlow drew a rail gun from his pack and fitted it with a rocket. The little handheld launcher, not much bigger than a concealable handgun, had the futuristic look of a weapon from the twenty-first century. It consisted of a grip, trigger, firing and guidance mechanisms, and a spindly rail for the launching of tiny, solid-fuel rockets—deadly little ballistic missiles the size of a pigeon egg. The thing *looked* futuristic, but in reality it was as archaic as a crossbow. Rail guns had enjoyed a brief spurt of popularity in the 1960s, then had been relegated to museums . . . mostly.

But that was before the perfection of microminiature warheads in the early 1990s and beam guidance devices about the turn of the century. Marlow's stint with WSL had given him substantial experience with rail guns. He had seen aircraft shot down and tank columns stopped by the little weapons.

Marlow raised the device, sighted it on Jack Logan, then changed his mind. The little missile with its explosive warhead would certainly kill the timecop. His flakwear would be no protection against a thing like this. But the explosion would damage everything around him, as well, including Marlow's own "soil-test equipment" crates, sitting on the flatbed.

He quickly thought of a solution and raised his sights. "I'll give you something to keep you occupied, timecop," he muttered.

Among the vehicles westbound on Maryland Avenue, he selected a black stretch limousine with flags on its nose. Some diplomat, out for a tour of the American capital. Mar-

low aligned the rail gun, sighted on the car's rear quarter—
the fuel tank—and set the guidance beam.

The little missile's launch was no more than a loud pop
and a touch of hot air. For an instant the rocket was visible,
out in front of the gun, dwindling as it accelerated. Then it
was gone, and a moment later the diplomatic limousine on
Maryland Avenue shook with internal explosion, flipped
over on its side, and erupted—a rising bright ball of
burning fuel. All around it, other cars skidded this way and
that, some colliding, others going off the road.

Nearer, in the construction area, workers lifted their
heads, turned to gawk at the spectacle beyond them, and
Jack Logan headed for the wreck at a dead run.

"It's called diversion," the Scavenger muttered to
himself as he put the rail gun away. "The second rule of
fundamental strategy."

In the north construction sector, Marlow flashed credentials, appropriated a team of electricians, and took
them into the tunnel. While they were modifying the overhead wiring beneath the Department of Labor building, he
returned to the south sector and inspected the newly in-
stalled lead shield in the newly dug hole there. Satisfied,
he had his crates unloaded from the flatbed and lowered by
sections into the hole. In this manner he assembled the
Manchurian Device and capped the cylinder over it. Metal
conduit spliced into an underground circuit completed the
triggering system.

When it was finished, he located the same job foreman and handed him a meaningless but official-looking
document.

"Here's your change order," the Scavenger said. "I've

finished here. Go ahead and pour your concrete. And thanks."

The bomb was in place, buried in concrete beneath the foot of a viaduct pier. It was assembled and live. The sealed components, originally designed for covert placement in the Soviet Union, were stable enough to last for thirty years—or maybe forty. Or the thing could be detonated within sixty seconds if he chose to. A simple telephone call to a certain coded number within the U.S. Department of Labor banks would trip a relay. From there an instruction code—delivered by telephone keys—would send an electromagnetic impulse through the conduit of Washington's Third Street tunnel lighting system, and the impulse would detonate the world's last remaining neutron bomb, within half a mile of the United States Capitol.

If and when this happened, only about one-sixth of the District of Columbia would become a hole in the ground, but the released radiation would make an instant graveyard of everything from Wheaton to Engleside, from Fairfax to Forestville—and as far downwind as its brief half-life permitted.

This had always been the design and the intent of the neutron bomb . . . maximum kill, minimum damage to real estate.

Bargaining power, Marlow mused as he watched the bomb site being buried in concrete while forming crews stood by to begin the footings of the pier. Now I have the mandate.

One more impulse remained—a small act of retribution. In afternoon sunlight, Felix Marlow followed his scanner's lead to the top of the FDA building and stepped out onto the roof, where a tall, dark-haired man in a TEC uniform stood at the north parapet, scanning the terrain beyond with electronic binoculars. As silent as a shadow, the Scavenger approached him, seeing his shoulders bunch as the agent realized—too late—that he was being stalked. With techniques learned in Weasel service, Marlow hit Jack Logan from behind, flipped him, lifted him, and threw him off the roof.

He stepped to the edge, peered over, and shrugged. There was no one there. Logan had activated the device returning him to his own time, as Marlow knew he would.

His work complete then, the Scavenger activated his own retrieval device. Around him, the dimensions of now distorted and coalesced, spiraling inward upon themselves to become a wormhole in time. Marlow managed one deep breath before the vortex closed around him, whirling him away into familiar nothingness.

For an instant—only an instant—Felix Marlow was part of the immaterial matrix of the wormhole. Then he rematerialized—strapped down, immobile, in an egg-shaped steel cage whirling dizzily between the prongs of a big, metal claw. The claw extended from the massive arm of a huge centrifuge, screaming around the confines of a stadium-size dome carved from the living stone of a subterranean cavern. At Marlow's emergence, in a momentary electromagnetic field crossing the dome, the centrifuge had a peripheral speed of 3,000 fps, exerting nine Gs of outward force.

For the first few seconds of deceleration, only the gyroscopic rotation of the cage protected him from this centrifugal extreme. But steadily, the spin decelerated, the roar of its passage dying to a whisper.

When the device came to rest at a boarding bay set into a stone wall, Marlow climbed out, dropped to the floor of the centrifuge chamber, and walked across to the great hub of the device. Within the hub was an elevator, which carried him upward to the sealed penthouse on top of Scofield Manor in the Blue Ridge Mountains.

Outside the penthouse, on a rooftop pad, a helicopter awaited him. On the receding slopes beyond, the foliage was just beginning to turn, sporting the colors of fall. Autumn was in the air—the autumn of the year 2007.

## TEC Headquarters
## September 2007

Jack Logan barely knew what hit him. Standing on the roof of a federal building in 1977 Washington, scanning the surroundings for sight of the Scavenger, he sensed a presence behind him and tried to pivot, but it was too late. The blow from behind was delivered by an expert, directly into the sensitive vertebrae just below his shoulders, and it stunned him. He was almost helpless as strong arms grappled him at neck and crotch, lifted him, spun him around, and threw him over the roof's edge.

It took all of his concentration in that split second to grasp his wrist unit and activate retrieval. As the pavement rose up to meet him, unimaginable forces spiraled into coalescence and he disappeared into . . . the cockpit of his timesled, huge gravities decreasing as the tachyon-propelled projectile decelerated along its launch track and slid to a halt at the dock.

The canopy opened, and launch techs appeared from the bay to help him climb out. Numb from the shoulders down, still stunned by the Scavenger's ruthless, expert attack, Jack Logan needed all the help he could get.

What he didn't need, right then, was Claire Hemmings, waiting for him in the bay with her systems-analyst expression and a pair of Science and Research techs to back her up. "I need a blood sample and vitals," she said. "You look like hell, Logan. Did the sled do this to you?"

"The sled's fine," he snapped, "and I'll be all right in a few minutes. I was hit from behind and thrown off a building, and my perp got away. Other than that and not knowing just what happened back there, I'm having a fine day!"

"Get that jacket off and make a fist," she said, unimpressed. "Can you walk by yourself? Where were you hit?"

"In the spine," he said, wincing as he removed his reinforced jacket and flak vest. "Just above center."

"You're lucky you weren't paralyzed," Claire decided, moving around behind him. "Any tingling sensations, persistent numbness, or sharp pains?"

"Only when I laugh," he growled, then flinched as she dug a businesslike thumb into the bruise between his shoulders.

"I guess you felt that," she said. "I'd say it's a moderate, temporary trauma, nothing more. When's the last time you slept, Logan? You're showing symptoms of exhaustion."

"Since when are you my nurse?" he growled. "I know what I need, and when I need it."

"Oh, sure. And what you need is an obsession over this Scavenger. God, you're stubborn, Logan. Do you think that guy could have nailed you from behind like that if you weren't running on adrenaline and exhaustion? Let's check your signs, then you're wanted in debrief."

"You never ease up, do you, Hemmings?" Logan glared

at her. For an instant he saw what might be real human concern in her eyes. But only for an instant.

"Not on the job," she said, breaking eye contact.

It was a frustrating debrief. Whatever had caused a point-nine ripple on the Dome, it had passed into history now. It was no longer a ripple. It had happened, and not been averted, and it had become part of the fabric of historic events.

Except for the explosion of a Jordanian Embassy vehicle on Maryland Avenue in October of 1977, with the deaths of a junior Jordanian official, his driver, a translator, and a Capital Tours guide, Jack Logan didn't know what the event might have been.

"We'll have to do an anomaly scan, Jack," Eugene Matuzek decided. "Easter, you set up the general overview. Use the sublimator sequence first. Maybe Logan can spot some changes there. When you've done that, Jack, go out for a cruise. You know the routine. Hemmings can go along with you to take notes."

"That might take all night," Claire protested. "Logan's out on his feet, Captain. He needs some rest."

"Well, do as much as you can," Matuzek ordered. "If this was the Scavenger again, we have to know what he did . . . why he was there in 1977."

"It was him," Logan said. "I'm sure of it."

"And the only thing he had in mind was to blow up Rasshad Beti's car? I don't believe that, and neither do you."

"ChronComp doesn't have anything significant on Beti," Dale Easter offered. "He was just an embassy clerk out for a drive that day. At least, that's all he was now."

"Does the name ring any bells for you, Jack?" Amy

Fuller asked. "You're the only one who'd know if Beti went on to do something important in the earlier history."

"None at all." Logan shrugged. "I never heard of him, or of those other dead people, either."

"Okay," Matuzek sighed. "Get on that anomaly scan as soon as we finish here. By the way, we got confirmation on Julie Price's data while you were out. There's no question about it, Felix Marlow is the one we're after. He *is* the Scavenger, and he's about as nasty a piece of work as I ever ran across. But we can't touch him in present time."

"We don't even have enough for a warrant to bring him in," Charles Graham said. "The law is still the law, and aside from a missing-person affidavit we don't have cause to arrest him even if we could find him . . . which we haven't, yet."

Matuzek nodded. "We'll have to nail him in the past, and bring him before Timecourt. Claire has an idea what his next treasure move might be, and ChronComp's running probabilities on it. Maybe that'll give us a strategy."

"That's not what I'm worried about." Claire frowned. "The Scavenger has a distinct behavior pattern, and part of it is that he always gets even, big-time. He's a thrill-killer in the worst sense of the term. When he's thwarted, he reacts dramatically and a lot of people die. It's like his ace in the hole. I'm afraid this time, whatever he's holding will be a doozy. He'll outdo himself to—"

"*Doozy?*"

"It's archaic slang, Logan. It means big . . . dramatic . . . memorable . . ."

"Have you been playing with the sublimator again, Claire?"

"Knock it off!" Matuzek snapped.

The systems analyst wrinkled her pretty nose at Logan,

then got back to the subject. "Dr. Easter thinks Marlow's had dealings with some nuclear stuff, sometime in the past. We know he's been a weapons trader, and we know he was in China—as a time jumper—about the time that rumor of a missing device surfaced."

Dale Easter looked up from his memos and nodded. "We might be looking at a cataclysm in the making, if we don't stop this guy. The captain was right. He's definitely a loose cannon, and he has ready access to time travel. He could plant a bomb somewhere, and nobody would ever—"

"He might have done it already," Matuzek growled. "There has to be some reason he went to 1977." The captain turned to Logan, thoughtfully. "Jack, put the site of the '77 encounter on your anomaly scan. Take a good look around there. Maybe there's something you'll see or remember."

In a corner of the briefing room, Bob O'Donnelly closed his memcorder. "In the meantime," he said, "Agent Deere wants another look at that Scofield mausoleum, out in the mountains. He wants me to go with him, so we're going back there as soon as he gets back from running some checks at the Bureau."

"What's he running?" Logan asked.

"Spook reports." O'Donnelly grinned. "He's trying to pin down reports of strange noises around Bucks Ridge."

## Washington, D.C.
## 2007

Serenity Arch was the newest of Washington's national monuments. And, like most of the statuary in the U.S. capital city, there were several versions of how it came to be and what it meant.

The official story was that the stainless steel arch soaring aloft in the east section of the Mall was a memorial to the decades-long Cold War, which had more or less ended in the nineties. The more generally favored version, though, was that the cryptic black-marble symbols at its crest were representations of a chair and a whip, and that the arch symbolized the Acts of Restraint in 2002, when the Internal Revenue Service was finally brought under constitutional restraints and made accountable for its behavior.

Either way, the Arch had become one of the most popular of Washington's edifices. Its observation deck, nearly three hundred feet above Madison Drive, was a fine place from which to view the panorama of the federal city at night. Every major building, monument, park, freeway, and thoroughfare glittered with light, showcasing the city as its designers had intended it to be, while darkness hid what many parts of it had become.

"My insertion point was over there." Jack Logan pointed, his voice slurred with exhaustion. "About where the triangle meridian is now. It was an open lot in 1977, between the thoroughfare and the freeway ramps. There was a construction project, just about where the ramps meet now. Workmen, machinery . . . excavating a trench along the east side of the Third Street tunnel entry "

"They were just building the tunnel, then?" Claire Hemmings asked.

"No, the tunnel was about three years old. This was a modification. They were sinking pilings and pouring support piers. That must be it, over there. The piers under the Independence Avenue embankments. They were just putting those in. It was kind of chaotic. There was a hassle over a change order on one of the pier excavations. But they were getting it done. Maryland Avenue, down there, is where the limousine blew up. And over there, south, that's where I got thrown off the roof."

"So do you see anything that's different now . . . any anomalies?"

Logan stifled a yawn. "Nothing significant. Maybe a little change in those highway embankments. I think Indy outbound was flat-sloped along there. I don't remember it having drain-offs. And shouldn't there be another monument over there by the Hirshhorn Museum? Where's the Antibac Shrine?"

Claire squinted up at him. "The *what*?"

"The *Antibac*. Memorial to the germ warfare casualties in Iraq and Kuwait, 1991. Saddam Hussein's 'blowing death' killed nearly four thousand . . ."

Claire was busy at her memcorder. "Never happened," she said. "Saddam Hussein played around with some nasty stuff in Iraq, but it was pretty much third-world tech. He never quite got it perfected."

"Well," Logan mused, "so much for the *insignificance* of Rasshad Beti. 'Embassy clerk,' huh?"

"Yeah, I guess Beti's death could have changed some things. He was Jordanian, not Iraqi. But then, King Hussein and Saddam Hussein had some common bonds. What if Beti opened a channel for biotics technology! You think that was the Scavenger's mission? To kill Beti before he helped Saddam get into the germ warfare business?"

"No, I don't." Logan frowned tiredly. "I think that was happenstance. It was a diversion. I had the feeling that I was being watched, and I remember a strange sound just before that car blew up. Kind of a high, quick whine, overhead. A projectile, I think. I was still at the construction site. He must have been over there, somewhere." He pointed.

"Do you think he shot at you and missed?"

"That doesn't seem likely, that he'd miss. Maybe he just wanted my attention. I thought at the time the explosion looked like a tach-beam hit, but now I'm remembering about Felix Marlow's safaris, back when he was young. He always favored odd old things like swords and crossbows for his games. Sort of an anachronist. I think, now, that he hit that car with a minimissile, like something out of the seventies."

Claire added notes to her memcorder, then gazed out across the vista. "If he was over there by the Indy, and you heard the projectile pass above you, that puts us right back to the construction site, where you were. He must have wanted you out of there—maybe out of the picture while he did something there. But what?"

"I don't know." Logan frowned, rubbing his eyes. "Let's cover that area again, then head in. Maybe ThinkTank's got some ideas."

Logan started for the elevator, his boots echoing hollowly on the flooring of the deserted observation deck, and Claire watched him go, then hurried to catch up. "Head in?" she demanded. "Logan, it's after midnight! You're stumbling around like a zombie, and you want to go back to work? When's the last time you had some sleep?"

"I'm all right." He yawned. "I've got to get that guy, Hemmings! I can't stop now!"

"He'll keep till morning," the systems analyst decided. "Right now I'm taking you home, and you're going to get some rest. The shape you're in, you're not doing anybody any good right now." She guided him into the elevator and hit the down button. At the landing, she turned toward the silver Gen-Em Trace sitting alone in the parking lot. "Get in," she said. "I'll drive."

"It's my car!" he protested.

"That's all right. It likes me better than it likes you. Get in."

### Bucks Ridge, Virginia

Cress hadn't seen razor wire in years, and he paused near the top of Scofield Manor to marvel at the sight of it here. From the ground, he hadn't even seen it—the loose floss of thread-size stainless steel wires girdling the building just below the top-floor sconces. From a distance, the floss seemed as insubstantial as trailing cobwebs. But this wasn't spider silk. This was hair-thin, razor-edged wire that could cut a man to pieces if he got tangled in it.

"Somebody really doesn't want these walls scaled," Cress told himself, backing down from the obstruction. Like a spider on a wall, the caretaker retraced his path, climbing down the sheer stone wall. On the ground, he went to the south gardening shed and found a roll of tar-backed burlap, which he strapped to his back. Then he returned to the wall and started upward again.

"This is like old times," he said to himself as the hard rubber soles of his boots found tiny footings in the stone, and strong fingers wedged into the crevices of seams and joints pulled him upward. "A solo climb, just out of plain, stinkin' curiosity."

Cress had been satisfied for a long time just to tend the grounds of the Scofield estate, keep the exteriors in good repair, and mind his own business. The pay was good, the work undemanding, and the solitude to his liking. Anywhere within the wide perimeter of Bucks Ridge, he could come and go as he pleased, answering to no one but himself, and with only old Raymond—who rarely showed up—to account to.

It had seemed like heaven on earth, for a long time, being caretaker of Scofield Manor. Mountain-born in central Wyoming, Cress had no family and no ties. He had knocked around here and there in his life, had experienced city life, military discipline, prison regimentation, and the harsh, suicidal thrill of paramilitary existence first as a freelance mercenary soldier and then as a penetration specialist with WSL.

He did his job, maintained his own quarters, found time for his books, and tried to mind his own business. The

rewards were peace, a growing prosperity from his accumulated wages, and a life full of the comforts provided by
money. Cress was not by nature a snoop or a criminal, and
the big, locked house dominating the estate held no particular interest for him.

For a long time.

But the solitude had been lonely at times, and the reclusive freedom grew thin. More and more often these days,
there was the helicopter landing on the roof, and he heard
those eerie, unearthly rumbling sounds that seemed to
arise from the mountain itself and came only when the
flier was present. More and more, Cress felt a growing curiosity about what went on in that stone mansion where
nobody lived.

The key, of course, was the penthouse, which he had
never seen except for the edge of its slate roof in the high
distance beyond the mansion's eaves.

Still, he controlled his curiosity and kept his notions to
himself . . . until the day the visitors had come with Raymond, and for the first time Cress had seen a portion of the
manor's interior. It was unlike anything he had ever seen,
and then the big man, FBI Agent Deere, had asked him all
those questions, and the two of them had found a picture
of Felix Marlow. Responding to Deere's questions, Cress
had told him what he knew of Marlow and how he felt
about him.

Marlow was a man Cress would just as soon have forgotten. A dangerous man, his instincts had always told
him—dangerous and unpredictable. Not a man to be
trusted.

Marlow was one of the reasons Cress had left the
Weasels. Even more than in the military, a mercenary had
to be able to count on those around him—to trust his bud-

dies absolutely. But Marlow was a crazy, and he seemed to infect some of those around him.

Cress could kill, when the pay was right and the orders proper. But it made his skin crawl to be around a guy who killed solely for pleasure. It made him always wonder who would be next.

The day B. T. Ericson, founder and commander of the WSL, was found dead in his bunk in the WSL camp outside a little Croatian village—impaled in his sleep with an African tribal spear—Cress had slipped away from the Weasels and never gone back.

From Serbia he had made his way to Ireland, then home to the U.S., and when this job as caretaker came along, it had been the answer to his prayers. But that was before he learned that Felix Marlow might be connected with the place. Now he needed to know what was going on, and so he climbed the wall for a look at the penthouse. It was tempting as he climbed to use the iron-laced windows and stone sills that were the outer faces of inside levels, but Cress had seen the intricate security of this place and he knew where the pressure plates and break-beams were likely to be. So he avoided the easy route and stayed to the sheer stone wall. An experienced mountaineer, he found it a relatively easy climb even without the ledges and braces the windows offered.

Arriving again at the razor-wire barrier, Cress used gardeners' cloth—heavy, tar-backed burlap—to bridge past it. Clinging to a hand-and-toe hold was easier here, among the caps and buttresses of the ensconced fourth level. Carefully, he placed his roll of cloth atop the uppermost fibers of the razor-wire floss, then dropped it behind, rolled it up and over, and dropped it again—binding a three-foot section of murderous wire into a harmless sleeve. A few feet beyond, he hoisted himself over the rustic eaves of Scofield Manor.

The penthouse—a long, low structure like a separate house built atop the house—occupied nearly a third of the roof area. Near it, connected by a railed walkway, was a helicopter pad. The rest of the aerie was a little walled yard with telescope mounts at its corners. A canvas-wrapped scope rested in one of the mounts, and after a close look at the exterior of the locked apartment he went to it and unwrapped it.

The view was breathtaking—fifty miles of Blue Ridge caps and crests through electronically enhanced lenses. He watched traffic on an interstate twelve miles away, looked down upon the rooftops of three little towns and a dozen rural residences ranging from farms to retirement retreats, then watched people in windbreakers playing golf on country club fairways two ridges over.

He saw people going about the day's business on the streets of little Dustin, then turned his scan on the road up the mountain. Someone was coming this way, and after a few minutes he saw who it was. The first car was Raymond's limousine. The one following it was a rental car, containing the FBI agent, Deere, and his young computer-genius sidekick.

"Maybe this time I'll have something to show Mr. Deere," Cress told himself.

There was no sign of anyone else approaching, so he put away the scope and studied the locked penthouse. It was alive with sophisticated security devices, but none he hadn't encountered before. In three minutes he was at the door, past the alarms, and it took him only a moment to open the lock and enter.

Somehow, he had expected ordinary furnishings in the

place. But it wasn't a residence, and didn't pretend to be one. Most of the interior was just empty space, but one room of it was a computer center. Banks of equipment and ranks of monitors seemed to fill the room, with the only human-type furniture being a work-surface table and a single chair.

"This is Farsight Trust," Cress told himself, identifying various pieces of equipment. "This is what Mr. Deere was looking for. Those blank ranges in the big computer downstairs . . . this must be the access terminal."

Raymond Scofield himself had said it: Show Mr. Deere anything he wants to see, as long as it has to do with the computer. Well, Cress nodded, muttering to himself, this certainly fit the category.

On an interior wall, behind the banks of slave computers linked to the megaframe below, was an elevator. Cress looked inside it and saw that the controls for the main house floors had been dismantled. But as he touched the panel a sound caught his attention. Three feet away, a shelf of reference books slid away, exposing a second, hidden elevator. Two lifts in the same shaft, and one of them was camouflaged!

For a moment, Cress hesitated about using the hidden lift. He was beginning to be a little nervous about his exploration. But when he opened its cage door and looked at the controls, he made up his mind. This was a dedicated lift. Unlike the other, visible one, it had not been modified for express use. No buttons had been disconnected. There had never been any for the various above-ground floors of the house.

The only stops identified on the panel were the penthouse and the basement, yet there were three buttons in all. The third one—the lowest one—was unmarked, but apparently below the basement stop. Giving in to curiosity, he stepped in, closed the portal, and pushed the button.

As the closed cage descended, Cress didn't hear the muffled whir of rotors above. A sleek, dark chopper swept in fast and low from the northeast. It hovered for a moment beyond the manor's north face as though inspecting the wrap of gardeners' cloth on the wire barrier there, then circled once, lazily, and put down on the roof pad.

"Yeah, I see him," John Davis Deere grunted as Bob O'Donnelly pointed out the flash of helicopter blades that swept momentarily past the distant, dark bulk of the great house on the ridge. "Maybe we'll get lucky this time, and catch somebody at home."

The FBI man took a tiny flip-top from his coat pocket and muttered into it. O'Donnelly grinned, knowing that the call would bring airborne reinforcements to close the back door up there. When Poppin' Johnny decided to talk to a person, he didn't want that person leaving before he was through.

The mountain road wound upward, and eventually the gates of Scofield Manor came into view. In the limousine ahead, Raymond Scofield pulled to a halt, got out, and turned off the electronic defenses. Then, without waiting for the two men behind him to catch up, he got in and drove the rest of the way to the fortress.

Scofield's getting tired of this, O'Donnelly thought. He doesn't like coming up here, but he has to. A trace warrant is a court order, and Raymond Scofield is a meticulous man. Still, I'll bet he wishes he hadn't ever agreed to be executor of Walter Scofield's estate.

"I wonder why he puts up with this," Agent Deere said,

as though reading his mind. "He said, himself, that he doesn't have anything to gain by traveling clear up here from Dustin every time somebody demands entrance. Why doesn't he just call that caretaker and tell him who to let in?"

There was no answer to that, so O'Donnelly ignored it. He wondered what Deere had found in the FBI's classified files—files that even ChronComp couldn't access—that brought them back here this morning. Whatever it was, Deere hadn't seen fit to mention it so far.

In the curving drive, they left the car and glanced upward at the roof. There was no sight of the helicopter on top, but they knew it was there.

Raymond was waiting for them at the door. "I do hope this will be your final inspection here," he said crossly.

Deere shrugged. "The warrant is to inspect Farsight Trust files, on site," he said. "We haven't been able to do that, yet. Where's Cress?"

Raymond opened the front doors, then stepped back and glanced around. "On the grounds, somewhere, I suppose. It isn't like him not to meet traffic at the gate."

"How did you happen to find him as caretaker?" Deere asked. "Did he apply for the job?"

"Well, no, not exactly," Raymond said, leading them into the reception hall. "He was recommended and I contacted him. Why?"

"Who recommended him?" Deere pressed.

"I really don't know. His name and references were in the estate file when I was appointed as executor. So I placed a call to him, he responded, I interviewed him and gave him the job. Is there something wrong, about Mr. Cress?"

"Just curious." Deere shrugged. "Let's go see that

computer again. We saw the technician land a few minutes ago, so we should be able to clear all this up soon."

When the secret elevator stopped—after a surprisingly long descent—Cress stepped out into a vast enclosure like nothing he had ever seen before. It was a huge, circular chamber whose walls and high, domed ceiling looked as though they were carved from living stone. Though well-lit and ventilated, the place had the feel of a deep, subterranean cavern.

He turned this way and that, marveling at what he saw around him. The place was an enormous, circular chamber, like the inside of a great, windowless building at least two hundred yards across. All around its vast wall was a single head-high shelf, receding to a farther wall that flowed upward and inward to become a seamless roof, which arched overhead and then downward, to form a wide, central hub of sleeved stone. The sleeving, seen closely, was more than a surface feature. It was great, vertical bands of copper coil, ranked edge to edge around a stone core. It looked like a giant, upright electromagnetic motor. The elevator shaft behind him was set into this core.

"It's a ring-space, a . . . a *torus*!" Cress muttered to himself, staring around at the vast, circular arena. "I'm inside a damned doughnut!"

Here and there along the distant wall, just above the shelf, were small, indistinct features like little rows of high, closed doors, and directly across from him a stepped pedestal fronted a row of glass windows. But the outstanding feature of the place was a huge, metal structure extending both directions from a great, fitted ring of dark steel. The ring was serrated, like the brushes of an electric motor. One end of the attached extension—a great arm of reinforced structural metal—extended outward almost to the wall, where huge claws of cast metal held an egg-shaped cage between delicate-seeming pincers, top and bottom. He walked partway around the hub and looked at the other end. It extended only about halfway across the chamber, but its end was a solid block of steel-encased stone the size of a semitrailer.

"Counterweight," he told himself, as shock gave way to recognition. "Like balancing spars on a free pivot. And a magnetic-coil engine. My God, this whole damned thing is a big centrifuge!"

Gaping and peering, Cress climbed through the massive structure of the arm and walked around the hub. Ducking under the counterweight arm he continued around, back to where he had started, and turned to the elevator—then stopped. Where the elevator opening had been was now nothing but a copper surface. The shaft had closed. The elevator was gone.

But Cress was no longer alone in the vast, silent cavern. The tall man who stood there, where the elevator had been, wore dark clothing that resembled a blast suit, armored and padded, right up to a helmet with a smoke-dark faceplate. He held a compact, spring-steel crossbow with the casual ease of long practice.

As Cress gaped at him, the man raised his faceplate. "It's been a long time, Cress," he purred. "You probably thought I'd forgotten about you, but I never did."

Cress gawked at him, recognizing a face from the past. Felix Marlow was older now, his features more craggy, but his eyes were still the cold, meticulous eyes of a born and trained killer. "Marlow," the caretaker gasped. "It *is* you!"

"I've been waiting for you to wake up, Cress." Marlow smiled. "I knew you would, eventually. And when you did, you'd do just what you always did best . . . snoop."

"How—how did you know?" Cress whispered. "The alarms . . ."

"Oh, you were very thorough," Marlow drawled. "Penetration was always your long suit, wasn't it. You breeched the defenses and bypassed the alarms—all but one. The razor wire was pressure-rigged, Cress. You got past it, but it told me that you had. No, no—" The crossbow came to point. "—don't be foolish, Cress. If you try to jump me, you'll just make things messy. You're fortunate, you know, that I was nearby when you tripped the alarm. I was only a few miles away, heading in. Otherwise you might have been trapped down here for days before I got around to you."

Cress had tensed himself for a rush, but now he relaxed. He remembered the Weasel assassin. He knew that a surprise attack would do no good. With cold fatality, he drew himself up and spread his arms, presenting his chest and his vitals. "You might tell me what this all means, Felix." He sighed. "This place, with its big computer and no one around, this . . . this centrifugal chamber, all this secrecy. What's it all about?"

Felix Marlow's smile was the grin of a cat at the kill. He snugged the crossbow to his shoulder and aimed it, casually.

"Of course, I'll explain it, Cress," he purred. "What's it all about? Why, it's about time."

The crossbow made hardly a sound as it released its bolt—only a small slap of cordage on the released, sliding leaves of stout, steel springs.

The deadly bolt went through Cress's breastbone and

imbedded its point in his spine. It quivered there, only its fletches showing. Cress stood for a second, then toppled, dead before he hit the stone floor.

# XIV

They were in the basement when the eerie wail began. It was as before—a deep, rumbling vibration of powerful subsonics that seemed to come from all around them, from everywhere and nowhere. But now, here in the deep basement of Scofield Manor, it was more. Now there was actual, audible sound in the blend, and it sounded like the rising whine of a huge electric motor. Up and up it went, climbing rapidly in pitch until all of them doubled over in pain, hands clamped to their ears.

Then, just as the scream reached ultrasonic pitch, it began to die away, receding until only a momentary subsonic rumble remained, then silence.

"Jehosaphat!" Poppin' Johnny gasped. "What the bald-headed hell *is* that?"

Bob O'Donnelly blinked, ashen-faced, and lowered his fists from his ears. "Sonics," he said. "I had ChronComp test the rumble we heard before. It was acceleration-deceleration subsonics. This had sonics and high-frequency whine mixed in, because we're closer to whatever it is."

"That's what I asked!" Deere spat. "What *is* it?"

"It's only a guess, but I'd say it's a timesled. Except that this one doesn't jump to temporal transfer and disappear. This one hits its field, then bounces back down the same track. How should I know what it is? Maybe we ought to find it."

Raymond Scofield had gone to his knees in the storm of sonics. Now he staggered upright, pale and frightened. "Find it?" he murmured. "How do you find a ghost?"

Deere turned to him, scowling. "There's no ghost here, Mr. Scofield. But there's something a lot worse. We have reason to believe that this place is a center of criminal activity, involving about a dozen major categories of felony. That sound you heard is somebody doing something extremely illegal. FBI records indicate that there have been eight reports of that noise, from outside witnesses, and every report corrcsponds to a known felony. These are *major* crimes, Mr. Scofield. Things I can't even talk about. But the key to them is right here. Now do I have your invitation to conduct a thorough search of this place, or do I have to order a general warrant and bring in federal marshals to do it?"

Raymond stared at him. "Criminal activity? Mr. Deere, this is an empty house. Nobody lives here, so how—"

"The computer," Bob O'Donnelly said. "The computer lives here."

"The computer is a machine! Machines don't do criminal activities!"

"But the people who use them do," Deere rumbled. "We think we know who it is, too. Your cousin's son, Felix Marlow."

"Felix . . ." Raymond Scofield took a deep breath and looked around at the megaframe banks as though seeing them for the first time. "Felix. Yes, I can believe that. Felix *would* be a criminal. We—the whole family—we tried to erase what he did, all those years ago. We tried, and the whole thing was so abominable that we tried to forget. But it's no good. It was never any good. Felix is worse than a criminal, Mr. Deere. He's *evil*! It was his behavior that drove Walter insane. And God help us, we all knew that, even if we never admitted it."

Deere's gruff demeanor became suddenly gentle. "Then we have to stop him, don't we?"

"Yes." Raymond nodded. "Yes, he must be stopped. As . . . as executor of the Walter Scofield estate, you have my permission to . . . to do whatever must be done, to stop Felix before he makes good on his threat."

Deere and O'Donnelly both frowned at the defeated man. "What threat?"

"The family knows about it," Raymond sighed. "Walter knew, and he believed it. That's why he turned away from everything. We all knew, but I suppose we just chose to forget about it—"

*"What threat?"*

"Why, the threat Felix made, before he . . . went away. He said he'd be back, and he'd get even. He said he'd get even with *everybody*. He said he'd own the world, Mr. Deere. He said he would acquire it the way a junk man acquires trash, and use it as he saw fit. He said . . . he said if he couldn't have the world, then nobody could because he'd destroy it."

"Destroy what?" O'Donnelly pressed. "The world?"

"The world as we know it," Raymond breathed. Suddenly the others noticed that there were tears in the old man's eyes. "Felix said that before he's done he'll have a way to destroy everything that matters. And you know . . . I believe him. All his life, Felix has made threats. And he has always made good on them."

"God," O'Donnelly whispered to himself.

"That helicopter up there," Raymond asked, "the one

that comes here . . . the computer service person. Is that . . . is it Felix?"

"Probably," Deere told him. "We'll know soon enough. I want to see that penthouse on the roof." Deere turned away, flipping open his palm phone. "Hypothesis confirmed," he told it. "One-A code to Graham, immediate relay to TEC and to chief of bureau. Alert all sectors. I'm going in on this end. The suspect may be on premises."

"Or he might not be," O'Donnelly reminded the agent. "That sound we heard . . . I think it's a timesled. He may have jumped to the past."

## TEC Headquarters

Dr. Dale Easter gasped, jerked upright, and nearly fell out of his chair when the lurid cover photograph on a thirty-year-old tabloid paper changed, right before his eyes. It was the October 7, 1985, issue of *Spotlight*. The primary picture on its cover montage was a muddy, long-lens view of strewn, hacked bodies lying in a littered alleyway. The stained brick wall in the background was streaked with graffiti and spray-paint art, and at least two uniformed policemen were visible in the foreground frame.

It was one of a stack of old publications Easter had gathered, from the time of the urban safaris in Washington's ghettos.

The bodies were indistinct, but obviously mutilated. They lay in a grotesque pile, as though dumped there in a load of trash.

He picked the tabloid up, glanced at it, then gasped and looked again. There were six bodies there, sprawled over one another like cast-off, broken mannequins covered in blood and tatters. Then, abruptly, the scene changed, and there were seven corpses. The one on top, a bearded man in coveralls, lay sprawled across the rest, with a few inches of fletched dowel protruding from his chest. Unlike the other bodies, this one was clearly defined and recognizable in the old halftone.

Easter blinked, steadied himself, and looked again, peering through his eyeglasses. Then, as though the tabloid was a catalyst, all the vague concerns he had been pursuing came together . . . and made sense. He sprang from the chair and headed for the squad room, waving his tabloid. He was halfway to Eugene Matuzek's office when alarms went off and the Dome came alive.

A sprinting tech cut across Easter's path, almost knocking him down, and turned to catch him by the arm. "We have a ripple, Dr. Easter," he said. "A big one. Level four and growing. It's pinpointed at 6:19 A.M. eastern time, October 6, 1985. Do you—"

"I know about it," Easter said. "Get the coordinates into the timefield and stand by. The captain will . . ." Just ahead, he saw Matuzek coming out of his office, heading for the briefing room. He ran to catch the TEC captain, herded him aside, and gave him a hushed, rapid report, brandishing his tabloid. Curious eyes turned toward them as people hurried by, responding to the ripple still spreading on the Dome. Few had ever seen Dr. Dale Easter so animated . . . so *agitated*! Among the scurrying crowds, others were heading for the briefing room, coming from various directions. With a nod to Matuzek, Easter moved to head off Jack Logan and Claire Hemmings, who had just arrived at headquarters. It had been a momentary item of discussion around the squad room—TEC's number one field agent and the beautiful, blond systems analyst, arriving at work together. The two were flint and steel, and though there was an obvious chemistry between them, it was volatile chemistry. More than a few quick wagers had already been made, just in the moments since their arrival.

Easter displayed his tabloid to both of them, then handed it to Claire. "Set up your sublimator for this date," the historian told her. "We'll aim for insertion in early afternoon, October 6, 1985. The Lincoln Heights area, right here in the city. ChronComp's already running peripherals. Matuzek wants you and Jack to make this jump together."

Then Easter grinned at Logan. "You'll want this one, Jack," he said. "The ripple is a level four. And this time we *know* it's the Scavenger."

## Bucks Ridge, Virginia

With backup on the way, Poppin' Johnny Deere set out to learn the secrets of Scofield Manor from the top down. Bob O'Donnelly was right behind him when the penthouse elevator—its seals overridden—opened into the house on top of the mansion, and the TEC historian gasped at what he saw there.

"This is more like it!" he said, flitting around among the computer equipment in the barren penthouse. "These are the access terminals. This is where we'll get the goods on Farsight Trust."

Deere glanced around, then went exploring. It took him nearly ten minutes to discover the camouflaged second elevator and determine that *its* lowest floor was well below the basement of the place. "I'm going down," he called. "Want to tag along?"

"You bet!" O'Donnelly crowed. "God, you ought to see the stuff that's in these files. This'll take months—by the way, where's Mr. Scofield?"

"Probably out looking for his caretaker," Deere said. "It's all right. He's not going anyplace." He turned to a wide window and pointed. In the distance, a trio of FBI and police helicopters were converging on the ridge, to take up surveillance until ground support arrived. "Nobody's going anyplace," Deere amended. "Come on, let's see where this deep shaft goes."

As the elevator settled at its lowest stop, O'Donnelly muttered, "Five hundred feet."

"What?"

"I've estimated descent," O'Donnelly said. "We're down about five hundred feet. That's pretty good depth, for a five-story building. Of course, we passed the basement four hundred feet back."

The outer door slid open, and Deere opened the cage. "Good heavens!" he breathed, peering out at the great, domed enclosure beyond.

"I knew it!" O'Donnelly laughed, scampering out into the vast, open vault. "Look at this place . . . this *machine*! Here's the centrifuge accelerator and the armature. I imagine the controls and temporal vector locks are behind that glass over there. And there has to be a—ah, there it is! Mr. Deere, look over this way! See the metal plates in the floor along there, and those capacitors along the ceiling? It's a timefield! Just like at TEC, but with a different configuration. A *centrifugal* track, with mega-amp electrical poles set to go zap at just the right instant. Well, so much for the sanctity of straight-track launching!"

Deere stood beside him, towering over him like a battleship over a yacht. "I guess," he said. "Very interesting. Where's Marlow?"

"This thing's on standby," O'Donnelly figured, turning this way and that, trying to see everything at once. "Smell the ozone in the air? The circuits are live. My guess is, Mr. Marlow has jumped to somewhen and hasn't returned yet. I sure wouldn't want to be in this chamber when this thing goes into retrieval rotation, though. Instant Mixmaster!"

"That's easy enough to avoid," Deere decided. "It's electric powered. All we have to do is find its plug and shut it down, while we look around."

Washington, D.C.
October 6, 1985
2:00 P.M.

"You want to flip a coin?" Claire Hemmings asked as she and Jack Logan waded out of the reflecting pool east of the Lincoln Memorial. "To decide who goes to the Treasury Department and who looks for the bomb?"

"You take Treasury." Logan shrugged. "The silver business is your idea."

"It isn't my idea!" She reached the rim of the pool and climbed out, pink-cheeked in the icy air. "It's one of the possibilities ThinkTank came up with, for the ripple. If Marlow got his hands on all that dumped silver stock when the market-corner failed, then he'd be interested in legislation that would alter the value of silver in our time.

"That's what the press conference is about, today. Senator Jacobs is plugging for silver standards, and public opinion is going to swing on that announcement. Just imagine, back on the silver standard. Just imagine the effect, if something happened to the senator today. That's why ChronComp rated this thing as a probability."

"And you understand all that? Like the stock markets and price value? You know about that stuff, don't you." Logan stiff-armed himself to the rim of the pool, swung out, and stood, letting his uniform and the gun at his hip shoo away curious passersby as icy water sluiced from him. Why can't they set that timefield more accurately, he wondered. Why can't they at least miss a pool of water?

"Of course, I understand it," Claire snapped. "It's basic economics!"

"So you take Treasury," Logan repeated. "I'll go see if I can find whatever it was that the Scavenger left here eight years ago. Bomb, or whatever."

"Easter thinks he planted a bomb," she said. "He was here . . . then . . . for *some* reason."

"And now he's back." Logan nodded. "Maybe to dig up something he buried in 1977, maybe to set off a bomb, maybe to get rich in silver stocks, maybe because this is the day his younger self arranged for all those people to be butchered . . . God! I hate multiple probabilities!"

"I'll take Treasury." Claire shrugged. She turned away, then looked back. "Logan . . . be careful. Take care of yourself."

"You, too, Hemmings." He watched her walk north, toward the Treasury Department building across Constitution Avenue, then turned and headed east. It was about a mile to the south end of the Third Street tunnel, and somewhere around there—in the midst of what had become a maze of roads, ramps, and trafficways—was where he had watched a public works crew dig a hole for a pier.

ThinkTank was certain now that the Scavenger had

buried something there, in 1977. Dale Easter had a frightening theory about what it might be. A neutron bomb, he said. One of the most terrifying and chillingly simple devices ever produced by a world obsessed with warfare and mass annihilation.

3:30 P.M.

"In a proper legislative body," the columnist Chase Lawrence wrote in this year of 1985, "nobody specializes but everybody is a specialist." Loren Jacobs, United States Senator, might have been a model for those words. A rarity among politicians, Jacobs truly held office for the benefit of the constituents and held his interests to be the interests of his state. Yet, by background, Jacobs was an expert in silver.

For nearly twenty years, Senator Jacobs had crusaded for a return to the silver standard for U.S. currency. In that time he had seen silver prices go from a regulated $1.29 per ounce to a free-market $25 to $30 per ounce, then skyrocket to nearly $60 when a group of investors attempted to corner world silver markets in 1983.

And during those years, the senator had seen the chaos of a national currency whose value was based upon nothing but the promises of a government. It was Jacobs's goal—almost his obsession—to resume the issuance of silver certificates, and return all United States legal tender to the steadying influence of a silver base.

Now, in 1985, the silver cartel had failed in its adventure, and silver stocks plummeted to $8.89 per share. It was the opportunity Jacobs had waited for, and he launched his "silver money" campaign anew, going head-to-head with the inflation brokers.

On October 6, 1985, the Jacobs-Studenham bill had its place on the Senate calendar, and Loren Jacobs was making one final appeal to the public. For his press conference, he chose the steps of the Treasury Department building in Washington.

The crowd outside the old building was small. The weather was nippy today, and economic measures chronically lacked the sexiness demanded by the sensationalist media. But the *Times* was there, as well as *The Wall Street Journal*, *Philadelphia Inquirer*, *Christian Science Monitor*, and all the major TV networks. Considering the subject, Jacobs was happy with the turnout.

At the top of the steps, above and behind the microphoned podium, a small, pretty blond in businesslike tweeds fiddled with a camera mount and watched the assembling crowd. Claire Hemmings didn't know what, if anything, the Scavenger had in mind for this event. But whatever it was, she intended not to let it happen.

"1985 . . ." the soundless voice in her mind intoned, as sublimator-enhanced recall scrolled within her. "1985— Ronald Reagan begins second term as U.S. president . . . Mikhail Gorbachev becomes general secretary of the USSR . . . Daniel Ortega becomes president of Nicaragua . . . Gorbachev and Reagan summit in Geneva . . ."

With a frown, she tried to still the distracting mental chatter. Her eyes roved the surroundings, expecting at any moment to see the telltale coalescence of a wormhole opening in time.

"1985 . . ." the speed-brief persisted. "1985—TWA airliner hijacked by Arab terrorists . . . Israeli aircraft bomb PLO headquarters in Tunis . . . Palestinians hijack the

*Achille Lauro* . . . robbers steal forty million dollars from the Wells Fargo Bank of New York . . . Mexican earthquake kills seven thousand . . . Colombian eruption kills twenty thousand . . . U.S. deficit reaches one hundred and thirty billion dollars . . ."

"Oh, shut up!" Claire snapped, under her breath. She was finding it difficult to concentrate.

"Pardon?" someone said, and she glanced around. Senator Jacobs had just stepped out of the building, flanked by several aides and Treasury staffers.

"Sorry," Claire said. "I was just—"

Quick movement in the crowd caught her eye, and she pivoted just as a man at the foot of the steps raised a revolver. With a gasp, Claire flung herself in front of the senator, reached for her own weapon, and was thrown back as someone else intervened, blocking her view. She heard a shot, then another, and someone large bumped her. She pitched backward, taking Senator Jacobs and two others down with her.

There was another shot, then shouting voices, and Claire squirmed upward, trying to see what was going on. At the foot of the steps, uniformed policemen had a man belly-down on the ground, holding him there while they wrested his gun from his hand. The pile of fallen people around her shifted, sorting itself out, and a strong hand helped her to her feet.

"Are you all right, miss?" a Treasury agent asked, looking her over with real appreciation. "Sorry I bumped you. I was kind of busy there."

"Senator Jacobs?" she asked. "Is he? . . ."

"He's fine," the T-man said, turning away. All around, chaos and panic were becoming the orchestrated procedure of a controlled incident. Someone had tried to shoot the senator, and failed. The only casualty was a Treasury security guard, with a bullet graze along his ribs.

At the foot of the stairs, the assassin was cuffed now and on his feet. Claire stared at him, incredulous. He was young, glassy-eyed, and red-haired, and he was no one she had ever seen.

"An acidhead," someone near her said. "High as a kite and running loose. At least, that's one they can put away for a while."

Through it all, there had been no sign of the Scavenger. In temporal terms, the whole thing was just a minor local incident.

### 4:15 P.M.

Rush-hour traffic was at its peak, and Logan was getting nowhere. For an hour he had grid-searched the area that, eight years before, had been a construction site. If there was a bomb—or anything—buried here, he realized, nothing short of major demolition and excavation was going to uncover it. Several times he circled around a particular column beneath the highway ramp rising from the Third Street tunnel, and his intuition told him that this was the place. Somewhere beneath that column, he felt, somewhere under the massive, sunken pier that supported it, was something that needed to be found.

But there was no way to get to it, short of destroying several million dollars' worth of federal highway.

As dusk settled over Washington, Logan made one more circuit, scanning the entire area with recorder lenses. The day was ending, and the city lights shone brightly all around him. On impulse, he traced sequences of lights from the site outward—strings of common-circuit over-head highway lights, traffic lights, walkway globes, even the row of ceiling lights visible now, leading into and through the Third Street tunnel.

He was just putting away his scanner when Claire Hem-mings appeared, darting across Second Street to join him at the triangle median. "I totally struck out," she said. "The Treasury Department thing was a false lead. Right time, wrong place."

"Me, too," he muttered.

She looked up at him, her eyes wide with concern. "So where does that leave us, Logan? By now that big ripple has spread to our own future. History has been changed, big-time. God knows what we'll find in our own time when we go back . . . or if there's anything left to go back to."

"I'm not going back," Jack said. "Our only chance of catching Marlow is here and now. Whatever he's come to 1985 to do, it has to be stopped or there won't be any 2007 to go home to. Can you read a lens scan?" He handed her his recorder. "This is everything I've seen here, so far. Maybe you'll see something I missed."

"I'll try," she said. "But I just realized something we *all* missed. It was in speed-brief, and it might have been a possibility. The Wells Fargo Bank in New York was robbed today, of forty million dollars. That's lost money now . . . right up the Scavenger's alley."

"That was in New York," Logan pointed out. "This is Washington, and this is where the ripple started—here and now."

"So what do we do?"

"We keep looking," Logan decided. "I have a feeling that Chinese bomb is right around here somewhere, maybe under that column over there. It . . . it *feels* like the right place. But we can't get to it. Still, there has to be some way to access it. Marlow wouldn't plant a bomb and not leave himself a way to set it off. Go through that scan. Maybe you'll spot something."

"And what are you going to be doing?"

"Slumming," he rasped. "There's one other possibility, remember? This is the night the hunters killed those people in Lincoln Heights. Felix Marlow set that up, when he was in his twenties. Maybe the Scavenger came back, to relive some old memories."

# XV

October 6, 1985
The Night of the Hunters
9:45 P.M.

Cold, erratic breeze dipped between tall, ranked tenements, carrying the smoke of drum fires here and there beneath a low, dark sky. Most of the street traffic was out of sight now, in this little universe of public-assisted housing. Those who had burrows to crawl into for the night had mostly holed up behind dead-bolt locks. All that remained in the open ways was the furtive, desultory night life of another failed experiment in federal socialism.

In a private loft overlooking the Anacostia River, the hunters assembled—six men in their thirties and early forties, and their guide, a tall, ski-masked young man known only as F, who had arranged for them the ultimate in urban adventures.

Bruno, the oldest at forty-three, had come down from Detroit for this night. Mario was from New York, Harold from Chicago, Jonathan and Blake from Los Angeles, and Chico from Miami.

They used only first names and kept their conversation to talk of hunts and trophies, of weapons and exotic game.

223

As they indulged themselves in their various passions—
a few sniffs of cocaine for the Californians, a joint or
two passed around, and the finest of liquors set out on a
folding table—there was more and more allusion to the
sensual highs of life . . . acts of dominance, the taking of
pleasure by force, and the hunt: stalking the perfect prey,
the smell of fear, the thrill of confrontation, the exhilara-
tion of the kill.

The six had this in common. They were wealthy, they
were bored, and they lusted for new diversions. There
wasn't much these six hadn't done, in their search for
pleasure.

Useless bastards, F thought as he catered to their comforts and directed their preparation. Useless, but intoxi-
cating in their arrogance, their lust for adventure. And
useful to me.

F had offered a new diversion, and men like these had
responded. Tonight's adventure would be his fourth safari.
Like those before, these clients knew him only as F and
had never seen his face. And like the others, these had paid
handsomely just to be placed on his list.

At 9:45 P.M., F unlocked a cabinet in the loft, exposing
two unmarked crates on a freight dolly. Without preamble,
he had the men open the first of these and pick out the
clothing that fit them. "Put it on," he said. "We have fifteen
minutes." There were dark shirts and trousers, pea jackets,
boots, light gloves, and ski masks. "Don't carry any personal items," he instructed them. "Put all your own
clothing, wallets, watches, rings . . . everything . . . in
those bags. They'll be waiting for you in the morning,
each at his own departure point. And remember, your fee
buys you one trophy kill apiece."

"What if I kill more than one?" Chico asked tauntingly.

F's gaze, behind his mask, was as cold as ice. "It's your responsibility," he said. "People die out there all the time. If an extra one or two get in the way, it's your decision. Just remember, though, this is a carefully planned hunt. If anybody screws it up, or does anything to bring trouble down on me, I'll remember."

When they were outfitted, F opened the second container. "Make your selections," he said. "Javelin, crossbow, sword, broadax, garrote, and a longbow. They're all here. And an assortment of knives, flashlights, and tack. Equip yourselves. We begin in five minutes."

Bruno hefted a broadax, his eyes glowing with excitement. "Beautiful," he muttered.

Mario grasped an exquisite, razor-edged sword, then straightened as F unwrapped a stubby Uzi semiautomatic with a folding shoulder stock and night-vision sight. "So who gets that?" the New Yorker snapped.

F snapped a clip into the Uzi, chambered a round, and slung the weapon from a belt swivel. "It's mine," he said. "I'm your guide and overseer."

When everyone was ready, Bruno poured bull glasses half-full of vodka and passed them around. "To the hunt," he said. They raised their glasses and drank, all except F. The guide stood apart, aloof and waiting.

Bruno handed him an envelope. "As agreed," he said.

The others followed suit, and F thumbed through the cash and slipped the envelopes inside his sweater. Then he looked from one to another of them. "Follow the directions, exactly," he said. "One kill per man, so choose your targets carefully. Stay together, and bring *all* the kills back here, to the alley behind this building."

"I got my trophy all planned." Chico grinned behind his mask. "I got me a taxidermist in—"

"Take your trophies in the alley, after the hunt," F said. Then with a sardonic shrug he opened the loft door and stepped aside. "It's ten o'clock, gentlemen," he said. "Your *jungle* awaits you."

As they filed out, Blake whispered to Jonathan, "Fifty thou' for a crossbow and a map? What's to keep us from takin' back our money an' doin' this on our own?"

Behind them, the Uzi whispered on its swivel. "It's been tried before," F said coldly. "You wouldn't like the outcome. You won't see much of me, after we leave here, as long as you follow the rules of the hunt. You know where to go, and each of you *will* find a target to meet your specifications. Don't expect to see me. You probably won't. But I'll see you . . . every step of the way. Now go, and good hunting."

## 10:15 P.M.

Blake and Jonathan took the lead for the first hunt. In a weedy, cluttered vacant lot behind a Salvation Army shelter they found Blake's hunting ground. It was a cluster of cardboard and chicken-wire shacks, where tattered people huddled around a pair of drum stoves in the chilly night.

In shadows, the hunters crept close and surveyed the group. After a moment, Blake picked out one of the silhouettes and pointed. "That's the one I want," he whispered. "That big buck over there, standin' guard like he was bull of the woods. I want him."

"You know him?" Bruno wondered.

"Never saw the bastard before." Blake shrugged.

"Then why him?"

Blake was silent for a moment, then he giggled. "Why not?"

Like scattering quail, the hunters burst into the little camp from three sides, shouting and threatening, kicking aside shelters, knocking over the fire drums. Ragged, terrified people scattered before them, and on the fourth side, the open side, Blake was waiting.

In a moment, it was ended. The street people were gone, all but one—the big man Blake had chosen as his prize. That one lay twitching on the ground, groveling and moaning, with a crossbow shaft buried in his upper chest.

They gathered around him, feral and excited. "He's not dead!" Blake hiccuped. "Kill him, somebody!"

"Do it yourself, asshole." Chico scowled. "He's your game."

"Use your knife!" Bruno growled. "Cut his damned throat!"

Jonathan turned away, raised his mask, doubled over, and was sick.

"Get over here, you faggot!" someone hissed. "We got to carry this garbage back to that alley. Everybody helps!"

Nearby, on a dark rooftop, F smiled grimly, watching through his night-vision scope. Psychotic fantasies, he mused. Blake had just meted out vengeance to a facsimile of a childhood bully. From his vantage, F could see the dark path where Mario would kill an old man who might remind him of his father, the vacant parking lot where Bruno would satisfy his curiosity about the "big high" of murder, the fire escape leading to the window where Chico would garrote a child, the dark street where Harold would chop down an out-of-work derelict, and the salvage yard where Jonathan would slay his dragon in the form of a sleeping wino.

And then F would watch them, unseen, as they collected their grisly trophies in a littered alley.

His contempt for his clients was a great, satisfying warmth within him—a warmth that he knew would lead him to bigger and better adventures in the future.

## 1:45 A.M.

They had done what they came for, and gone away. F took one last look at the deserted loft, satisfied that he had left no traces of the gathering there, then descended to the alley one last time to stand over the mutilated remains of six murder victims. The thrill-killers had been thorough, if clumsy. They all had their bloody trophies of the hunt.

But now Felix felt abruptly angry. He sensed that something had gone wrong, something had been overlooked—something critical, somewhere. In the distance, he heard police sirens, and his anger solidified. It was too early! It meant that someone—obviously one of his clients—had done something stupid. At that moment, Felix knew instinctively that another hunt had begun. A hunt of a different kind.

Somehow, the police would come to him now, and they would interfere. Police always interfered. They were meddlers, and they would ruin everything. He scowled, controlling his anger, then squared his shoulders and turned away. It didn't matter that much, he decided. Enough money and the right family name would erase any problem, just as it always had in the past.

Felix Scofield was untouchable.

With a last, lingering look he walked away, to disappear into the trails and warrens of these tenements he had studied so well. He would hide and observe for a while, then go home, to Georgetown. Once more, he knew, the Scofield name would have to be evoked, and something told him this would be the last time.

After this, it would be time for a career change. F would disappear. Felix Scofield would disappear. Then there would be time to seek new opportunities as Felix Marlow.

Behind him, in the vacant alley where the hunters had left their kills, a patch of nothingness swirled, coalesced, and shifted. Out of nothing, an older, harder Felix materialized—tall, lean, and craggy, dragging the body of a bearded man whose curiosity had cost him his life.

This Felix, the older one, paused and looked at the pile of safari victims, allowing himself a moment of fond remembrance. Then, with a heave, he lifted the body of Cress and added it to the grisly pile.

The sirens were near now, and on the grimy walls of the stamp-molded PHA buildings were dull reflections of flashing lights.

"Meddlers!" the Scavenger growled, remembering his rage of twenty years before and feeling it again. "Why must there always be meddlers!" He fought down his anger, clearing his mind. This was all in the past, just as the man who had called him Ice was in the past. For now, there were other things to do—the thing he had programmed his time-jump coordinates for before Cress had interfered.

Not far from here, just about now, a lost treasure was being transferred from one vehicle to another. Forty million dollars in lost treasure, looted just today from a bank in New York City!

With a last glance at the long-ago scene of his first real venture, he turned toward the quiet end of the alley . . .

and stopped, gaping at the man who stood there, blocking his path.

"It's really true," Jack Logan said sardonically. "The criminal really does return to the scene of the—"

The stunned surprise lasted only for an instant. Then with a quickness the timecop could never have expected, Felix raised his crossbow, released its quarrel, and darted into a dark, empty doorway, charred by recent flames.

The crossbow bolt barely missed Logan as he ducked aside, and his laser-sight dot touched the Scavenger's shoulder too late to fire. He crouched, ran for the dark doorway, and vaulted past it as a muffled shot sounded from inside. He heard the bullet flick past him, and its impact as it hit the wall beyond. Then he whirled, dived, and was inside. He heard the bullet flick past him, and its impact as it hit the wall beyond.

Another quarrel whined past, then the crossbow itself clattered against a wall as Felix changed weapons.

Thread-fine beams of laser sights played crazily in the darkness of the fire-gutted building, each seeking the source of the other, then both flicked from sight and a shadow moved among shadows. Like a sprinting ghost, Felix emerged for a vague instant, to disappear again into the pitch-black of a burned-out stairwell. His feet crunched on cinders, and somewhere above a fire door creaked on its hinges.

Logan was only a few steps behind. By dim light through hollow windows, he found himself in a central hallway, where the doors of empty apartments stood at intervals along both sides. He passed the first two, whirled for a glimpse of the third, and ducked as a shot from across the hall showered burnt splinters from the frame above his head. Hitting the floor he rolled, sighted into the opposite room, and heard ripping, splintering sounds from there. He lunged, crossed the hall low and fast, and felt the whine of a shot that missed him by an inch.

There was a moment of silence then, and retreating footsteps somewhere overhead. As Logan spun into the dark room he heard breaking glass, not far away, and followed the sound. The apartment was empty, but there was a gaping hole in its ceiling where the charred remains of old flooring still showered from above, a sifting veil of ash and plaster dust.

With a muttered oath, Logan sprinted across the littered floor, leapt to the opening, and pulled himself up through it. He was in another abandoned unit now, one floor above, and his senses told him he was alone. He whirled, seeking, and saw the broken window in the next room. The Scavenger had gone that way!

I have to get him now, Logan's mind raced. If he gets away, he'll trigger that bomb Claire is looking for. I've got to nail him before he can do that!

But, his reason reminded him, if I get too close and miss, if I panic him, he'll simply retrieve back to our time, and disappear.

With renewed stealth, Logan gained the window, looked out, and knew where the Scavenger had gone. He was climbing, heading for the roof. As Logan spotted him he disappeared around a vertical corner.

Logan raced back to the stairwell and fought his way upward, through the litter of the only exit anyone had had when this building was torched by hoodlums, months before.

Through the long hours of evening, Claire Hemmings had traced and retraced Logan's search area south of the

Third Street tunnel. She memorized the site, both as she saw it now in the city's lights and as Logan's lens scan had seen it earlier in daylight. She had focused her search on that same highway support column and had the same intuitive feeling Logan had mentioned—that the reason for Scavenger's earlier visit to this scene was *right here*, if only it could be seen. It was after 10 P.M. when she noticed an odd thing about the support.

As the headlights of vehicles on the nearby Washington Avenue ramp swept over it, the base cap at the bottom of the structure showed slight irregularities—little bulges unlike the bases of other columns around it, as though this one had been different in its construction, then modified to fit the original highway plan.

In frustration, she walked around the base, stooping here and there to touch it. She would have given a year's pay right then for a few seconds of ChronComp's time, to check out the old work orders on this project. But Chron-Comp was almost twenty years in the future. This was 1985, and the massive trivia files that were part of the big computer's memory base hadn't even been assembled until after the year 2000.

Then as a thought struck her, she stood bolt upright. The files hadn't been assembled yet, but the data that was in those files existed . . . right where ChronComp would find it when the compilations began.

With sudden decision, Claire sprinted across to the pedestrian lane facing Second, and hailed a taxi.

"D.C. Public Works," she told the surprised cabbie. "Municipal building." As the Beacon Cab cruiser headed north across the Mall, Claire wondered what Captain Matuzek would say if he knew that TEC's systems analyst was, at this moment, on her way to commit felony breaking and entering at the city hall building of the nation's capital.

In the public works section, she burrowed through data on local road and highway projects until she found the one she was looking for, then traced its project codes to the hard-copy repositories in a basement vault.

Buried there, unnoticed for these intervening years, she found change orders on details of the old tunnel-ramp projects, and ran these through the department's division accounting ledger.

"Got it!" she whispered finally, staring at an official-looking paper that the inventories could not match. It was a bogus change order, and it told her where and how the bomb—she knew with certainty now that the thing *was* that missing Manchurian neutron device—was buried.

It was nearly midnight when Claire Hemmings emerged from the closed municipal building. She knew what the device was now, where it was, and had a pretty good idea how it was meant to be triggered, from a great distance away.

A simple telephone call to an existing number, followed by a number code, would set the thing off.

Again she ran through the recorded views in Logan's scan, and just at the end of it—where the view panned away along rows of overhead traffic lights diminishing into the Third Street tunnel—she found inspiration.

"I've got it!" she muttered to herself. "Now all I have to do is find a way to disable a conduit system before that killer decides to keep his threat."

Thought of the ice-cold killer Logan was seeking, the man they called Scavenger, was like a shiver of dread. "Take care of yourself, Logan," Claire whispered. "Take good care of yourself."

# XVI

In the cold, dark hours of October 7, 1985, two travelers from the future played a deadly game of hide-and-seek on tenement roofs.

Felix Marlow, the Scavenger, placed his laser sight on the fire door of the stairwell two hundred feet away, and when the door opened he fired, and fired again. But there was no one there. Then as he raised his head, searching, a bullet shattered a cornice stone beside him and showered him with shards. The flattened slug screamed like a banshee as it ricocheted away in the darkness.

Marlow fired again, at a tumbling shadow, then pushed off from a ventilator shaft and sprinted across frosty tar to leap out over the void between buildings, to the next roof. There he rolled into the cover of a cornice, aligned his gun, and waited. But the tenacious shadow behind him didn't come from where he had been. Out of the corner of his eye he saw Jack Logan sail across the twenty-foot gap a dozen yards away, to his right.

Rage engulfed the Scavenger as a bullet from the time-cop's weapon seared across his left arm, numbing the fingers of that hand. "I'll make you a bargain, cop!" he shouted as he scuttled backward, into cover. "One life for nine million! Come out where I can see you, and maybe I won't wipe out everybody within two hundred miles!"

He listened for a response, and heard nothing. He sensed that the meddler was moving again, but he couldn't tell where he was. "Do you hear me?" he screamed. "I'm putting an end to this! Last chance!"

This time there were faint, scuffling sounds, and Marlow shifted his own position, sprinting to the cover of a framed skylight.

He waited, listened, and raised himself slightly, and a voice directly behind him said, "Freeze, Marlow! Let it drop, and don't move!"

Marlow froze, but only for an instant. Beneath him, his numb left fingers found the time-return stud on his belt and twisted it.

Logan flinched as a vortex of nothingness opened just at his feet—the dimensions of physical reality swirling lazily, coalescing, falling in upon themselves . . . and then it stopped. The world steadied, and he was still where and when he had been. And so was Felix Marlow, crouched wide-eyed and stunned beside a skylight frame.

Logan struggled to recapture his equilibrium. The time traveler's retrieve had failed! Its signal had gone out into the timestream, and a wormhole had presented itself, but the sequence was incomplete. He's lost his link, Logan realized. He can't go back because there is no mechanism in the future —his future now—to receive him!

"Drop it, Marlow," he growled. "You're under—"

With a scream of rage, the Scavenger came upright, whirled, and threw himself through the skylight, into the darkness below.

"Damn!" Logan muttered.

With only a moment's hesitation he followed, rolling into a ball as he crashed into broken furniture below.

It was an empty apartment, with an open door. As Logan got to his feet, he heard hasty footsteps somewhere, a shout and a shot, then somewhere below another door crashed open, and he knew that Marlow had escaped the building.

Cold dread crept up Logan's spine, dread more chill than the night wind on barren rooftops. With a policeman's instincts, he tried to put himself in Marlow's place, to see through Marlow's eyes, to think Marlow's thoughts. With sick certainty, he knew what the killer's next move would be, and his eyes narrowed.

The Scavenger had no tolerance for frustration. When thwarted, his schemes and games interrupted, he reacted with deadly intent.

Matuzek was right. Marlow was a loose cannon, and now his last retaining link with reason was gone. He had tried to escape from 1985, to return to his own time, and his retrieve had failed. How that could be, Logan didn't know. A timesled launch was always retrievable. The retrieval was part of the sequence of Kleindast technology. Like a wound spring, a time-launch had its own kinetic force, and the act of retrieval was simply the unwinding of the spring.

But that was timesleds. Logan recalled what Amy Fuller had said about other possible configurations—other technologies with their own laws and limitations. The kid with the lottery scheme had used a particle collider and a roller-bearing plate, and achieved the equivalent of Q-velocity in a timefield. So maybe Marlow's mechanism was some other system, too.

Whatever it was, Marlow was trapped. And like a cornered weasel, he would react. The Scavenger would play his hole card now, if he could.

On a nighttime street outside the tenement rows, Logan looked all around and played a hunch. At a dead run, he headed for the nearest island of light—a service area with a phone booth.

From fifty yards away, he saw that his hunch was right. There was a man in the open booth, and that man was Felix Marlow. He stood there in plain sight, making a telephone call. As Logan sprinted around the curve, heading for him, Marlow lowered the telephone receiver, then tapped a few more times at the number pad. That done, he stepped out of the booth, smiled coldly at the approaching cop, and bent low in a formal, theatrical bow.

"You're too late, cop!" he said. "Fifteen seconds now, and *boom*!"

"Drop your gun, Marlow!" Logan commanded, bringing his own weapon to point.

"You go to hell," the Scavenger said casually. "Five seconds. Four. Three. Two . . ."

All the street lights dimmed momentarily. Somewhere behind Logan, distant alarms echoed across the sleeping city. As though in response, a police siren sounded abruptly, very close by. Logan flinched, glanced around, and in that instant Marlow dropped to the ground and opened up, rapid-fire, his gun blossoming with little flares that spat bullets. One of them took Logan dead center, driving into his flak vest, knocking him backward. He grunted with shock, rolled, and came up to return fire, and hesitated. Marlow was running again, zigzagging away into the shadows, howling obscenities. He was heading back into the tenement rows.

The countdown had come and gone, and the world was

still here! Scavenger's annihilation device—like time retrieval—had failed!

With an effort, Logan got to his feet just as a police cruiser braked to a halt beyond the phone booth.

"I'm police!" Logan shouted, flashing a badge. "TEC special agent, in pursuit. The man I'm after is a murderer, armed and dangerous. He's headed into those PHA buildings!"

"We saw him," a cop answered. "He went through that gate over there. Are you all right? We saw you go down."

"Vest," Logan said. "Thanks." He set out at a run, following where Marlow had gone.

Behind him, a policeman asked, "What the hell is TEC?"

His partner glanced at him. "What?"

"What he said," the first repeated. "He said *TEC*. What is that?"

"Something federal." The partner shrugged. "In D.C., what else?"

In a neighborhood where gunfire is a nightly occurrence, people don't throw open their windows to see what's going on. They bolt their doors, turn out their lights, and stay low, hoping as always that it will all just go away.

The Lincoln Heights area stood dark and silent now, the only visible life the police cruisers homing in on the east end, where lights flashed and flashlights waved this way and that, searching.

Marlow knew that the timecop was behind him. A dozen times he had twisted and cut back through these littered alleys and trash heaps, trying to lose him. But the

cop was unbelievably tenacious. Now Marlow's screaming rage went unchecked, his twisted mind half drowning
in its own spite. Frustration rode him like a clawed mon-
ster, and like a rabid animal he seethed and ran, twisted
and turned and ran again, going in erratic circles among
the tenement rows.

His retrieval system had failed, and he was stuck . . .
trapped in this time and place. And then, at the end, even
his retaliation had failed him. He had dialed the number,
punched in the code . . . and nothing happened!

Now, wild with rage and fear, he dodged and ran, scurrying from shadow to shadow while a remorseless fate
closed in on him from behind. He had lost his crossbow,
and his laser gun was empty, and he ran.

Rounding a dark corner, he heard the cop closing in on
him. The man was younger than he, and in top physical
condition, and he was relentless.

Marlow ducked behind a trash bin, puffing and wheez-
ing, then scurried out and darted across a weedy vacant
lot. Just ahead lay a heap of refuse—broken furnishings,
old car parts, and filth—high enough to hide behind, and
he went for it.

He was within a few paces of the welcoming shelter
when a dark figure emerged there, coming upright out of
the shadows.

"Help me!" the Scavenger gasped. "A million dollars if
you hide me, help me get away!"

The dark figure, masked and still, stared at him, then
chuckled.

"Sorry, old man," a purring voice said. "I have no time
for you right now."

"No time? . . ." Marlow stepped closer, and abruptly he

recognized the mask, the dark pea jacket. He was looking at *himself*! Himself of twenty years before . . . that
younger self just finished with his last urban safari.

"I know you!" the Scavenger shrilled. "Felix! Felix,
look at me! I'm—"

"That's too bad." The younger Felix cut him off. "You
know me, so you've just run out of time. Good-bye." In
the shadows, the shadow shifted and a night-sight Uzi
sang its song of parting.

It was a tired, bedraggled Jack Logan who made his
way back to central Washington, to where lights flashed
red, white, and blue in a seethe of activity surrounded by
police barricades. There were emergency vehicles there,
and power company service rigs, and the entire northbound section of the Third Street tunnel was blocked to
traffic.

In the curious crowd behind police barricades, Logan
asked a man what was going on.

"Damned if I know," the man said. "All I've heard is
bits and pieces. They say there's a fire engine tangled up in
the tunnel. A *stolen* fire engine. Can you believe it, somebody stealing a ladder truck right out of the DCFD main
barn, then driving it through the tunnel with its ladder up.
Tore out the lighting conduit half the length of the tunnel,
then got crossways and wedged itself between the rail-
ings. She must have been crazy, is all I can say."

*"She?"*

"Sure. It was some woman. Can you believe it? One
little blond dumpling doing all that? They're out looking
for her, now."

\* \* \*

At the west reflecting pool, between the Lincoln Memorial and the Washington Monument, Logan found Claire Hemmings waiting for him.

"That tunnel—" He pointed eastward. "I guess the conduit was the trigger?"

"I think so." Claire nodded. "How about the Scavenger? Did you find him?"

"I found his body. He killed himself. Shot himself to pieces with an automatic weapon."

"It's about time," she said. Then she looked him over critically, noticing the ragged pock on his chest, where his flakwear had stopped a bullet. She reached toward him, and he backed away a step.

"Yes, dammit, I can feel it," he growled.

Claire nodded, almost smiling. "You look like hell, Logan. I think you need some rest. Let's check in, then go to your place."

*Read on for a sneak preview of*

# FACES OF INFINITY

Book Two
of
The Gates of Time

by
**Dan Parkinson**

He stood at the very lip of the maintenance sconce, seven feet beyond the observation deck railing and more than three hundred feet above the tiny strip of halogen-lighted pavement that was a city street at night.

Defeated, destitute, and sick at heart, he was beyond desperation. He had reached the end of his rope. A man bereft of hope, he had come here to make an end of humiliation, an end of the disappointments of a world where only cynicism could thrive.

Cold, erratic wind shoved at him, pushing him this way and that. It pasted his stained, torn tuxedo pants around his trembling legs and toyed with his thinning gray hair. He had lost his glasses, but he didn't need them. He knew where he was going, and he wouldn't be reading again. Nothingness . . . perpetual sleep . . . was a simple step ahead. Not even a step. All he had to do was lean into the wind.

They said I'd be a smash on Wall Street, he thought with bitter irony. My formulas. My theories. My wonderful little discovery . . . God! What an innocent I've been! Let my guard down. Hell, I never even had it up. Everybody's looking for a new idea, they said. Invention is the magic wand that makes it rain money. Sure, it rains money! But only for the swindlers and the cheats. Invention? Innovation? That isn't what business is about nowadays. It's about packaging and marketing and delayed option clauses. Used to be about building a better mousetrap . . . didn't it? Now it's the bottom line and nothing else. Sharks in a feeding frenzy, scavengers feasting on the scraps.

Who the hell are these people? he asked himself, as astonished as when he had first asked it. I don't know these creatures. If this is their world, then *where is my world*?

Management will love this, they said. A lamp that lights itself! Dynamism from gravity! How wonderful! Perpetual energy. A breakthrough. The classic better mousetrap! Commerce will beat a path to your door. Just wait till management sees this!

What management? There's nobody out there but accountants and lawyers and beady-eyed MBAs. There aren't any *managers* anymore! Just the terrible triad. Don't buy it, just take it . . . Just sell it, don't make it . . . If it isn't broke, break it!

They beat a path, all right, he thought. But it wasn't commerce at the door. It was slicksters and thieves. Sharks.

In the uncaring wind, his face contorted with the pain of lost ideals. Tears of frustration and defeat glistened in his eyes. There was nothing left. They had it all now. Well, not quite all. They had left him his IRS audits . . . and his mounting debts.

Slowly he rocked back and forth, feeling the shift of his own inertia each time he teetered toward the distant street below. But he didn't look down now, at the almost-deserted depths. Instead he raised his anguished eyes heavenward, where low clouds hung dull and somber, pierced by the taller buildings beneath them.

Somewhere below, within secure walls, deals had been closed . . . like doors slammed in his face. Innocent and enthusiastic, he had come to the party, only to find his life's work already dissected and parceled out, with no share left for him.

"Sorry, David," they had said through their plastic smiles. "But that's business."

"This is what it comes to, Irene," he muttered, his voice thin against the cold, playful wind. "A whole life's work, a life spent believing that if you do the right thing, everything will be all right. At least you don't have to be here to see this, now.

"I'll be a smash on Wall Street, they said. I'll bet not one of those bean-counters would know how to calculate the exact impact down there. But then, why should they care about the force generated by 150 pounds of spun-off profit potential falling 323 feet? Inertia conversion doesn't matter to anybody. Hopes and dreams and ideas don't matter. Only money matters."

Direct conversion of gravity to photoelectric energy—a simple reversal of the direction of kinetic flow. This was his life's work. But did they want to see its results? No, only to control the investment potential it would generate. Three hundred and twenty-three feet of free fall, and he wouldn't even light up when he hit.

"Good night, Irene," he breathed.

He closed his eyes tightly and rocked forward, giving himself to the wind. Just for a moment, he told himself bleakly, he could lose himself again in pretense. This time he would pretend he was flying.

He leaned, felt his weight shift to his toes at the edge of the glass-and-steel precipice, and his dinner jacket snugged sharply around his shoulders.

"Very messy," a high, reedy voice behind him said. He almost lost his footing, swiveling around to look.

The person holding his coattail was tiny—not much more than four feet tall. She—somehow he knew it was a she, though her head was as hairless as a fresh, pink egg—had both feet braced against the little wall of the sconce and was gripping his coat with both hands. The little garment that covered her from neck to feet, like a pilot's jumpsuit, revealed no particular contours. But it was her eyes that held his attention. They were the biggest, darkest eyes he had ever seen.

"You might want to reconsider this," she urged, struggling to hold him against his own inertia. "You'll almost certainly change your mind on the way down, and just imagine how you'll feel. At that point it will be too late."

"It's already too late," he shouted, angry at the interruption. "It's all over! Everything! Let go!"

"I can't," she piped. "My hands are cramped. I'm stuck. Do you want to kill me, too?"

A gust of wind staggered him and he reeled, his arms windmilling for balance. "Will you turn me loose?" he demanded.

"I'd like to," she assured him. "Just give me a minute. You might not mind splattering yourself all over that paving down there, but I'd just as soon not. Have you ever actually seen what surface impact does to a human body? It's disgusting!"

"It's your own fault! You grabbed me!" He wrenched at

his lapels, trying to free himself of the restraining jacket, and felt her tug falter.

"My feet are slipping!" she shrilled. "Help me!"

The wind and the height caressed him, inviting him to peaceful oblivion. But if he went, she would go, too. With a thin cry of frustration he threw himself back, and down. His right knee collided painfully with a scaffold anchor, his hand skidded on wet metal, and his face scraped against rough, tar-bedded pea gravel. He lay stunned for a moment, then groaned as protesting pain coursed down him—first his bleeding face, then the deeper, throbbing traumas in his wrist and his knee.

Beneath his bulk, something small squirmed and protested, then pulled itself free. Little feet scuffed on the pea gravel, and a little face not quite like most faces leaned close to study him.

"You're a mess," she decided. "But you'll live."

"Get away from me!" he whimpered, abruptly aware of his pathetic position. He lay bruised and bleeding on a cold, damp rooftop, with all the grim determination of moments before—the agonizing resolve to just once, just one last time, take his fate into his own hands and do something right—fading away. He had been ready. Now he was uncertain.

"I can't even jump off a stupid building!" he moaned. "Simple thing like that, and I can't get it done!"

"You're a pretty sorry specimen, all right," the little person agreed. "I think you should reconsider your whole life, if you're that unhappy with it."

"That's what I've been doing!" he grated. "What right did you have to interfere?"

"None, I suppose." She shrugged. "But after traveling farther than you can imagine just to see you, then chasing you all the way up here, I didn't want to lose you before I at least give you my card."

"Your . . . your card?"

"Yes." She produced a little white business card from somewhere and handed it to him. Unbelieving, he squinted at it in the light of a rooftop sign, and she held out a pair of glasses to him—his own glasses.

"You dropped these in the elevator," she said.

With his glasses in place, he peered at her. "Who . . . who or *what* are you?"

"I'm just a Whisper," she said casually. "But you don't know about Whispers, of course. We haven't happened yet. Just read the card."

Beneath an odd little logo—like two parentheses joined by an elongated X—were the words:

ANYWHEN, INC.

—Excursions, Tours, Sightseeing—

Adventures in Extratemporization

KT-Pi, rep.

—HAVE A NICE TIME—

Sitting on the cold, damp roof, thirty floors above city streets, blood dripping from his cheeks, his violated knee aching, his bruises throbbing fiercely, he stared at the innocuous little card.

"What?" he said finally.

"It's another option." The strange little person beside him gave another shrug. "You might want to look into it. Have you ever been to Kansas?"

# About the Author

**Dan Parkinson** is the author of many westerns and successful TSR fantasy novels. He has also written *The Gates of Time*, an exciting science fiction series in which a time-travel agency is the center of drama and action.

# DEL REY® ONLINE!

## The Del Rey Internet Newsletter...

A monthly electronic publication e-mailed to subscribers and posted on the rec.arts.sf.written Usenet newsgroup and on our Del Rey Books Web site (www.randomhouse.com/delrey/). It features hype-free descriptions of books that are new in the stores, a list of our upcoming books, special promotional programs and offers, announcements and news, a signing/reading/convention-attendance calendar for Del Rey authors and editors, "In Depth" essays in which professionals in the field (authors, artists, cover designers, salespeople, etc.) talk about their jobs in science fiction, a question-and-answer section, and more!

Subscribe to the DRIN: send a message reading "subscribe" in the subject or body to drin-dist@cruises.randomhouse.com

## The Del Rey Books Web Site!

We make a lot of information available on our Web site at
www.randomhouse.com/delrey/

- all back issues and the current issue of the Del Rey Internet Newsletter
- sample chapters of almost every new book
- detailed interactive features of some of our books
- special features on various authors and SF/F worlds
- ordering information (and online ordering)
- reader reviews of upcoming books
- news and announcements
- our Works in Progress report, detailing the doings of our most popular authors
- bargain offers in our Del Rey Online Store
- manuscript transmission requirements
- and more!

## If You're Not on the Web...

You can subscribe to the DRIN via e-mail (send a message reading "subscribe" in the subject or body to drin-dist@cruises.randomhouse.com), read it on the rec.arts.sf.written Usenet newsgroup the first few days of every month, or visit our gopher site (gopher.panix.com) for back issues of the DRIN and about a hundred sample chapters. We also have editors and other representatives who participate in America Online and CompuServe SF/F forums and rec.arts.sf.written, making contact and sharing information with SF/F readers.

## Questions? E-mail us...

at delrey@randomhouse.com (though it sometimes takes us a little while to answer).

# 🖋 FREE DRINKS 🖋

Take the Del Rey® survey and get a free newsletter! Answer the questions below and we will send you complimentary copies of the DRINK (Del Rey® Ink) newsletter free for one year. Here's where you will find out all about upcoming books, read articles by top authors, artists, and editors, and get the inside scoop on your favorite books.

Age _____ Sex ❑ M ❑ F

Highest education level: ❑ high school ❑ college ❑ graduate degree

Annual income: ❑ $0-30,000 ❑ $30,001-60,000 ❑ over $60,000

Number of books you read per month: ❑ 0-2 ❑ 3-5 ❑ 6 or more

Preference: ❑ fantasy ❑ science fiction ❑ horror ❑ other fiction ❑ nonfiction

I buy books in hardcover: ❑ frequently ❑ sometimes ❑ rarely

I buy books at: ❑ superstores ❑ mall bookstores ❑ independent bookstores
❑ mail order

I read books by new authors: ❑ frequently ❑ sometimes ❑ rarely

I read comic books: ❑ frequently ❑ sometimes ❑ rarely

I watch the Sci-Fi cable TV channel: ❑ frequently ❑ sometimes ❑ rarely

I am interested in collector editions (signed by the author or illustrated):
❑ yes ❑ no ❑ maybe

I read Star Wars novels: ❑ frequently ❑ sometimes ❑ rarely

I read Star Trek novels: ❑ frequently ❑ sometimes ❑ rarely

I read the following newspapers and magazines:

| | | |
|---|---|---|
| ❑ *Analog* | ❑ *Locus* | ❑ *Popular Science* |
| ❑ *Asimov* | ❑ *Wired* | ❑ *USA Today* |
| ❑ *SF Universe* | ❑ *Realms of Fantasy* | ❑ *The New York Times* |

Check the box if you do not want your name and address shared with qualified vendors ❑

Name _____
Address _____
City/State/Zip _____
E-mail _____

timecop

PLEASE SEND TO: DEL REY®/The DRINK
201 EAST 50TH STREET, NEW YORK, NY 10022 OR FAX TO
THE ATTENTION OF DEL REY PUBLICITY 212/572-2676